THE BOY
MADE THE
DIFFERENCE

THE BOY
MADE THE
DIFFERENCE

MATT BISHOP

Matador
9 Priory Business Park,
Wistow Road, Kibworth Beauchamp,
Leicestershire. LE8 0RX
Tel: 0116 279 2299
Email: books@troubador.co.uk
Web: www.troubador.co.uk/matador
Twitter: @matadorbooks

ISBN 978 1838594 879

British Library Cataloguing in Publication Data.
A catalogue record for this book is available from the British Library.

Printed and bound by CPI Group (UK) Ltd, Croydon, CR0 4YY
Typeset in 11pt Minion Pro by Troubador Publishing Ltd, Leicester, UK

Matador is an imprint of Troubador Publishing Ltd

To the braves of the Lighthouse and the Broderip

AUTHOR'S NOTE

Is *The Boy Made the Difference* a gay novel? No, in 2020 there is no such thing as a gay novel, or a straight novel for that matter, nor should there be. Rather, it is a novel in which some of the characters are gay and therefore sometimes do gay things.

But *The Boy Made the Difference* is set not in 2020 but thirty years ago, when life for gay men was terrifyingly dominated by HIV/AIDS, which cruel disease was wiping out part of a whole generation of us. HIV/AIDS exists in our midst still, of course it does, especially in the developing world, but it is rarely now a rapidly terminal disease in the developed world thanks to the invention of anti-retroviral meds in the mid-'90s. Almost no one in the developed world under the age of about forty-five therefore has first-hand experience of what it was like before their invention.

It was like the First World War. Young men were dying in hospital beds as young soldiers had died in trenches three-quarters of a century before. But, as a wife and mother observes in one of the later chapters of *The Boy Made the Difference*, unlike the heroes of the Somme and Ypres, who were rightly revered and decorated, the boys and men who died of HIV/AIDS only thirty-odd years ago often faced their deaths despised and rejected, and sometimes entirely alone.

Over the past ten or fifteen years very few (if any) new novels have been set against that narrative backdrop, and increasingly I found myself wanting to read one. Specifically, having worked thirty-odd years ago as a home support volunteer (aka "buddy") for London Lighthouse, at the time the world's largest HIV/AIDS centre, and having helped too many men and boys cope with the ravages of their destructive and disfiguring disease, often breathing their last breaths in the Broderip Ward of the Middlesex Hospital (now closed), I wanted to read a celebration of their magnificent courage, woven into a moving, gripping, entertaining and sometimes rollicking story of everyday familial stoicism. Eventually, I decided to try to write one myself. *The Boy Made the Difference* is my attempt.

I should make clear, however, that *The Boy Made the Difference* is a work of fiction. Yes, I drew on experience when writing it, as all novelists do, but none of the characters is based on anyone I have ever met and none of the events depicted ever took place.

There are many people I must acknowledge. First and foremost, I want to thank my mother, Bernardine Bishop, the author of five critically acclaimed novels, a phrase-maker *nonpareil* when speaking as well as writing, who taught me to love reading. I will donate any proceeds from sales of *The Boy Made the Difference* to the Bernardine Bishop Appeal (part of the wonderful cancer charity CLIC Sargent), which was set up in her honour after she died of cancer in 2013.

I was born into a very literary family. My mother's mother, Barbara Lucas, was a novelist, as was her aunt, Viola Meynell. My great-great-grandmother, Alice Meynell, was a poet – and a suffragist, too. Her husband, Wilfrid Meynell, my great-great-grandfather, was a writer and editor. So I am very far from being the first published author in my family, but in my teens I became the first person in my family to come out as gay. Wilfrid Meynell's cousin, my cousin four times removed therefore, was the painter Henry Scott Tuke. He was not out. He would not have known what "out" meant. But he was manifestly gay, as just one glance at any of his beautiful paintings will tell you.

Finally, I would like to thank my husband, the incomparable Angel Bautista, and also John Allert, Lauren Bailey, Lucy Bergonzi, Catherine Bond Muir, Josh Brandon, Rachel Burnett, Fern Bushnell, Caryl Churchill, Stuart Codling, Steve Cooper, Joe Downes, Kate Gray, Cass Green, Rainbow Haddad, Penny Harrison, Sharon Hendry, Moira Hunter, Philippa Iliffe, Emma Jacobs, Fabio Marcolini, Gina Miller, Sophie Missing, John Olliver, Martin Ouvry, Josephine Parnas, Natalie Pinkham, Michelle Pugh, Sathnam Sanghera, Carrie Stammers, Steven Tee, Jeremy Thompson, Desmond Tumulty, Jack Wedgbury, James Wharton and John Woods, who encouraged me or advised me or cajoled me or helped me in any number of other ways.

PART 1

SATURDAY 22 APRIL 1989

CHAPTER 1

AN INDEX FINGER BECKONING
RHYTHMICALLY AND PERSISTENTLY

R ex fancied Jill rather enjoyed arguing with him. Ever since they had been married, he had always thought that she was, if not quite spoiling for a fight, then too often too eager to make conspicuous the virtue of her efforts to tolerate his many apparent idiocies. Yet she found it easy to treat others with patience.

He found her irritating, too. He conceded that she was intelligent in her way, and he remembered that she had once been rather beautiful, yet he could see neither quality in her now. But she ran the domestic aspects of their life well, she was a good mother, and, by and large, she had learned to mind her own business where his work and play were concerned. Yet, when they were alone together, her

3

face sometimes tended to take on a testy scowl, in which configuration her features appeared to settle gratefully, and there was no word other than "fat" to describe the shape of the once lissom girl he had married nineteen years before.

She was cross today because he had stayed on the phone for too long after she had shouted, "Lunch is ready." Had Danny been eating with them, instead of being out playing football, she would not have been so liverish. Indeed, by the same token, had Danny been with them, Rex might well have rung off earlier. But Jill had heated up the remains of last night's Chinese takeaway for herself and Rex, and he had thought it would not matter much if he were to begin to eat his half of it a couple of minutes after she had begun to eat hers.

In fact the interval had been longer than that, albeit not much longer, and, by the time he had entered the living room and had sat down, she was sitting sullenly in front of an empty plate.

"Yours must be cold by now. I've finished mine," she said.

"I'm sure it's fine. Thanks for heating it up for me."

A silence developed, which was broken by Jill.

"Why can't you just come when meals are ready, like normal people? Why d'you always have to delay? Shall I put it in the microwave again for you?"

"No, of course not. I'm eating it, aren't I? It's fine. It was only a couple of minutes, and I…"

"It was six minutes. You took six whole minutes to ring off. I'd finished mine before you'd so much as deigned to appear. To whom were you speaking anyway?"

Ah, it was going to be one of those conversations, thought Rex. Jill's use of the word "deigned" confirmed it. "To whom" was discouraging, too.

There was another pause. Rex took a mouthful of lukewarm chicken chow mein.

"Well, it's very nice," he ventured.

"It *was* very nice," Jill replied. She scooped up her plate, knife and fork, and disappeared into the kitchen.

"For fuck's sake," muttered Rex.

"What did you say?" said Jill, hurrying back into the living room.

"Nothing," replied Rex.

"You did. You said something. I heard you."

"Well, if you fucking heard me, why the fuck did you ask me what I fucking said then?"

"Oh, lovely. Swearing like a trooper. Beautiful. I cook your lunch, you don't bother eating it 'til it suits you so to do, then you thank me by effing and blinding at me."

"I doubt that the quality of this debate will improve with longevity, so I'm going out," said Rex, who stood up, strode briskly out of the living room, grabbed his bomber jacket from the hallway coat hooks, and walked out of the house, slamming the door behind him. Jill neither followed him nor attempted to prevent his departure.

He was not sure where he would go. He looked at his watch. It was 12.55pm. He did not fancy going to a pub, an obvious bolthole, because he and Danny had agreed to play snooker later and he wanted to be on form for that; a rake of beer would not help. Danny had become a pretty good snooker player lately, and, although Rex was a little shamefaced about minding being beaten by his eighteen-year-old son at a sport that he himself had taught the boy to play, the truth was that he did mind. Danny had won the last time they had played – three-nil as it happens – and Rex wanted to avenge that defeat today.

Rex had come to the end of Manor House Drive, which, although he had to concede to his more mickey-taking friends was an incongruously grand-sounding name for a residential street in Willesden Green, was also, he insisted, the poshest road in the London Borough of Brent; and it probably was. He turned right onto Brondesbury Park, right again onto The Avenue, and began to walk faster.

It was a fine day, warm for April, and he shook off his jacket and slung it over his right shoulder, his right index finger hooked through the hanging-loop inside its collar as he walked on, now swaggering a bit, into Wrentham Avenue.

He knew where he was going now, and he quickened his pace again. He crossed Chamberlayne Road into Clifford Gardens, slowing slightly to check his reflection in the window of a betting shop on the corner. Not bad for thirty-seven, he reckoned. He had always been sporty, had played football well as a boy, and had recently embraced tennis, which he hoped would be the vehicle via which he would remain fit well into middle age. His hair was neither as thick nor as unvaryingly brown as it had been ten years ago – of course not – but it was receding in a uniform direction, from his forehead backwards, and he had it cut regularly and often, in what his barber called a "Bruce Willis". Indeed, when Rex and Jill had seen *Die*

Hard at the cinema a few months ago, he had been pleased to observe a distinct resemblance between himself and the Hollywood star, which similarity was made all the more gratifying by the knowledge that he, Rex, was three years the elder of the two.

He walked into the betting shop, glanced at the TV monitors, saw that the hare was about to run prior to the 1.07pm at Crayford, grabbed a betting slip, scrawled "£100 win trap 1" on it, and ran to the counter, paying with two £50 notes which he unfurled from a thick-ish wad that he pulled from the left front pocket of his jeans as the six greyhounds set off. The dog in trap one was badly baulked at the first bend, dropped to the back of the field, rallied somewhat, but finished only fourth. Rex screwed up his betting slip, tossed it onto the floor, and strolled back out into the sunshine. Winning was great, he reckoned, but even losing was fun. It was the punting itself that he enjoyed.

He crossed College Road into Bathurst Gardens, congratulating himself on the discrepancy in opulence between the dowdy bay-fronted Edwardian terraces he was passing and the kempt six-bedroom detached with double garage and abundant gravel in which he, Jill and Danny lived on Manor House Drive.

He arrived at a mini-roundabout, turned left into Wrottesley Road, then right onto Harrow Road. He looked about him, this way and that, then sauntered into the gents' on the corner.

He took his position at the urinal, and unzipped his flies. He had not come in for a piss, but he pissed nonetheless. He always felt a comforting sense of rectitude at this point: if a policeman were to question his motives, as an alibi incontrovertible he would be able to point smugly at the blameless pale-yellow torrent cascading out of his dick and splashing onto the porcelain below it.

He finished pissing, but remained in position. He looked about him. He was one of seven men present, and it was already clear, or at least very likely, that none of them was motivated by the need to empty bladder or bowels. A couple of them were leaning separately against the farthest wall, watching. Two more were at other urinals. Both the cubicles were occupied and locked, and the elderly man inside one of them was from time to time standing on the toilet seat and popping his head over the partition to look down at the presumably seated occupant next door.

Rex did nothing for some time, other than listlessly knead his cock, allowing it to become semi-erect. One of the wall leaners approached him, leant over, and proffered a tentative backhand towards his groin. Rex batted it away. The advance was too clumsy, and too conspicuous, and the man was anyway unattractively overweight.

Rex tucked his softening dick back into his pants, zipped up, left the erstwhile wall leaner at the urinal, and strolled slowly across the room, taking a position in a corner by the washbasins. There was no one here whom he found remotely appealing. But he was in no rush.

He looked at his watch. It was almost 1.30pm. Depending on how long this took, he would have to come up with an excuse for Jill. Perhaps he would pop in at a pub on his way home after all, for a swift half but no more, so as to be able to tell her that he had gone for a drink, a claim that the smell of lager on his breath would corroborate, if she noticed it. Maybe he would attempt to hug or even kiss her as soon as he saw her, so as to make sure she caught a telltale whiff of Hofmeister. If she also regarded his beery lunge as an amorous bid for forgiveness, and welcomed it as a sign of contrition, so much the better.

He had been cottaging since his teens. He had never admitted it to anyone, but he was not ashamed of it. He was not gay, he thought, and perhaps not even bisexual. He was nothing like John Inman or Larry Grayson, he had fancied women in the past, he still fucked Jill every Saturday night – or perhaps every other Saturday night – but he liked messing around with guys, too. His sex life was therefore a sporadic one, consisting of unadventurous and mechanical fortnightly couplings with his chubby wife, interspersed with clandestine fumblings with strangers in men's toilets. But he had become accustomed to it, and it suited him. He hankered for love affairs with neither women nor men, and neither did he want more or better sex with Jill.

He worried about being caught, though. He had read stories in the *Willesden and Brent Chronicle* about local chaps being arrested, charged, tried, found guilty and even briefly imprisoned for gross indecency in public conveniences, and he had noticed that not only were the men's names published, but their addresses, too. He cursed the singularity of his silly forename, and not for the first time found himself wishing his parents had called him John or Mark or Paul. It was possible that a trial of a John

Davis or a Mark Davis or a Paul Davis might not attract much attention, but a trial of a Rex Davis, especially a Rex Davis of 67 Manor House Drive, would be distinctive indeed.

Perhaps the danger was part of the reward. A few years ago he had read an article in *The Lancet* that had put forward the theory that habitual risk takers' brains contained fewer dopamine-inhibiting receptors than is the norm, dopamine being the neurotransmitter that makes human beings feel pleasure, meaning that such people are predisposed to pleasure-seeking even when seeking pleasure is plainly unsafe. Such fellows – for they are mostly men, apparently – tend to like adventure sports, drive cars or ride motorbikes faster than most other people, enjoy gambling large stakes, and recurrently place themselves in compromising positions when looking for sexual thrills.

Rex wondered about this, but not for long. Besides, there was nothing he could do about it. Perhaps his brain was awash with dopamine, perhaps it was not. All he knew now was that he was feeling horny. One of the cubicle doors had opened, and the elderly man was edging his way out, ostentatiously buttoning up his flies as he did so. Rex moved fast, faster than the others caught napping, and slipped into the momentarily empty cubicle almost as the old boy was sidling out of it. Rex bolted the door, hung his jacket on a protruding rivet on the overhead cistern, pulled his jeans and pants down to his ankles, and began to masturbate, taking in the homoerotic, anatomical, genital and even diagrammatic graffiti on the cubicle walls as he did so.

As was the case in most cottages these days, council workers were in the habit of boarding-up glory holes here more or less as soon as cottagers had bored them. Rex had never made so bold as to create a hole in a cubicle partition himself – a tiresome, lengthy and hazardous chore surely – but he had many times availed himself of the amenity created for him and others by braver souls. Today, sure enough, a fresh aperture had been cut, a roughly circular opening of about two inches' diameter, and through the hole his neighbour had extended an index finger, which now beckoned him rhythmically and persistently.

Rex was hard now, and he wasted no time. He pushed his dick through the hole, and, gritting his teeth in dreaded readiness for the gay-basher's machete chop that he had always feared but had never come, instead felt the familiar sensation of moist, welcoming lips. The guy on the other side of the partition knew what he was doing, and Rex did not take long to come. As he did so, his partner did not flinch; their conjunction was completed efficiently and without spillage.

Rex pulled up his pants and jeans, zipped up, put his jacket on, unbolted the cubicle door, and walked over to the washbasins. Laboriously and carefully he soaped his hands, and washed them at length. He was motivated not so much by a craving to rid himself of germs – although, now that his ardour had been sated by orgasm, the seedy filthiness of these places had the power to disgust him as much as to enthral him – but by the desire once again to be seen to be engaged in an activity for which purpose the building and its facilities had been designed. In other words, if a policeman were to enter now, he would be found to be doing nothing more unusual than washing his hands.

He shuffled over to a wall-mounted roller-towel unit and began meticulously to dry all his fingers and both his thumbs, waiting three times for the click that indicated that the mechanism was ready to dispense more towel roll, and duly using four lengths of it as he did so.

While he was waiting for click number three, he heard a cubicle door being unbolted and opened behind him, and the sound of footsteps – presumably those of the man who had recently so efficiently fellated him. Rex did not look over his shoulder at his departing accomplice, but instead continued to stare at the roller-towel unit and finish drying his hands. There was no need, nor even any desire on his part, to put a face to the encounter.

Rex checked his reflection in the mirror on the wall above the washbasins – his carefully trimmed designer stubble looked particularly crisp today, he thought – and walked out into the street, turning towards home. As he looked ahead down Harrow Road, he stopped dead. About fifty yards in front of him, walking rapidly away from him and now turning left onto Wrottesley Road, was a young man whose back view he recognised: red baseball cap worn jauntily backwards, black puffer jacket, faded blue jeans hugging slim hips, white trainers, bulky blue sports bag, and an unmistakable gait. Rex turned away and began to walk rapidly in the opposite direction from the young man.

Chapter 2

"Hi Mum, Dad," Danny shouted as he opened the front door and let himself in.

"Darling, you're home," Jill replied, walking out of the kitchen into the hallway, beaming.

"Yeah, that's obvious, ain't it?"

"Very funny, darling. How was football? Don't say 'ain't.'"

Danny laughed, hanging his puffer jacket on a coat hook, popping his baseball cap on the banister newel, then climbing the stairs, dragging his sports bag behind him, step by thumping step.

"I asked you a question, Danny. Where are you going?"

"It was OK. We lost one-nil. Toilet," Danny shouted from the first-floor landing.

13

He pissed, washed his hands, brushed his teeth, flossed, gargled mouthwash, then walked back downstairs, leaving his bag on the landing.

"Where's Dad, Mum?"

Jill removed Danny's baseball cap from the banister newel and hung it on a coat hook. "I've no idea where you father is. Dump your kit in your dirty-clothes basket and put your bag away."

"I will, later. We're s'posed to be playing snooker in a bit."

"Well, I don't know where he is."

"How come?"

"Leave it, please, Danny."

"Ah, you've had a row."

"I said leave it, Danny, please. Did you score?"

Danny paused. "Er, no. I told you we lost one-nil. How could I have scored? Well, unless I scored an own goal, and I never." He chuckled again and gave his mother a hug, which she reciprocated.

Jill was not a football fan, or indeed a devotee of sport of any kind, but she was proud of her son's athletic prowess. Nonetheless, Danny had been momentarily thrown by her question. After all, he had scored, if serially bringing to orgasm five penises in a toilet cubicle on Harrow Road, his ministrations invisible to their owners, could be described as scoring.

He felt he was OK with being gay, a consideration whose validity was franked in his mind by his being immutably and increasingly horny for cock, but he was pleased that he was what he gathered was called "straight-acting". He had

14

been aware of his attraction to his own sex since puberty, which was a good five years ago now, but he had come out to only one person, his best friend, Kimberly Coleman, a fellow sixth-former at Hampstead Comprehensive. That had been easy enough, because Kimberly had conceived that she might be a lesbian and had shared that notion with only one person: Danny. Their gayness was their secret. Neither of them could imagine how gay men or lesbians ever dared to come out to straight friends, colleagues or neighbours, let alone parents. They realised that Elton John and Boy George were gay, and they had heard rumours about Jimmy Somerville and even George Michael, but it was easy for millionaire pop stars. It appeared to be OK for female tennis players, too, such as Billie Jean King and Martina Navratilova. They were allowed. Normal people were not, really, at least not in the world that Danny and Kimberly inhabited. When Rock Hudson had died of AIDS four years ago, Danny had sat in silence during the TV news reports, his tummy in knots, while his father had guffawed about it, delighting in referring to AIDS always as "arsehole-injected death sentence". Jill had scolded Rex's uncouth witticism, but she had added, "Such a handsome man. We all thought he was a real dish back in the day. Silly bugger only had himself to blame, though, running around after queers, pathetic really."

"Well, at least you didn't score an own goal, darling," said Jill, while Danny walked into the living room, switched on the telly, and tuned it to *Grandstand* on BBC1, where was revealed ice hockey instead of the world championship snooker he had been hoping to find. He knew next to nothing about ice hockey but nonetheless contentedly watched the players sliding around, thudding into one another, presumably hunky when stripped of all that padding, Danny imagined. "Any chance of a cup of tea, Mum?" he shouted.

"I'm making us one already," Jill called back from the kitchen.

Danny fell asleep. Jill brought him his tea, set it down on the coffee table in front of him, but did not wake him. She drank hers alone in the kitchen.

*

"Hi, Jill," called Rex, opening the front door the best part of an hour later, which greeting woke Danny up. He reached out, lifted his cuppa to his lips, and tasted then spurned the now tepid liquid.

"Hi, Dad," he shouted, without turning his head in his father's direction, his gaze once again trained on the telly.

"Hi, son," said Rex, hanging up his jacket, walking past the open living room door, and raising a hand in greeting, unseen by Danny. He stopped for a moment, hesitated, turned, took a step back towards the living room, stopped again, then turned again and walked on towards the kitchen, where he knew Jill would be.

"Have you calmed down now, Rex?" she asked.

"Yeah, stress, I think, work's been tough lately, as you know," Rex replied, walking up to Jill and essaying a hug, which she endured, albeit twisting her head away from his attempted kiss.

"Your work isn't as tough as mine, never has been. Isn't it a bit early to be drinking?" she asked rhetorically, shrugging herself loose of his embrace to study his face from an improved vantage point, the better to discern whether he was actually drunk. He was not, she decided. She enjoyed drinking, sometimes to excess, but she adhered strictly to a rule that she had made for herself: no alcohol before 6.00pm except on Christmas Day. Having said that, it was very rare that the clinking of ice cubes being dropped into a large gin 'n' tonic could not be heard in the Davis kitchen by 6.01pm on every other day of the year.

Rex ignored the question, satisfying himself that his alibi had been successfully established and unwilling to be drawn into a conversation in which he might be required to provide further details of his recent whereabouts. He walked back into the hallway, and leant on the banister rail, where he stood still, thinking. The truth was that he had drunk quite a lot more than the tactical swift half he had planned to have.

*

After Rex had left the Harrow Road toilet, he half-walked-half-ran to the nearest pub, finding the College Park on the corner of Scrubs Lane, a large and run-down establishment full of Irishmen in dirty workmen's uniforms braying at one another over pints of Guinness, and West Indians in oversized beanies and tams playing dominoes. It was not his kind of place at all. But he drank two pints of Hofmeister and two double whisky chasers in short succession, in an effort to calm his nerves.

They did not do the trick. There was no getting away from what he had just done, what he had unwittingly been party to. He saw that his hands were trembling, and he felt his shirt clinging, clammy, to his back. He looked around him wildly. What would these men think of him if they knew what he had just done with his own flesh and blood? They would probably lynch him, he reckoned, and he could not blame them.

But the question that was troubling him most grievously was whether or not Danny had recognised him. Surely – oh, please god – he had not. The only part of his body that the boy had seen had been one he had never set eyes on before, definitely not in an engorged state anyway, and certainly could not therefore recognise. On the other hand, if Danny had turned and looked to his right as he had walked from cubicle to street, he would have seen his father's back view while he was washing his hands. Would Danny have done that, or would he have instead hurried out, head bowed, the better to make a rapid and discreet escape?

Within an hour Rex would know. Danny would be either normal or in some kind of a state. It would be immediately clear. Rex began to pray that Danny had not seen him, then chided himself for doing so, not only because he was an atheist but also because, selfish though he often suspected he was, he understood that from an objective point of view there were other issues just as important as whether or not he had got away with yet another sexual indiscretion, albeit the daddy of all sexual indiscretions. He shuddered: "daddy" was not a word he wanted even to frame in a thought right now.

"What the fuck was Danny thinking of?" Rex exclaimed – and he realised that he had cried the exclamation out loud, the quartet of Rastafarians on a neighbouring table briefly pausing their game of dominoes to cast him perplexed and pitying stares.

"Cheer up, it might never happen," a barmaid chirruped, gathering up his empty second pint jar as she passed.

"It just has," Rex replied, staring into his second whisky glass. She shrugged and walked on.

He knew that he would have to go home soon. He was aware that he would have to try to pick up his life where he had left it. But nothing in his cosy, if duplicitous, existence felt normal any more. He briefly toyed with the idea of suicide, but dismissed it just as quickly. He could stamp on a spider easily enough, but he had been frightened to kill a mouse when Jill, horrified, had pointed one out to him in their kitchen some years ago. She had had to tackle it herself, breaking its back with a well-aimed swipe of her broom, then carrying its corpse by the tail to the dustbin outside. He had been impressed. No, he felt sure he could never kill an animal as large as a human being, not even himself. He would not dare. Despite being a risk taker he was also a slave to his own cowardice, he knew that, but he consoled himself with the thought that most people put themselves first when the chips were down.

A pretty but rough-looking woman in her late teens or early twenties walked up to the bar, and began talking to the landlord, a large Irishman incongruously holding a hurley. Rex could not hear what the young woman was saying – she looked nervous and was speaking quietly, her eyes darting to left and right – but the landlord's Kerry brogue was one that carried naturally, and it soon became clear to Rex and the men sitting near him that the girl was a stripper who was about to strut her stuff on the bar top. Rex's neighbours began whooping and hollering. Rex drank up, stood up, and left.

*

Rex relaxed his grip on the banister rail, to which he had been clinging for some minutes, and stood alone beside it for a few seconds more. He could see Danny's back view, where he was sitting on the sofa, watching telly. Suddenly, another ghastly realisation hit him: Danny must also have sucked off the old man whose place he, Rex, had taken in the cubicle. He felt overwhelmed by the freakish hideousness of the position into which he had so suddenly been thrust. Jill passed him, carrying three teacups on a tray. "You OK?" she asked him.

Rex shook his head from side to side like a wet dog emerging from a river, and walked into the living room after her. "Yeah, yeah, fine. Hi, Danny," he replied.

"Hi, Dad."

"I didn't know you liked ice hockey, son," Rex ventured.

"I don't really, but there's nothing else on."

"The snooker should be on again soon," said Rex.

Jill put the tea tray on the coffee table, picked up her teacup, sat down on the sofa next to Danny, and quickly engrossed herself in the *Radio Times*. A silence developed.

"Ah," Jill began, "after this silly sport..." – she waved a disdainful hand at the ice hockey – "... there'll be horse racing, then snooker at 4.00pm. And snooker continues on BBC2 after *Grandstand* comes to an end on BBC1."

"We playing snooker later, Dad?" Danny asked.

"Maybe, yeah."

Danny did not reply.

"How was your football?" Rex asked, the quietude between them becoming unbearable for him. He sat down on an armchair.

"It was OK."

"You win?"

"No."

"What was the score?"

"One-nil."

Rex was slowly beginning to feel just a little less dreadful. Danny's replies were the frugal ejaculations that were his usual conversational fare whenever his parents attempted to chat to him while he was watching telly. The signs of inner anguish surely they were not. Rex decided to tease for more evidence. "I've been in the pub. I'm a little bit pissed. Don't tell your mother..." – Jill looked up, sighed theatrically, smiled thinly, then returned to the *Radio Times* – "... but, OK, yeah, I guess if you want to play snooker later then, yeah, why not?"

Danny looked up at his father, and grinned. "Yeah?"

"You fancy it? You'll probably win. I'm a bit pissed, as I say."

"I'd probably win even if you were sober," Danny replied.

"Cheeky sod," said Rex, reaching over to clip the boy around the ear, but gently.

"Oi, Dad, leave off," Danny yelped, but he was laughing as he said it. "OK, yeah, let's play a few frames."

Rex felt an overwhelming sensation of relief – Danny's wry, cheery, unembellished responses were encouragingly normal – and he was becoming therefore increasingly confident that he had got away with his crime, his abomination, his violation. Assuming he had done so, there and then he resolved to cast the afternoon's terrible incident from his mind for ever. Yes, that was what he must do. His life would be unliveable otherwise. There was no point in his trying to cope with the many horrific problems it had hurled at him – at the two of them, at the three of them actually. No, the issue of Danny's sexuality, a subject to which Rex had never given any proper thought before, and which he had never discussed in any detail with Jill – they had both assumed their son was straight, in the usual way, and that Kimberly was a girlfriend whose status in his life he was as yet too shy to share with them – would have to go hang. Specifically, the challenge of learning that he had a fellow cottage queen for a son would have to go hang, too.

"You two boys off out to play snooker then?" asked Jill, walking out into the hallway with her empty teacup.

"Yeah, come on, Dad," said Danny.

"Let me watch the horse racing first, it's Ascot, then the snooker, for a bit anyway, it's the world championship," Rex replied. "I need time to sober up. But, yeah, we'll play snooker in a bit, deffo. We said 6.00pm, didn't we?"

Danny nodded. Rex found horse racing boring unless he had had a bet on it, which he had not, but the booze was beginning to make him sleepy, and he fancied doing nothing for a bit. He dozed off, as did Danny, his second catnap of the afternoon. They slept through the transition from horse racing to snooker, and were awoken by Jill at 5.40pm, by which time *Rolf Harris Cartoon Time* had replaced sport on BBC1.

"I'll get your snooker cues," she said, fetching them from the umbrella stand by the front door, where she had placed them temporarily, and extending both her arms, handing Rex's expensive aluminium cue case and Danny's cheaper nylon jobbie to their respective owners. She tossed Danny his baseball cap, correctly guessing that he would not have remembered where he had put it, nor have noticed that it had moved.

Rex yawned, but Danny was already on his feet. Rex stood up. Jill watched them as they gathered their jackets, opened the front door, and walked out of the house, over the gravel and onto Manor House Drive. "Let's stroll, I'm probably still over the limit. It's not far and the fresh air will sober me up," she heard Rex tell Danny as they paused outside the garage. Yes, Rex could be a pain, he was undoubtedly self-centred, and she might have hoped for a more passionate husband, but he earned a lot of money, her parents and friends liked him, and he was a sound and dutiful father to the sweet, friendly, good-natured son he had given her, and for all that she was thankful.

She went into the kitchen and began to mix herself a large gin 'n' tonic.

CHAPTER 3

A TELEPHONE CABLE STRETCHED ATOP
A LATE-VICTORIAN OAK WRITING TABLE

Jill took her gin 'n' tonic into the living room and sat down on the sofa. It was 6.01pm. *Rolf Harris Cartoon Time* had been succeeded on BBC1 by *MacGyver*, an American serial, which she watched abstractedly for a few minutes.

She drained her first gin 'n' tonic. She was feeling peckish, so she went into the kitchen where she decanted a few handfuls of salted peanuts into a bowl, made herself another gin 'n' tonic, put the lot on a tray and took it into the living room. She wished she had told Rex and Danny to be home by 8.30pm, so that she could plan for them all to have dinner together at that hour prior to watching *Yes Minister* at 9.30pm, which she and Rex both adored; but she had forgotten to do so. Perhaps they would come home at about that time anyway. They would surely be hungry, after all. Did snooker halls serve snacks? Jill did not know.

She decided to put a wash on, so that it would be finished, their damp clothes hung out on the drying rack in the scullery, by the time she began to cook dinner. She found the churning drone of the washing machine annoying and preferred to time its operations for when she did not have to be in the kitchen. She went upstairs to collect the dirty-clothes baskets, and saw Danny's sports bag where he had left it on the landing. She unzipped it, then stopped. Instead of the jumbled and mud-spattered football kit that she had expected to have to tackle, and had tackled so often, she found his shirt, shorts and socks absolutely pristine, neatly folded, alongside a dry towel carefully rolled, and his clean boots, shin pads and jockstrap tucked tidily alongside. They were exactly as she had organised them for him this morning. The Tupperware box in which she had packed his lunch was now empty, however, save for a few crumbs.

She heaved the dirty-clothes baskets downstairs and put a wash on, leaving Danny's sports bag on the landing, open, its contents unmolested. She made herself a third gin 'n' tonic and began to drink it on her feet, in the kitchen, leaning her back against the fridge door.

It made no sense. If Danny's football match had been cancelled, where had he been between 9.30am and 2.00pm? And why had he not revealed that it had been cancelled? Why, indeed, had he said that his team had lost one-nil?

Or had he been a substitute, and had not played at all, instead sitting in his kit on the subs' bench throughout the match, and therefore not getting it dirty? Perhaps he had been too embarrassed to admit to that humiliation, frustrated as he would have been not to be included in the initial eleven that had taken the field, and doubly disappointed not to have superseded one of them for the second half? But he was too good a player for that to be likely. Besides, even if it were the case, why was his kit stowed exactly as she had arranged it for him? Danny was an eighteen-year-old boy; even if he had wanted to, he would not have been able to unpack, wear and repack his kit as neatly as had she, a forty-one-year-old wife and mother, given to paying extravagant attention to presentational detail.

She glanced at the clock. It was 7.20pm. She went upstairs, putting the dirty-clothes baskets back in their places as she went, one in her and Rex's en-suite bathroom and the other in Danny's bedroom, picked up Danny's sports bag, zipped it shut, and carried it into her and Rex's bedroom, where she set it beside their bed on her side. She then went downstairs, hung out the washing, and began to make dinner.

She regarded herself as a decent cook. Tonight she was planning chicken kievs with rice. As she readied her ingredients – a process she was proud to call *mise en place* – she wondered whether she should confront Danny as soon as he and Rex arrived home, but she quickly decided not to. If Danny's explanation turned out to be one that he would be embarrassed about, she would prefer to hear it without Rex present. Rex would be no help and might even mock their son, teasing him for having lied about being a substitute, perhaps even taking the opportunity to regale them with stories of the footballing glories of his own youth. No, she would bide her time. She pre-heated the oven and poured herself a fourth gin 'n' tonic.

She was aware that her default attitude to Rex was to expect little from him and thereby remain sanguine enough when he failed to deliver more than she had anticipated, and she had long ago abandoned any hope of being positively surprised by anything he might say or do, particularly when it was directed towards herself. However, he was nice to Danny, and he had founded and still owned and ran an eponymous publishing house – RED Publishing Ltd, denoting Rex Everton Davis – but it was duller than it sounded because it produced only trade magazines, read exclusively by professionals who plied those trades, such as *Tractor Accessory Trader*, *Geo Drilling Review*, *Packaging World* and even *Parking Weekly*. Jill had often wondered how the hapless staff of the latter found material enough to fill an entire magazine on the subject of parking fifty-one times a year (there was no issue in Christmas week), but at a recent dinner party Rex had described it as "seriously remunerative" so they clearly managed it and their readers evidently lapped it up in healthy numbers. Indeed, RED was more profitable than quite a few publishing houses that produced magazines one had actually heard of, which was how they were able to live in a house that had been valued recently at £600,000 and drive a new top-of-the-range BMW (him), an immaculate '60s Chevrolet Corvette Sting Ray (him), a new Suzuki sports motorcycle (him) and a nearly new Volvo estate (her).

Equally, although Jill worked hard to try to make her Camden Passage antiques shop a money-making concern, the truth was that it was solvent at best and sometimes even made a loss. Without the money that Rex brought in, it would be an unsustainable self-indulgence; but she loved it. She specialised in nineteenth-century campaign furniture, military chests, trunks and gentlemen's club and hotel furnishings. In the past she had bought items because she had fallen in love with them at auction, had duly paid too much for them, and could not then sell them without making an embarrassingly sizeable loss. They had therefore been parked at 67 Manor House Drive and had passed into daily use there, where Rex sometimes tutted at them, feeling they jarred with the more modernist furniture that dominated their abode, and which he favoured.

She had opened the shop a year or so after Danny had started primary school, finding her days suddenly home alone almost unbearably unstimulating. Indeed, some months before that, she and Rex had had something of a relationship crisis, or blip, a result of her having had a brief affair with her personal trainer, Jaden Carpenter, a brawny Tobagonian five years her junior. When Rex had found out about it he had not been noticeably upset, but his pride had clearly been wounded and he had therefore vehemently insisted that she discuss it with no one; but he had said nothing whatsoever about it otherwise, with only two exceptions. "I s'pose he's got big muscles and a massive rock-hard cock," he had observed with a sneer on the day of his discovery, to which dual suggestion she had responded with a shrug and more tears, thereby managing not to reveal either that his guess had been accurate on both counts or that his very description had sent a ripple of wistful rapture through her body and soul. The next day he had added, without preamble, "And don't you ever even think about having a personal fucking trainer ever again." Without specifically demanding it, he had assumed that she would end things with Jaden, and she had; immediately. Over the next few weeks Rex had sulked a bit, and had gone out alone a lot, but he had said no more. Life had returned to normal surprisingly quickly, without any determined effort being made by either of them to repair whatever fractures in their relationship had tempted Jill into Jaden's arms. But that was thirteen years ago now, and she and Rex had never once discussed the matter since.

Rex had always been a handsome man, lean but well muscled even as a teenager, and Jill had fancied him rotten when they had first met, on 16 June 1970, her twenty-third birthday, when he had been only eighteen. He and a pal had journeyed to north London from the Wirral, where they had both been raised and still lived, to see the first Test Match between England and the Rest of the World, which would begin at Lord's the following day, and had been the last to leave an impromptu post-pub party that Jill and her flatmate Linda Norris had thrown in their Gospel Oak flat, which the two boys had attended solely as a result of having been playing pool with some of Jill's and Linda's friends at closing time. Nonetheless they had slept with Jill and Linda that night. Linda had neither seen nor heard of her fleeting paramour thereafter, but four months later Jill had discovered that she was pregnant, and had tracked Rex down to inform him. When they had heard about it Rex's parents had been furious, Jill's very upset. At the insistence of his father, a lower-middle-class Tory who admired Enoch Powell and loathed what he called "the permissive society", Rex had done the decent thing by offering to marry Jill almost at once, to which suggestion she had in some desperation and under pressure from her parents agreed. A small wedding had taken place before her bump had become visible, and their parents' friends and neighbours either did not notice that Danny had been born only five months after the nuptials, did not care, or were too polite to mention it.

Rex never therefore went to university, a deprivation that he minded at the time but had accommodated since by becoming not only professionally successful, and therefore rather rich, but also a prodigious reader of non-fiction, often at work, where he would shut his office door and immerse himself in an improving text for a couple of hours or more, leaving the running of his company to a small number of capable lieutenants. He challenged himself always to answer more questions than did Jill, a history graduate, whenever they watched *University Challenge* or *Mastermind* together, and he almost always succeeded. His knowledge was truly general, hers unusually specific, her forte nineteenth-century English architecture, furniture, pottery, chinaware, glassware and jewellery, although she was not bad on English literature of the same era and, a stubborn enthusiasm of hers, English grammar and syntax. She was no better on music or art than he was, and hopeless on science and sport, while geography was a total blind spot for her. Rex often chided her for what he called her directional dyslexia, which he had read was an actual thing.

Jill always drank while she cooked dinner, and the reminiscences that her solitary drinking triggered usually engrossed her. They had done so this evening, right enough, except that she had been plagued all the while by her concerns about Danny's spotless football kit. She glanced at the clock again. It was 8.10pm. She fried the chicken kievs for three minutes each side until they were golden-brown, then put them on a baking tray and popped it into the oven. She laid the table and opened a bottle of red Le Piat d'Or, which she placed in the middle of the table to *chambrer*, another culinary Frenchism she favoured. If Rex and Danny came home when she hoped they would, they would be eating at about 8.35pm, she calculated.

"Jill?" Rex called by way of a greeting, opening the front door at 8.40pm, hanging his jacket and leaning his cue case against the wall as he entered.

"Good," Jill responded, shouting her reply from the kitchen. "Dinner's ready. Let's eat."

She carried all three plates into the living room, one in each hand and the third balanced on her forearm in the manner of professional waiting staff, and lowered them onto the table where she had set places for them. "Where's Danny?" she asked.

"Oh, he went to Kimberly's," Rex replied.

"But I thought we were going to eat together. I've cooked. Look, there's his plate."

"Well, you didn't tell us."

"What d'you mean, 'You didn't tell us'? We always eat together on a Saturday evening."

"Not every Saturday evening."

"Every Saturday evening unless one of us has prearranged something else, always," she said, her voice rising in volume.

"OK, OK," Rex replied, and went to the downstairs loo.

Jill was not very drunk, but neither was she remotely sober, and insobriety always emboldened her. She stood outside the toilet door and began to address it.

"Ridiculous. Why can't you ever just be normal? We've had two meals today, and you've messed up both of them, one way or another. You should've told Danny to come home with you. If you weren't such a selfish prick you'd have known I'd be cooking for us all."

Jill swore rarely, and only when she had not only been drinking but was also ready for a row. "Come out of there and sit down," she said. "Let's eat it now or it'll get cold. I'll heat Danny's up when he gets home."

"He's an adult, you know," Rex replied, flushing the toilet, washing his hands and opening the door. "I don't know why it's such a disaster, or indeed my fault, that he decided to pop in on his girlfriend – er, on Kimberly – on his way home. He can think for himself, you know. And he won't be long."

"He's our child," Jill replied. "You're his father. You're my husband. Both roles involve duty. All you had to do was say, 'Home time now, please, Danny.' But oh no. You couldn't do that. Even the simplest things you always manage to fuck up."

Rex considered telling his wife to pipe down. She was being stupid, after all. But he did not have the heart for a shouting match with her, especially not now. He was feeling good. Despite the lager and whisky he had drunk earlier, he had beaten Danny three-two, both of them playing well, and they had enjoyed their match. Danny had compiled a fifty-four break in their second frame, which had pleased him immoderately, but Rex had gone for and potted a risky long red when Danny had tucked him up on the baulk cushion in the final frame and had then made a break of thirty that had included two flukes and had won him frame and match. Moreover, they had chatted amiably throughout their two and a half hours together, and Rex was now absolutely certain that Danny had not seen his back view at the washbasins earlier that afternoon.

He sat down at the table, where Jill had already begun eating. "This is lovely. Veal escalope, is it?" Rex asked, tucking in.

"No. Not even close. Chicken kiev. I don't know why I bother," Jill answered.

"Danny'll be along soon, I'm sure," Rex replied.

"You never know with Danny these days," said Jill.

Rex allowed a pause to develop, considered, then decided not to respond to this conspicuously peculiar remark.

"I said," said Jill, taking a large swig of Le Piat d'Or, "you never know with Danny these days." She glared at Rex over the top of her wine glass, awaiting an answer.

"I don't know what you mean. He's a good chap," he replied.

Jill realised she had now embarked on a subject that she had intended not to broach until she could speak to Danny alone, but she had found herself unable to resist bowling Rex this googly, if only to unsettle his irritating *sang froid* in the face of her anger with him.

"You used to play football, didn't you?"

Rex did not respond.

"I just said – so listen and answer, please – I just said, 'You used to play football, didn't you?'"

"I did indeed, but d'you mind me asking where you're going with this?"

"Well, did you ever play a football match and afterwards your boots, socks, shorts and shirt were as clean as a new pin, as though they'd been starched for a Persil ad?"

"Obviously not."

"Exactly," said Jill, and took their dirty plates, knives and forks into the kitchen.

"It's *Yes Minister* in a mo," Rex shouted after her, but she did not answer.

Rex was unnerved. She could not know what Danny had been doing instead of playing football, even if she had rumbled the falsehood of that alibi, but perhaps she had something else to unburden herself of, and as sure as eggs is eggs he did not want to hear it. No, it could not be what he dreaded it just possibly might be – there was no way she could know about *that* – but, even so, he did not want to be having a *tête-à-tête* with her about Danny's internal world, not now, not today, probably not ever. Any such conversation would be too dangerous for him for the foreseeable future; it was a case of least said soonest mended. So it was that he was relieved when he heard Danny's key turning in the front door, and he duly sprang up, the better to make sure that he would not have to suffer part two of whatever inquisition Jill had in mind without their son's magically pacifying presence. "Hi, son," he said, greeting Danny in the hallway, taking his cue case off him, and leaning it against the wall alongside his own.

Jill skipped out of the kitchen to greet Danny, and whipped his jacket and cap off him as though she were a footman in the lobby of a swanky restaurant. "I'll heat up your chicken kiev, darling," she said.

"Great. I love your chicken kiev, Mum," Danny replied, which triggered Jill's first smile for some hours.

"Where've you been, darling?" she asked, walking back into the kitchen to plate up Danny's dinner.

"Er, I called in on Kimberly," Danny replied.

"I told you that," said Rex.

"How is she, darling?" said Jill, ignoring Rex's interjection.

"Fine, fine," said Danny, sauntering into the living room and sitting at the table as Jill set down a steaming plate in front of him.

"*Yes Minister* is just about to start," said Rex, and walked over to the telly to retune it to BBC2. He and Jill sat down on the sofa and began to watch. Soon, Jill was chuckling. But shortly after that she was snoring, slouched on the sofa, her head tilted way back on its backrest, her fleshy neck exposed inelegantly.

"I'm going to bed," said Danny, already rising as he spoke.

"Night, son," Rex answered, and continued to watch Paul Eddington's and Nigel Hawthorne's excellent, if stagey, portrayals of Whitehall tomfoolery. Jill was still asleep. Rex was pleased to find that he could lose himself in the comedy, despite his roller-coaster of a day, and at one point he guffawed, which awoke his wife.

"Where's Danny?" she asked, sitting up.

"Bed," said Rex.

"Oh, OK," said Jill. "I'm going to the loo."

Since she wanted more than a pee, she shunned the ground-floor toilet, instead climbing the stairs so as to use the main bathroom, whence odours would not permeate downstairs. As she did so, she saw that Danny had taken the upstairs phone into his bedroom, the late-Victorian oak writing table on which it usually lived on the landing now bare save for a telephone cable stretched atop it and disappearing under Danny's bedroom door, beneath which no light was visible.

Jill knew that she should not snoop on her son, but her curiosity got the better of her. Besides, the coast was clear. Rex was absorbed in *Yes Minister*, and as she approached Danny's bedroom door she could hear his voice, whispering but animated.

She knelt, pressed her ear to the keyhole, and began to listen. She soon divined that Danny was talking to Kimberly. He was beginning an anecdote – no, a saga. He giggled often, and she heard him saying, "It was fucking awesome" and "I totally loved it" and "I promise you I ain't exaggerating". Jill listened intently, and what she heard, which took Danny nearly twenty minutes to relate in lurid detail, horrified her. She began to cry. When she realised that her sobs might be audible, she crept away from Danny's bedroom door and went to bed.

CHAPTER 4

A RED NISSAN BLUEBIRD
IN A QUEEN'S PARK SIDE STREET

Danny had not popped in on Kimberly after playing snooker with Rex, although that is what he had told his father he was going to do. No, when Rex had hailed a black taxi outside the snooker club on Kilburn High Road, near which Kimberly lived with her parents, Danny had headed straight for the Harrow Road cottage, a thirty-five-minute walk that he had done in less than half the time by running it, eager to experience a repeat of his morning's sexual diversions. However, he had found it closed, and had therefore jogged home disappointedly, arriving three-quarters of an hour or so after Rex had done.

Since then, however, Danny had been aching to tell Kimberly about his latest sexual escapade. They shared almost everything with each other – and, having no one else to talk to about sex, or even gayness, Danny relished their heart-to-hearts. As for Kimberly, she took vicarious pleasure in her friend's developing sex life, was awed by his increasing intrepidity, and was unsqueamish about even its most graphic details. In turn she shared her private hopes and fears with him, including her increasing certitude that her life would be complete only when she had found herself a pretty and adoring girlfriend. She had not yet had sex with anyone, female or male, although she had snogged a couple of drunk girls at a recent party in Maida Vale and had found the experience more sensual than they had appeared to have done. They had been playing to the gallery, mostly leering boys, she had thought.

Danny was not a virgin. He had messed around with a couple of his male schoolfriends when they had simultaneously fallen victim to the burning exigencies of early teenage horniness, but that kind of horseplay had petered out once those mates had gained the confidence to turn their attentions to girls, who were the actual objects of their desires. Between the ages of fifteen and eighteen, therefore, Danny had had a thin time of it, a three-year libidinal interregnum characterised by masturbation and loneliness, countervailed only by his friendship with Kimberly and his love of snooker, tennis and, in particular, football, into which he had thrown himself with effort and enthusiasm. He had become a classy outside-right, the star of his school's first eleven, for which he played on Wednesday afternoons and Saturday mornings, and, as a result of the advocacy of a jobbing West Ham United talent scout, John Shaw, had recently begun to play for the amateur Hackney and Leyton Sunday League team, Ordell Arms FC, based in Bow, which was captained by the same John Shaw. Danny found playing for the Ordell Arms eleven more demanding than school football because Ordell's opponents tended to be teams made up of big, strong, experienced men. But he did well against them. Although only a wiry five-foot-eight and therefore neither physically imposing nor good in the air, Danny struck the ball powerfully and was skilful, fit, quick and nimble, so much so that he often embarrassed the tough adult defenders whose vain efforts to tackle him he made look clumsy. After playing in the Hackney and Leyton Sunday League, in fact, school football felt too easy, and he enjoyed ogling his hefty Ordell teammates in the post-match showers more than he did his schoolmates, too.

He had first had full penetrative sex only four months ago, on New Year's Eve, with an athletic and sinewy Tamil minicab driver from Sri Lanka, in his late twenties or early thirties, whom Danny knew only by his minicab call sign, Three-Eight, by which appellation he had heard the controller address him on the base-to-cab radio. Three-Eight had made his intentions plain early in the journey from Trafalgar Square to Manor House Drive, letting his left hand graze and then settle on the inside of Danny's right thigh while hooking third gear as he braked for the Marble Arch roundabout at the north end of Park Lane. At nudging 4.00am he had parked his car on Lonsdale Road, an industrial side street in Queen's Park that was a hive of commercial activity in the daytime but was frequented only by cats and foxes at night, had leant across to recline the front passenger seat on which Danny had been sitting, and had invited Danny to take off his shoes, jeans and pants, adding that he would waive the fare if he complied. Danny had agreed, the waived fare neither here nor there, and, although it had hurt despite Three-Eight's applying liberal amounts of KY Jelly so as to ease his passage, he had found the experience of being fucked like that exhilarating. He had told Kimberly all about it the next day, allaying her one concern with a quick and easy lie when she had asked him whether Three-Eight had used a condom, and his heart had skipped a beat whenever he had spotted a red Nissan Bluebird since. It was Three-Eight who had told him about the Harrow Road cottage, which he had now visited a dozen times or more, albeit never with as prolific success as this morning.

He had finally been able to confess the day's high jinks to Kimberly from his bed, the best part of twelve hours after they had taken place, lying naked and aroused, the phone receiver tucked into the crook of his neck, giving her lively descriptions of all five cocks. He had then carried the phone back to its place on the landing, had gone back to bed, had had a wank, and had fallen asleep.

Meanwhile, his father had nodded off on the sofa in the living room, the telly's post-National Anthem hum-hiss failing to stir him, while his mother had been lying awake in their bedroom, teary eyes wide open, gradually sobering up.

Eventually, at some time after 2.00am, Rex had awoken, glanced around him, got up, switched off the telly, turned off the living room lights, and walked upstairs to his and Jill's bedroom. As he had opened the door, to his surprise he had found her sitting up, propped up by two pillows, her bedside light on.

"Something truly terrible has happened, Rex," she said to him, burst into tears, and held her arms out to be hugged. Having been initially panic-stricken by her greeting, he observed her gesture with relief: even if the "something truly terrible" was that she had somehow found out about Danny's depravity from some as-yet-unknown source, she could not have discovered his part in it, else she would certainly not be looking for him to console her, still less embrace her. He kicked off his shoes, flopped onto the bed beside her, and put his arms around her. She hugged him tightly, in silence, then eventually pulled away and sat up again.

"Our son is a, er, he's, er, a homosexual, Rex," she said, staring straight ahead of her.

"Go on," said Rex, after a pause that he thought would be interpreted as evidence of shocked concern.

"But it's even worse than that. He's a pervert. Disgusting behaviour. Oh, you wouldn't believe it if I told you. Oh, Rex, I'm sorry for being so snappy earlier – I'd had a few gins before dinner – because, I tell you, we're going to need each other's support now. Believe me, we really are."

"OK, love."

"Look, Rex, there's only one way to tell you this, and that's simply to tell it to you, in one breath, so please don't interrupt."

"OK."

"Well, as you know, my suspicions were raised when I found that he hadn't used his football kit. Here it is, as clean as a whistle..." – she reached down and grabbed Danny's shirt and shorts, spreading them out on their duvet – "... and that was odd, I thought, because why had he told us he'd played football when he obviously hadn't? Anyway, when I came upstairs a few hours ago, to go to the loo, which I still haven't done actually, I saw that he'd taken the phone from the landing into his bedroom. Is it on the landing now, by the way?"

"I think so. I dunno."

"Darling, would you go and check?"

Rex got up, opened their bedroom door, and peered down the corridor. He then closed the door and returned to Jill's side. "Yes, it's there."

"Right, well, he must have put it back. But it was in his bedroom earlier, and I heard him talking to Kimberly. I heard everything he said. That girl's no good for him, by the way. We need to end that friendship."

"Why? Oh well, we can come back to that. But, anyway, he'd just seen Kimberly, so why did he have to ring her?" Rex asked.

"He didn't see Kimberly this evening, Rex. That was another lie. He went to, er, to a public lavatory on Harrow Road, but it was closed."

"Why on earth would he do that?" said Rex, congratulating himself on his ability to play dumb so well.

"Because he'd been there this morning, instead of playing football – the match had been cancelled at the last minute because the pitch was waterlogged, you see

– and on his way home he'd gone to this public lavatory, this cottage, he calls it, and he'd locked himself into one of the cubicles and he'd, er, oh, Rex, I can hardly bear to tell you…" – Rex coughed – "… because you'll be so disappointed in him. I don't want to make you hate him, or even be disappointed in him, as I admit I am, very."

Rex decided now was the time to begin to sound noble, masterly even. "Tell me as much or as little as you like. Tell me now or tomorrow or whenever. Danny is our son. We aren't ever going to hate him, whatever he's done."

"Oh, Rex, you're so good, I'm so sorry I'm often so horrid to you."

"Don't worry about that now."

"Well, er, oh, Rex, there was a hole in the wall of the cubicle, and he sat there for two hours waiting for men to poke their penises through it, and when they did he gave them all, you know, er, oral sex."

"All?"

"Well, yes, all. But the number of men is hardly the point, Rex, is it?"

"I guess not," said Rex, but for him in fact it was, because the word "all" rather than "both" had imparted the one significant bit of information of which he had not already been fully aware.

"If you must know, there were five of them, filthy bastards," said Jill, and she began to cry again.

Rex fell silent, then reached over and held Jill's hand. Eventually he said, "OK, look, love, let's get some sleep. It's after 3.00am. Things'll seem better and clearer in the morning. Come on."

Jill paused, then sighed. "To be honest I'm amazed you're not angrier. I thought you'd be furious. I was even frightened you'd march straight into his bedroom and chuck him out on his ear right now. I know you aren't fond of queers. But, OK, you try to get some sleep. I doubt if I'll get any." She kissed him chastely on the lips, switched off her bedside light, and rolled onto her side, her back to him. He undressed and did likewise, his back addressing hers, a clear foot between them. Despite its being Saturday night, they did not make love. Soon Rex was snoring lightly. Jill got up and went to the loo.

CHAPTER 5

A FLAKED SMEAR OF DRIED BLOOD
ON HER RIGHT KNEE

At 6.40am, having barely slept at all, Jill stopped trying to count sheep, sat up, listened for a few moments to Rex's slow, rhythmic breathing, but decided not to wake him. She stood up, put on a dressing gown over her nightie, tiptoed downstairs, and walked to the kitchen.

She felt tired and slightly hungover. She boiled the kettle. She ambled to the French windows that led to the back garden, and looked out. The sun had risen less than an hour ago, and the sky was a pale grey-blue flecked with red. It was what Jill would usually have thought beautiful, but not today. Nothing was beautiful today. She made herself a mug of Maxwell House, tapped a Hermesetas into it, stirred it a couple of times, and began to sip it, standing up.

She had had a bad dream, an alarming nightmare in fact, which she tried to piece together as she drank her coffee. She could not recall it all, but it involved her having murdered a little girl. The killing itself had not been part of her dream, only its aftermath, her sickening guilt, and the grim realisation that she would have to give herself up to the police. She shuddered, shook herself, then walked to the living room, where she began carting last night's dirty plates, cutlery and glasses to the kitchen. She dropped a wine glass on her third trip, and it shattered noisily on the stone kitchen floor tiles. She took a dustpan and brush from the cupboard under the sink, lowered herself ponderously onto all fours, and began to sweep up the shards. She knelt on one, and it cut her right knee, which began to bleed. She tried and failed to fight the urge to cry, and used the brush to flick the last small fragments of glass into the dustpan. A tear dropped onto the floor in front of her. She swept that up, too.

She heaved herself up, tipped the broken glass into the bin, and put the dustpan and brush away. She licked her finger and rubbed her cut. It was still bleeding, but slowly; it would heal without the need of a plaster. She looked at the clock. It was 7.10am. She switched on the radio, which was tuned to LBC, on which a presenter and a pundit whose voices she did not recognise were arguing about what was being referred to as the Hillsborough disaster, in which nearly a hundred Liverpool fans had been crushed to death during an FA Cup semi-final between their team and Nottingham Forest the previous weekend. Jill retuned to Radio 1. She did not want to hear about death, or indeed football, this morning.

She was pleased to hear Rex's heavy footsteps on the staircase about half an hour later, however. As he entered the kitchen, already dressed in a white sweatshirt, black jeans and white trainers, he hugged her, holding her for a few seconds, and said, "You OK, love?"

"Not really," she replied.

"No," he said.

In silence she made him a mug of Maxwell House, and another for herself. As she did so, he stood behind her and massaged her shoulders.

"What are we going to do?" she said, handing him his coffee. They sat down together at the kitchen table.

"Well, I didn't say much last night, because it was late, but, yes, obviously, he's a filthy little shit," Rex replied. "But, even so, do we actually have to do anything? I know it's a worry – a big worry – but is there anything to be gained from, you know, actually doing anything? I dunno. What are you s'posed to do when you find out your son is a queer?"

"It's not so much the queer thing, Rex. Not to me it isn't, anyway. OK, yes, that's an issue, of course it is, but he's only eighteen and he may well grow out of it. Having said that, the way he was talking to that little trollop Kimberly last night, it seems he's kind of, you know, set on it. There was no reticence in his voice, no uncertainty, no trepidation. It was all just graphic details about, well, cocks and cum." Rex thought it best to gasp.

"Oh, I'm sorry," Jill went on, taking his hand in hers. "I s'pose that was a bit crude of me. But that's the language he was using. It was revolting, to be honest. And she was

49

obviously lapping it up, and encouraging him, because he kept giggling at whatever pathetic nonsense she was saying, which of course I couldn't hear."

Rex released Jill's hand and walked to the French windows. "Lovely day," he said. "Ironic, really."

"Yes," Jill replied.

A silence developed. "But d'you see what I mean about maybe not doing anything?" said Rex suddenly. "I mean, let's look at it logically, dispassionately. What would we do if we did something anyway? I mean, what would we actually say to him? You know, 'We've discovered that you like sucking strange men off in toilets, so could you stop doing that, please?' I don't know if that would be effective. It might even be counterproductive."

"Perhaps," Jill replied, "but we need him to stop, don't we? Rex, it's awful, revolting and dangerous. And he's just a child. God knows what's possessed him. Also, there's the issue of AIDS."

"I hadn't thought of that," Rex lied. "Can you get it from, you know, oral sex?"

It so happened that Rex knew very well that most medical experts now agreed that you almost certainly could not, but he had decided to maintain a position of scandalised, baffled, kindly innocence, and he was going to stick to it. For many years he had subscribed to *The Lancet*, which was posted to his office along with a couple of dozen or so other trade magazines, not because he was particularly interested in medicine but because he liked to see what he called "the competition", and *The Lancet* was in his opinion the trade magazine *nonpareil*. He knew, therefore, that his preferred blow-job role, the receiver, was regarded as a zero-risk activity as far as HIV was concerned. Danny's role was only slightly riskier, and even then only if the blow-job giver had cuts or sores in his or her mouth, gum disease or an oral venereal disease, or had had recent dental work, which Danny had not.

"I don't know," Jill answered. "I thought I might ask Dr Mukherjee. If Danny got AIDS I'd die. I really would. Well, he'd die..." – she began to cry again – "... and I'd want to die then, too. Sorry but it's true. I must stop crying. Maybe asking Mukherjee isn't such a good idea. Muslims take a dim view of homosexuality."

"He's Hindu. I don't know if that makes him less anti-gay though."

They laughed, which surprised them both, especially Jill.

"What a thing," she muttered. "It probably does make him less anti-gay, yes, but he's still probably pretty anti, I'd have thought." Another short silence developed. "It's like when people lose loved ones in accidents. Or disasters such as all those football fans getting killed the other day. They always say, 'You never think it's going to happen to you.' Well, that's just how I feel now. Why did this have to happen to us?"

"Yeah, I know," Rex replied.

"I might ask Bernard," said Jill. Bernard Culpepper, a tweedy bachelor in his late fifties, had worked as an assistant in Jill's antiques shop for the past eight years.

"Is he a bender?" asked Rex, silently commending himself for using a term so *passé*.

"Well, I've never actually asked him, but he obviously is," Jill replied. "He shares a flat with another man. They're both rather, you know, effete. Queers, definitely, yes, both of them. But I don't know whether Bernard actually has sex with Geoffrey, I think the man he lives with is called. Yes, Geoffrey. I've only met him a couple of times. No, on second thoughts, I don't think I could ask Bernard about oral sex."

"Or indeed about cocks and cum," said Rex.

"Or indeed about them, no," she replied, "although I'd rather you weren't so flip about it." She stared at him for a while. "Oh, I wish to hell I knew."

"You wish to hell you knew what?" Rex asked.

"If what our son did has put him at risk of getting AIDS, of course." She began to cry yet again, then quickly wiped her eyes with the back of her right hand.

"I'm going out to get the papers," said Rex.

"Oh, don't yet, please. What if he comes down?"

"What d'you mean?"

"Well, if he comes down while you're out, what'll I say?"

"Nothing. Just be normal. But he won't."

"He might. He's got football today, I think. In – where is it? – you know, that place in Essex."

"Bow," said Rex. "Bow isn't in Essex. It's in Tower Hamlets, which is a London borough. But they play in Hackney actually: Hackney Marshes. That isn't in Essex either. Directional dyslexia, Jill."

"I see," she replied, ignoring one of their staple in-jokes. "The East End, is it?"

"Yeah. I'll only be a minute. I'll be back before he's up," said Rex, and walked out of the house, opened the door to the double garage, got into his BMW, fired it up, and drove off towards Willesden High Road.

Jill washed up and began to listen to the radio, which had been on, ignored, throughout the time she had been chatting to Rex. The current number one, 'Eternal Flame' by the Bangles, was playing. Jill liked it, and admired Susanna Hoffs' strong, sweet voice. But the ballad's melody was too doleful for her today, and she switched off the radio before it had finished.

Rex returned with *The Observer* and the *News of the World*. "Why've you bought that rag?" Jill asked him, spying the latter under his arm.

"Danny likes it," Rex replied.

"Does he? He's never told me that."

"Well, he does. He told me last night."

"When?"

"When we were playing snooker. Some of the Ordell Arms guys read it apparently. Does it matter?"

"D'you think he looks at page three?"

"Maybe. Dunno. That's *The Sun*, not the *News of the World*. He says he likes it for the sport."

Jill frowned. "In all the upset of last night I forgot to sort his football kit for him. I haven't made his packed lunch, either. But are we going to let him go out this morning, to play football, I mean?" she asked.

"I don't see how we can stop him. And, as I say, maybe we should do nothing. I certainly don't think we should be too hasty. A knee-jerk reaction is rarely a good one."

"Well, I don't know if he…" Jill began, but she stopped speaking suddenly, having heard the sound of Danny's light but speedy footsteps on the stairs. She looked at the clock. It was 8.15am.

"He's up early," said Rex.

"Must have football obviously," Jill replied as Danny entered the kitchen. "Darling, good morning. You're dressed. I'll make brekkie."

"Not for me. I've got to go. Football. Where's my kit? I can't find it."

"Oh, er, yes," said Jill. "I'll go and get it."

"No, I'll get it," said Danny urgently. "Just tell me where it is."

Jill did not want to tell Danny that most of his kit was laid out across the duvet on her and Rex's bed, so she walked briskly out of the kitchen into the hallway and trotted up the stairs, shouting behind her, "No, I'll get it for you, darling. Rex, make Danny a quick cup of tea before he leaves."

"Ain't got time," Danny replied.

"Don't say 'ain't'," said Rex, which injunction Danny showed no sign of having registered.

Jill darted into her and Rex's bedroom, closed the door, and quickly but neatly repacked Danny's kit. As she did so, she briefly clutched his shirt to her face, breathed in, and kissed it. She then walked downstairs and handed him his repacked bag.

"Ordell Arms kit?" he asked.

"Oh, sorry, no, school kit," Jill answered.

"No, Ordell Arms today, Mum," said Danny.

"Oh, it must be in your chest of drawers, darling. I washed it last week. I haven't had a chance to make a packed lunch for you."

"Right. I never looked there, I only looked in my wardrobe," said Danny, sprinting out of the kitchen and running up the stairs two steps at a time. He flew into his bedroom, rummaged through his drawers, gathered his Ordell Arms clobber, and bolted back down to the hallway, where Jill was now standing, his bag at her feet. She removed his school football kit – shirt, shorts and socks – and took the Ordell Arms counterparts from him, folding and packing them.

Rex appeared with the *News of the World* and a £10 note, and handed both to Danny.

"Something to read on the trains, and a tenner to buy yourself some lunch," he said. "Keep the change."

"Thanks, Dad. Bye, Mum, Dad," Danny replied, grabbed his puffer jacket and baseball cap from the coat hooks, put them on, hugged Jill, and scampered out of the house.

Rex and Jill walked back into the kitchen, where Rex had spread *The Observer* over the table and had been reading the sports section. He sat down and continued doing so.

"How long does it take to get to Stepney?" Jill asked him.

"What?"

"Stepney. How long does it take to get there?"

Rex looked puzzled. "Oh, Hackney. Directional dyslexia again, Jill. It's miles away. But I think they meet in the pub first, which is in Bow. The nearest station is probably Bow Road. Jubilee Line then District Line. An hour or more, I reckon, maybe even longer on a Sunday."

"Oh. Bow. Yes," Jill mumbled, then added, "I love him so much."

"You've cut yourself," said Rex.

"Yes," said Jill, bending forward to look down at the flaked smear of dried blood on her right knee. "It's nothing." She stood upright again. "Oh, I forgot to tell you, last night I had a horrible dream I killed a little girl."

"Well, you didn't. It was only a dream."

"I know that. I've been wondering what it means, that's all."

"It means nothing."

"It must mean something. All dreams mean something."

"It means nothing at all."

She stared at him, then said, "I think I'll have a bath."

CHAPTER 6

COTTON SOAKED IN COLD MUD,
SUFFUSED WITH ADOLESCENT SWEAT

While Jill was lolling in a deep Badedas-infused bath, and Danny was on the tube en route to Bow Road, Rex continued to leaf through the various sections of *The Observer*. He felt a bit sorry for Jill. He was still moderately fond of her, in his way, even though he could no longer remember what it felt like to fancy her and had never been in love with her. But he realised that, despite not being aware of his part in what she had heard Danny confessing to Kimberly, she was taking it rather worse than he was. He was now taking it rather well. Certainly, he no longer felt it would be necessary, even if it were possible, which it surely was not now that Jill knew the half of it, to try to banish it from his consciousness for ever, as he had vowed to do only yesterday.

Besides, on reflection, it was understandable that Jill would be more upset than he would be. After all, cottaging was hardly foreign to him; no, he regarded it as harmless, if illegal, fun. He was also secretly but confidently of the view that sex between two (or more) men was raunchier and therefore better than sex between a man and a woman, and he felt he was well placed to make that judgment, so on one level he was not specifically displeased that his son was already enjoying it, and would presumably continue to do so for the rest of his life, even if it was an activity about whose appeal they would never be able to compare notes.

However, unlike Jill, Rex had worked out that Danny had evidently had quite a bit of sexual experience already. The expertise with which the boy had brought him to orgasm had told him that much. That being the case, Rex wondered whether Danny had gone farther with men than to conspire in the kind of entanglements that were ergonomically practicable via a glory hole, and whether, if he had, he or his partners had used condoms. But, again, he did not share these speculations with Jill, and neither did he dwell on them.

She came downstairs, having put on a blue dress that was gathered and belted at the waist, thereby making her plump form look what she liked to refer to as "pleasantly Junoesque". She had washed her hair, which she dyed auburn and wore long for a woman of her age, and had put on the expensive vintage white-gold diamond-clasp two-strand pearl choker that Rex had given her three Christmases ago. She had chosen a pair of gold court shoes, which matched the choker.

"You look nice," said Rex.

"Thank you, darling. I didn't want to slouch about in my dressing gown all day just because of what's happened."

"Good for you."

The phone rang. Jill almost always answered it hurriedly when Danny was not in the house, a habit that she had fallen into when he had first begun to go out on his own. She was not an inveterate worrier, but she fretted if ever he was late home, and she had always told him to ring if he thought he was going to be. By and large, he did.

"Hello?" Rex heard her say from the hall.

There was a pause. "It's for you. It's Terry."

Rex stood up and went to the phone, passing Jill coming back the other way. "Hi, mate. What can I do for you this fine morning?"

Terry Morrison was RED's advertising director, and Rex's most senior right-hand man at work, but they were friends as well as colleagues. "Exactly. It is indeed a fine morning. So d'you fancy playing tennis?" Terry asked. "As you so rightly say, it's a perfect day for it."

Rex pondered. Undoubtedly, Jill would prefer him to stay with her today, given her emotional state, but the truth was that he would much rather play tennis with Terry.

"Yeah, fine, when?" he replied.

"To be honest, I took a punt on it, hoping you'd be available, so I've booked for 10.00am. OK with you?"

"Perfect."

Rex and Terry were both members of South Hampstead Tennis Club, which boasted five well-maintained floodlit all-weather courts and a lively bar. It was not actually in

South Hampstead, but was rather in Milverton Road, which was a four-minute walk from Manor House Drive. Nonetheless, Rex usually drove there, and would drive there today. Terry lived two miles north, on Dollis Hill Lane.

"Listen, love, I'm going to pop out for a game of tennis with Terry."

"Oh, are you?"

"Yes. I won't be long. I'll be back long before Danny is. Why don't you go out to lunch with one of your friends? It'll do you good. Ladies who lunch and all that."

"What time will you be home? To be honest I'd prefer it if you stayed, after all we've been through, I mean, and…" But she did not complete her sentence, for Rex was already running upstairs to change into his tennis whites and fetch his racquet.

He had left his BMW on the gravel when he had returned from having bought the papers this morning, parking it alongside Jill's Volvo, which lived permanently outside, there being space in the garage only for Rex's two cars and one motorbike. He hopped in, and roared off down Manor House Drive, faster than he had driven the same Tarmac this morning. He turned left and left again, and parked up outside the club. He decided to wait in his car for Terry rather than go in on his own.

He reflected on how sanguine he was feeling now, and registered for the first time that, as long as he was going to get away with it, which he surely now was, just as he had got away with so many episodes of sexual recklessness before, he was going to be able to put this latest one behind him and move on, even if he would never entirely forget it. Yes, the incestuous element was shameful and shocking, yet he no longer felt either shocked or ashamed. Rather, he felt unlucky. It had been a terrible mischance – no one's fault – but the unhappy result was that he would never be able to go to the Harrow Road cottage ever again, for fear of encountering Danny there. He toyed with the idea of transferring his patronage to the Kilburn Lane cottage, but it was less cruisy than the Harrow Road one and was frequented by an annoyingly large number of straight men wanting to piss. Besides, how was he to know that Danny did not also cottage in Kilburn Lane?

Rex spotted Terry parking his Ford Scorpio across the road, and he got out of his BMW as Terry and his nineteen-year-old son did likewise, each carrying identical expensive carbon graphite racquets. "Hi, mate, where's Danny?" said Terry.

"Football," Rex replied.

"Oh. I've brought Todd. I thought you were bringing Danny. I thought we were going to have a four, you know, Morrisons versus Davises, father and son versus father and son."

"Sorry, mate, I didn't realise, you never said."

"No. I kind of assumed though. Oh, never mind. There's bound to be someone decent looking for a game. Let's go in."

The three of them walked into the club and headed for the bar, where a handful of members were having coffee. It was early yet, not quite 10.00am, and two of the five courts were free. Terry was forty-four, but he was lean, fit and rangy, and he took his tennis very seriously. He addressed the room. "Any of you chaps fancy making up a four?" he asked. "Not you lot…" – he bowed theatrically at three women sitting at a nearby table – "… we want a serious men's doubles." The women laughed.

"I don't mind," said a voice from behind them, and up strode Kenyon Jenkins, the club chairman's nephew.

"Great, good chap," said Terry. "You play with Rex. You know Rex, don't you?"

"I think we've met, yes," Kenyon replied, but he was not sure that they had. Rex was certain that they had not. The four of them walked to the nearest of the empty courts in two pairs, Rex alongside Terry in front, Todd and Kenyon a little way behind. Terry was talking about Hillsborough, but Rex was not listening. The two lads behind him clearly knew each other, and were chatting animatedly about what Rex could not quite make out. He wished he could.

The truth was that he found Kenyon astonishingly attractive: he was probably in his mid-twenties, six-foot-one or -two, had broad shoulders and a narrow waist, a strong, chiselled, clean-shaven face topped by a golden, tousled undercut with a carefully textured quiff; he was coltish but graceful, ethereally tanned, and his smile was coruscating, revealing white, even teeth.

Terry won the toss and served. He was a very good player, the best of the four, the other three capable but much of a muchness. Todd made too many unforced errors, for which his father scolded him angrily – "Come on, boy!" – but they nonetheless won six-four six-three.

Rex had been distracted throughout by Kenyon, who had stage-whispered amusing asides every time Terry had snapped at Todd. He had also shouted "Shot!" or "Well played!" whenever Rex had won a point for them, always accompanying such exclamations with an open, friendly grin and sometimes a high five. When Rex had served, Kenyon had gone to net, crouching in readiness to volley, legs apart, his well-knit butt encased in tight, short, white shorts, and Rex had sometimes had to bounce the ball an unconscionable number of times in order to refocus on his serving. "Come on, Rex," Terry had shouted more than once.

After their match, they repaired to the bar. "Losers pay," said Terry happily, and Rex bought Diet Cokes for them all. Thirsty, they finished them quickly, and didn't stay long. "I'll run you back to your uncle's if you like, Kenyon, OK?" Terry suggested as they all made to leave. "That's Gladstone Park Gardens, right?"

"Yeah, that's right, thanks, that'd be great," Kenyon replied.

"Good," said Terry. "I'll give you a lift then."

"Or I can," Rex offered.

"No, no," said Terry. "You're already practically on your doorstep here. We're going Kenyon's way. Gladstone Park Gardens is only a stone's throw from Dollis Hill Lane." Rex had to concede that it was.

"Bye then," he said, and watched them climb into Terry's Scorpio and speed away.

Rex was horny now. He was sorely tempted to go cottaging, but he felt he could not. OK, Danny had said he was playing football, and should therefore now be more than ten miles away, but football had been the cover story that the boy had used mendaciously to explain his absence while he had been messing about for a couple of hours in the Harrow Road cottage only yesterday; how could Rex be sure that he was not doing the same thing, in the same place, today? No, it was too much of a risk. But, there was no getting away from it, Kenyon had made his balls ache. He felt sexy, frisky, tetchy even, and he badly wanted to come.

He drove home. He found the house empty, and a note on the kitchen table: "Am having lunch with Linda. See you about 3.00pm. Love, Jill xxx". Rex looked at his watch. It was 12.30pm. He went upstairs and jerked off into the toilet pan in his and Jill's en-suite bathroom, his mind's eye full of visions of Kenyon's taut backside.

*

Danny had arrived at Bow Road at just after 9.30am. Kick-off was scheduled for 10.30am, so he was in good time. He walked to the Ordell Arms, which was closed for business until 11.00am, and knocked at the door. It was opened by the landlord's wife, who admitted him without a word. He found the captain, John Shaw, and half a dozen other players already there. Within fifteen minutes all eleven were present, and they climbed into various of their cars and drove to Hackney Marshes. They were there in ten minutes.

As they got changed, John spoke to Danny. "The team we're playing, Rilcrest Green Man, are a bunch of nasty bastards. They'll probably try to kick you all over the park. But don't worry. Just do your thing, run rings round 'em, and I'll make sure you come to no harm, OK?"

"OK," said Danny, and smiled.

Rilcrest scored early, the result of sustained pressure on the Ordell defence. Out on the right wing, Danny spent much of the first half-hour watching his defensive teammates trying to limit the damage, and wondering when he was going to get a touch. A couple of times the Ordell centre-half had hoofed the ball up the middle, but it had always been cleared by the Rilcrest defenders.

After about forty minutes an Ordell clearance soared over Danny's head, and he began to sprint for it. It turned out to be a perfect through-ball, the result of luck not judgment, and Danny saw that, although he had been on-side when the ball had been kicked, he had outpaced his marker and was now running towards the Rilcrest goal with only the goalkeeper to beat. The ball fell in front of him, the left-back launched himself into a lunging slide tackle that missed its target, and Danny was through. Still running fast, he tapped the moving ball with his left foot, teeing it up for his favourite right, then chipped the keeper to level the match.

Nothing – really, nothing – ever gave Danny so visceral a buzz as scoring goals, and this was a great goal. The elation was wonderfully multi-faceted. Goal-scoring involved bottle, vision, skill and the responsibility of finishing a move begun by, or involving, teammates who were depending on the last bit of the action being done successfully – brilliantly even. And Danny had done his bit. He jogged back past the centre line, his arm aloft, and John patted him on the back as he passed him. The referee blew his whistle for half-time.

John passed around orange quarters, and Danny ate his contentedly. Why was it always orange quarters? And why did they always taste so good halfway through a football match? "Listen, lads," John said, "all we have to do is mark 'em tight, tackle 'em hard, and don't let 'em score again. Whenever you get a chance, hoof it up the right wing and this kid'll do the rest. He's that quick. He's that good. He may not do it every time, but he only has to do it once again and we'll win, as long as we don't concede another goal."

The second half started quietly, and it was now raining hard. Danny began to feel chilly. It was alright for defenders and midfielders, he often thought; they were always on the move and never therefore had a chance to get cold. But it was different for strikers. For long periods you were walking and watching, hoping for a break. Sometimes it came; often it did not.

At about eighty minutes Ordell were awarded a free kick in the centre circle, the result of a Rilcrest foul. Danny ran ahead, looking for space, but the Rilcrest left-back was in dogged attendance, lumbering around behind him. "Don't you come flash with me, you little cunt," he said at one point. Danny tried to ignore the remark, but it had scared him.

The Ordell free kick floated into the Rilcrest penalty area, and was headed back by their centre-half. It landed at Danny's feet, about twenty-five yards out. The foul-mouthed full-back was upon him immediately. As he approached, Danny nutmegged him, instinctively seeing the gap between his legs and popping the ball through it, nipping past the big man, who turned and began to run back at him. Danny knew he would be angry, but that was a problem for later, for now he was about twenty yards out, and he had a clear shot at goal. He drilled the ball hard and low, about a foot high, and it went in off the far post, making the goal net ripple satisfyingly as it did so.

Danny turned, both arms in the air, to find the Rilcrest left-back right in front of him. Danny put his arms down, sensing that a triumphant celebration would antagonise the brute further, but the man swung at him and planted a punch right between his eyes. John ran over and nutted the Rilcrest man, and the referee sent them both off. Danny walked to the touchline, his nose bleeding heavily. As play restarted, only nineteen men now on the field, his assailant was yelling at John about thirty yards away, but, although they pushed each other a few times, they did not come to further blows. Danny lay down on his back just off the pitch, in a bit of pain, but happy. After a short while he heard the final whistle blow, and his teammates carried him back to the dressing room.

Under the hot showers Danny's nose stopped bleeding, but it still ached. "Nice pair of shiners you'll be getting there, me ol' china," said John, and he splashed him playfully, his big, flaccid dick swaying pendulously as he did so. "But well done, good game, two great goals, fan-fucking-tastic. Let's all have a couple of pints back at the pub."

Danny was not much of a drinker, but he drank today. In fact he drank five pints of Carling Black Label, all of them bought for him by his teammates, the Ordell Arms staying open illegally behind locked doors for players and other regulars well after Sunday afternoon closing time, and he was pissed when he began his tube journey home. He was still quite drunk when he finally rolled in at nearly 5.00pm.

*

Jill's day had been rather less eventful than had either Rex's or Danny's. Lunch, at D & G's, a superior Greek restaurant beside Willesden Green station which was her favourite local eatery, had dragged, because Linda had wanted to talk about her non-existent love life, whereas Jill had been hoping to confide in her old friend about the Danny situation. She had decided against that as soon as Linda, looking woebegone, had sat down opposite her. A problem shared was sometimes a problem doubled, Jill reflected, for, although Linda was kind and clever, she was also a gossip.

After a starter and a main but no dessert – a rare Sunday lunchtime omission for Jill – she had driven home, arriving about an hour and a half after Rex had finished masturbating.

"Hi," she said, finding him glued to the San Marino Grand Prix.

"Gerhard Berger's had a massive shunt," he replied, excitedly. "I think he's going to be alright, but, fuck, it was a big one."

"I'll make tea," she replied.

"Senna's going to win this now," he replied.

"Are they?"

"He, not they. Ayrton Senna. He's a person, not a team. He's a Brazilian racing driver. The best in the world actually."

"Oh."

She went into the kitchen, and returned with two mugs. "Thanks, love," said Rex. "OK? How was lunch?"

"It was OK. Well, Linda was a bit of a pain actually. How was tennis?"

"Yeah, it was OK. We lost." Rex was momentarily struck by the similarity between this conversation and the conversations they had had with Danny the day before.

"Who's we?"

"Oh, me and this guy called Kenyon. We played Terry and Todd."

"Kenyon? That's an odd name."

"Yeah," Rex replied. "Nice guy, though, actually."

"Good. I s'pose Danny'll be home soon."

"About 4.00pm I reckon, not yet," said Rex, noting that it was only 2.30pm.

"Have you had lunch?"

"I'm fine. I made myself a cheese sandwich."

"It's raining out," she replied. "Should one of us pick him up from the station?"

"No, he'll be OK," Rex replied.

Jill went into the kitchen, and ate a Twix. Rex watched the remainder of the Grand Prix, then seamlessly transferred his attention to world championship snooker, which followed. The twenty-year-old Scot, Stephen

Hendry, whose dapper little arse Rex found himself ogling as he stooped to take each shot, was playing the experienced Willie Thorne in a second-round match, and was in stupendous form. He had carved out a good lead by the time Danny arrived home, wet and woozy.

"Hi, Mum, Dad," he said, and dropped his bag in the hallway. He entered the living room. "I'm soaked, Dad. I'm going to have a shower. We won two-one, by the way, and I scored both our goals. I nutmegged this big left-back and he got so narked he punched me in the face. It was brilliant."

As Danny scurried up the stairs, Rex called out, "That's great, son. Well done. But take your shoes off. Don't trample mud all over the stair carpet." Danny wriggle-kicked his trainers off as he continued his way upstairs, allowing them to rest where he had discarded them, a couple of steps apart from each other. Jill hurried over from the kitchen and gathered them up, putting them on the doormat to dry.

She looked at his sports bag for a few seconds, then unzipped it. She plunged her hands into it, and for the first time in her life she was grateful for the yucky, if familiar, sensation of fingering cotton soaked in cold mud, suffused with adolescent sweat.

CHAPTER 7

A FEW ROGUE SHOWER-WATER DRIBLETS
SLIDING DOWN ONTO HIS CHEEKS

Jill returned to the living room from the kitchen, where she had been putting on a wash. "While he's having his shower," she said to Rex, who was reading *The Observer* colour supplement on the sofa, "you and I need to work out what we're going to say to him when he comes down."

Rex made no reply for a few moments, then rested his magazine on his lap. "Give him a break, Jill. He's excited about having scored two goals, and he got punched in the face by some defender he obviously outclassed. Good for him."

"Oh my goodness! Is he OK?"

"He's having a shower. Of course he's OK. Anyway, as I said this morning, what he did in that public bog is repulsive, stomach-churning in fact, of course it is, but we don't know what to say to him, so I think we should say nothing."

Jill got up from her armchair and sat down next to him. "Look, darling," she said, "it's difficult for you, I understand that. It's difficult for me, too, very difficult. But we can't have our son behaving like this. We just can't. It's appalling. Surely you see that?"

"I do, and I've just described it to you as repulsive and stomach-churning. I can put up with poufs if they keep out of my way and mind their own business – each to his own and all that – but to be honest I don't want to even think about what they do in bed or, for fuck's sake, even worse, in public toilets."

Jill winced. "Yes, but it isn't just 'poufs', or 'they', is it? It's our son. What used to be remote and foreign to us is now part of our life. It's a chicken that's come home to roost."

Rex frowned, so Jill added, "Look, I can tell you're upset by all this, and I am too…" – she leant over and gave his shoulder a squeeze – "… but, however appalled we are, we can't just ignore it and hope it goes away. We've got to protect him from AIDS or prison or both…" – she swallowed, paused and carried on – "… because, I mean, doing things like that in public lavatories is illegal apart from anything else, I assume."

"It must be, yes," Rex replied, and resumed his reading. It was undoubtedly the case that Jill's harrowing discovery had significantly moderated her quotidian incivility towards him, anxious as she was to enlist his support, and as a result their home life had suddenly become more agreeable. Moreover, if Danny was gay, he was secretly gay, and very far from being a screaming queen. That was a good thing, too. All the boy was doing, after all, was covertly fooling around with a few willies, and who really gave a tinker's cuss about that? Not Rex. He would not have wanted what had happened to happen, but his efforts to remove himself from his version of events were proving more and more successful as time went by. It was going to be OK.

"Well, if it's illegal," Jill went on, "then it's obvious we've got to stop him doing it. Imagine if he were arrested. Just imagine the disgrace, Rex."

Rex had indeed imagined the disgrace, many times over many years, but from his own perspective. He had also been thinking about it over the past twenty-four hours, from Danny's. It bothered him less. It would be embarrassing if his son were apprehended for gross indecency, of course it would, but Rex had come to the conclusion that it would not be life-altering in a fundamentally injurious way; not for himself, anyway. Besides, Danny was too young, surely, to be imprisoned for such an offence, since, at just eighteen, he was under the age of consent for sex between males, which twenty-one. If he were caught in a compromising position with a boy of his own age, their wrists would be slapped, but that would be all. If his accomplice were an older man, that older man would go to prison for molesting a minor. Both scenarios would be regrettable, but life would go on much as before. Nonetheless, he needed to reply. "OK, Jill, look, I don't know the solution and I don't think you do either. He'll probably grow out of it. I'm sure I've heard that teenage boys sometimes go through this phase. It usually passes."

"Well, you didn't. We conceived Danny when you were his age."

"I know that. I didn't say all teenage boys go through this phase. Some do, though."

"Did you?"

"Of course not. I was too busy shagging you."

Jill got up and walked into the kitchen. She looked at the clock. It was 5.55pm. She began to mix herself a gin 'n' tonic. "Are you having a drink?" she called back to Rex.

"No, thanks."

Danny appeared, barefoot, wearing low-slung hip-hugging jeans and a tight black T-shirt that made his slim, thewy torso look positively skinny. His thick black-brown hair was still wet, and the damp locks of his fringe hung over his already blackening eyes, a few rogue shower-water driblets sliding down onto his cheeks. He had had a shower followed by a bath, and his long soak had sobered him up. He switched on the telly and sat down next to Rex. *The Animals Roadshow* had just started on BBC1. Danny stood up again and changed channels to BBC2, where the evening's snooker coverage was just beginning. He returned to the sofa, next to his father. Soon, Jill returned with her first gin 'n' tonic of the evening. "Oh, look at you, darling," she said. "Your eyes. Are you OK? Are they painful?"

"I'm fine, Mum. Don't make a fuss. Eddie Charlton versus Tony Meo, Dad. Boring. I hate Eddie Charlton."

The phone rang. No one moved. Eventually, Rex got up, walked to the hall, swiftly returned, and said, "Danny, it's for you; Kimberly." Danny got up and went to the phone.

Jill waited until Danny had begun speaking, then glared at Rex. "What?" he replied. Jill said nothing, but swallowed a slug of gin 'n' tonic.

Danny returned and sat down again. "She's coming round in a bit," he announced. Jill grimaced again, unseen by Danny, who had begun enthusiastically to tell Rex the story of both the goals he had scored that morning. "Good stuff, son," Rex replied.

Again, the phone rang. "Someone else's turn," said Rex. Jill got up.

"It's for you," she said to Rex.

"Who is it?" he asked.

"Dunno."

Rex walked to the hallway to take the call. "Hello," he said.

"Hi, Rex. It's Kenyon, you know, from earlier. Tennis. I hope you don't mind me calling you."

"Not at all," Rex replied, careful to temper the excitement in his voice, which trick he only partially succeeded in pulling off.

"Well, what it is, is, I was talking to my uncle just now – Nigel from the tennis club, right? – and I told him I'd played with you, Terry and Todd this morning, and he said you've got a '67 Corvette. Well, that's my all-time favourite car. Honestly, it really is: the 'mako shark'. I'd love to see it. So I asked my uncle for your phone number, so that maybe I could arrange to come and have a look at it some time. But only if and when it's convenient, of course."

"I didn't even know you liked cars," Rex replied.

"Oh, I *love* cars, especially from a styling and design point of view, and old Corvettes look dead cool," said Kenyon.

"Well, you can come now if you like. It's stopped raining and it'll be light for another couple of hours."

"OK, if you're sure, yeah, that'd be great. D'you mind if I bring my camera?"

"Not at all. Course I'm sure."

"Thanks so much. See you in about twenty minutes."

Rex walked back into the living room. "Kenyon's coming over to look at the 'Vette," he said.

"Who's Kenyon?" Danny asked.

"Chap I played tennis with this morning. Made up a four with me, Terry and Todd. Nice guy. Turns out he's a petrolhead."

"A what?" Danny asked again.

"A petrolhead. It's Australian slang for someone who's a car nut."

They watched snooker in silence for a bit. Finally, Jill spoke: "I'll start making supper, we're having lamb."

"It'd be great if you could make a bit extra for Kimberly, Mum…" – Jill heard but did not reply – "… how the hell did Charlton miss that blue off its spot?"

"You know he's nearly sixty," Rex replied.

"I know, but still."

The doorbell rang. Rex sprang out of his chair, crossed the hallway, and opened the front door.

It was Kimberly. "Danny! Kimberly!" Rex shouted, took the Corvette's ignition key from the wall-mounted cabinet in the hallway and walked past her onto the gravel. A wet afternoon had become a dry evening, and, although there was a nip in the wind, the sun was bright and still warm. He opened the garage door, heaving it up and over the vehicles inside, climbed into the Corvette, and fired it up. Its big V8 spluttered, coughed, then caught, after which he kept it revving for a couple of minutes, before gently letting the revs drop, then lifting his foot off the gas altogether, and allowing it to idle. He selected first gear and edged the car forward into the driveway, parking it neatly in a far corner, next to the new palisade fencing, so as to give Kenyon enough space and a photogenic background for his snaps. Finally, he reversed his BMW into the space hitherto occupied by the Corvette, but left the garage door open so that Kenyon would be able to see all his automotive toys.

He walked back into the house, and into the living room, where Danny and Kimberly were chatting, Danny now ignoring the snooker and Kimberly teasing him, saying his developing shiners made him look like a badger. She was wearing black and white Converse All Star High Tops, baggy faded jeans that she had turned up to her mid-calf and in which she had ripped holes in both knees and the right thigh, and a black and white crop top, covering her nugatory breasts but exposing her equally flat navel and abdominal muscles.

Jill joined them at the same time, and sat down. "Hi, Mrs Davis, Mr Davis," Kimberly said, and smiled at them both.

Jill did not reply, but instead drained her second gin 'n' tonic.

"Why d'you cut your hair so short?" she asked, waving her empty glass in the direction of Kimberly's crew cut.

"Oh, dunno, I like it," Kimberly answered, while Danny flicked his mother a quizzical glance.

"I think she looks good like that," he offered.

Jill went into the kitchen and began to cook dinner. Once she was out of earshot, Danny and Kimberly giggled. "Don't mind Danny's mum," said Rex. "She's already under the influence of Mr Gordon and Mr Schweppe." They all cracked up.

"Wow!" shouted Kenyon from the gravel outside, an exclamation that startled all three of them. Rex walked out to greet him, grinning. "Wow-wee, she's a beauty," Kenyon purred, now crouching beside the driver's door to examine the left side pipe, and stroking its aluminium cover. "Go on, fire her up."

Rex climbed in, floored the throttle, and turned the starter. The engine roared into life. Rex gunned it a few times, pinging the tacho needle around the dial as he did so, then let it idle again. "Sheesh! That's so awesome," said Kenyon, bouncing on his heels, "You can't beat the sound of a '60s muscle car's V8."

They opened the bonnet, which in deference to the car's country of origin Rex was pleased to note that Kenyon knew to call the hood, and the young man cooed over the orange cam covers, each of them adorned with the word "Chevrolet" picked out in large silver italics. "D'you mind if I do a few pics?" he asked, taking his expensive new camera out of its bespoke case.

"Sure thing," said Rex, allowing an unintended transatlantic twang to infect his pronunciation, which he hoped Kenyon had not noticed. Kenyon had not. He took more photographs than Rex had expected him to – a lot more, in fact, from many angles, for some of them asking Rex to hold aloft a big circular silver-coloured light-reflector – and the operation took almost half an hour. He used six rolls of Kodachrome slide film, and apologised halfway through. "I'm bracketing like fuck," he said at one point, grinning. "Costs me a bloody fortune."

"I bet," Rex replied, but, not being a photographer, he had not understood Kenyon's quip, even though he had recognised that it had been one.

"I want to make the most of this gorgeous light, you see. I'm doing a post-grad in photography at Middlesex Poly. Ideally, I want to be a car photographer when I, er, grow up." Again, he flashed a smile in Rex's direction.

"Great," said Rex. "I might be able to give you some work, or work experience, or both, or whatever, if you like. I run a magazine publishing company, you see." Rex neglected to mention that the RED portfolio included no car magazines.

"Wow, that would be awesome," said Kenyon, standing up from his final crouch and beginning to pack his camera body, lenses and film into their cases. "Oh, actually, one last pic, but this one's just for me, would you mind?" And he handed Rex a Pocket Instamatic, kicked off his flip-flops, took off his shirt, chucked it to one side, and lay across the Corvette's hood.

Rex swooned momentarily, then pulled himself together. Kenyon was wearing the shorts in which he had played tennis this morning, but nothing else, and the majority of his tightly muscled and well-tanned body was consequently now on display. Better still, as he arched his back so as to recline atop the front of the Corvette – to which sacrilege Rex would usually have objected – his abs clenched bewitchingly. "Take plenty," said Kenyon, laughing and shutting his eyes against the low sun, "and finish the whole film if you like, but crop out the number plate if you can, please." Stupefied into mute acquiescence, Rex did as he was told. One eye closed and the other squinting into the Instamatic's viewfinder, he did not notice Kimberly leaving. Neither did he observe that she was upset, or that she stared uneasily as she passed, first at Kenyon, and then at himself, soundlessly keeping to the curved flagstone walkway so as to avoid crunching the gravel with her footfalls.

"Right, all done," Kenyon announced. "Sorry I took so long."

"No prob. Fancy a drink? Or even a bite to eat? I think my missus will have got dinner ready by now. My son and his, er, girlfriend are eating with us tonight, but five can feed as easily as four." He put his arm around Kenyon's bare shoulders, and guided him into the house. It was a smidgen before 8.00pm.

*

Unknown to them, while Kenyon had been engrossed in the Corvette and Rex had been engrossed in Kenyon, Jill had had six large gin 'n' tonics in the kitchen. At about 7.45pm she had tottered into the living room, a leg of lamb, two pounds of roast potatoes and a baking tray full of carrots and parsnips seasoned with honey and thyme all juicily roasting in the oven, ready to be served about half an hour later.

She had sat down, had turned to Kimberly, and had said, slurring her words slightly, "Would you mind giving Danny and me a minute, please? He and I need to talk, and, actually, yes, I think it'd be best if you go."

"Mum, what's up?" Danny had asked, a mixture of irritation and concern clearly discernible in his tone.

"I'll tell you in a minute, darling. Kimberly, please go home," Jill had replied. Kimberly had shrugged, muttered, "Bye then, Danny," and had pootled out.

"Mum, what's up?" Danny had asked again. "Why are you being rude to Kimberly? She was invited to dinner with us and now she's got to just walk home on her own."

"Is that girl your girlfriend?"

"She's got a name actually. Kimberly. Why d'you ask?"

"Is she or isn't she?"

"No. She's my girl friend, two words, not my girlfriend, one word. We're, you know, best mates."

"Look, darling, I love you very much. All I want is for you to be happy. So, look, I have to ask you, d'you sometimes think…" – she lifted her seventh gin 'n' tonic and put away an inch of it – "… that perhaps you like boys more than girls?"

There had been a long silence. The longer it had continued, the more clearly Danny had realised that a flat denial would have been decreasingly convincing. And yet he had been unwilling, unable even, to answer with a quick-fire one-word lie.

Eventually, he had said: "Mum, how can I know? I'm only eighteen."

"My poor, poor darling," Jill had replied, and had begun to sob.

"It ain't 'my poor, poor darling'," Danny had snapped. "It ain't a case of that. I'm OK. Leave it, Mum, please. I wish you'd never started this. Why the fuck did you say anything about any of this?"

Jill would usually have ticked Danny off for swearing, but this evening she had not. "Because I love you and I want you to be happy, darling, that's why. Have you had sex with another boy, or man, yet?"

"Mum!" Danny had howled. "That ain't none of your business. And you're only asking me cos you're drunk. I love you very much but drop it, please."

Jill had squinted at her son awhile. "Look, Danny, I may know more about what you've done than you think I do, so please don't lie to me. There's the issue of the law, you know, never mind AIDS."

Danny had not replied, but he had begun to sob, albeit silently.

"Look, darling, I know what you did yesterday, when you said you were playing football, which you weren't. I know, OK? Don't ask me how I know, but I know. I know everything."

"No, you don't. I did play football yesterday – and today, too."

"No, darling, you didn't. Well, you played football today, yes, but not yesterday."

"I did," Danny had whispered, and had then fallen silent. Jill had taken another swig of gin 'n' tonic and had then stared at Danny's melancholy countenance with a mixture of devotion and disgust that had felt unpleasant and alien to her.

*

Rex and Kenyon walked into the living room, but Jill was still studying Danny's face, oblivious to everything and everyone else. Finally, she spoke, firmly but evenly. "You didn't, darling. You spent yesterday morning fellating five strangers' penises in a public lavatory on Harrow Road."

Simultaneously, Jill and Danny became aware that Rex and Kenyon had arrived among them, Kenyon standing magnificent in only his tennis shorts, a wild-eyed Rex alongside.

"Oh, for heaven's sake," said Jill, dropping her glass and flooding her lap. She ignored the spillage. "Rex, a word." She stood up and took her husband by the elbow, leading him into the kitchen and shutting the door behind them. "Why the hell did you think it was appropriate, or helpful, to bring that, er, male mannequin into our house, after everything that's happened? Are you stark staring mad? Danny and I are having an important conversation about you know what, and the arrival of a half-naked Adonis certainly isn't what we need right now."

"He's not half-naked."

"He is. Tell him to put his shirt on, assuming he has one. If you won't, I will." She marched back into the living room, to find Kenyon standing in the middle of the room, still shirtless, and Danny sitting cross-legged on the floor, his head, bowed, in his hands.

Rex had followed her. "What the fuck's the matter with you?" he barked. "You're massively embarrassing Kenyon, you're annoying me big time, and you've really upset Danny. Why?"

"Because someone had to," Jill replied.

"Someone had to embarrass Kenyon, annoy me and upset Danny? Are you fucking serious?" Rex bellowed, his voice now enraged and thunderous.

"I'm going to bed," said Danny, and bolted upstairs.

Jill looked about her, emitted a long and shapeless wail, said, "Well, I'm not staying down here with you two clowns," and set off for bed herself.

Rex and Kenyon listened to her heavy footsteps as she began to clump up the stairs, followed by a sudden percussive arpeggio as she fell back down them. "I'm OK, just fucking leave me alone," she mewled as she righted herself and began to mount the staircase once again. The two men waited, silent and still, until she was out of earshot, and it was Kenyon who spoke first.

"Is she OK, d'you think? Shouldn't we help her?"

"Oh, yeah, I'm sure she's OK. Drunk, that's all."

"OK. Good. Well, not good, sorry, but you know what I mean. And are you OK?"

"Yeah, thanks. I'm so, so, so sorry about all this. Look, by all means leave if you want to, I certainly wouldn't blame you, but I need a drink and you're welcome to have one too if you like." He walked into the kitchen, Kenyon following, and poured them each a stiff Scotch. He tapped a couple of ice cubes into both tumblers, and said, "Thrice distilled single malt Auchentoshan. Good stuff. Chin-chin."

They both took a sip. "Wow, nice," said Kenyon.

"Yeah, very."

"I feel a bit of a spare prick. I'll leave if you want me to."

"No, look, stay. It's not even 9.00pm and I'm fucking angry to be honest. With Jill, I mean. It's nice to have someone here. Oh, and that lamb must be ready. I'm starving. Let's eat." And, with that, Rex switched off the heat, put on Jill's oven gloves, opened the door of the oven, and lifted its contents onto the worktop. He fetched two plates, filled them, noting that everything was by now a little overcooked, particularly the potatoes, which were a bit too crispy, and put both plates on the kitchen table. They sat down. "I'm going to get us some decent vino," he said, stood up again, walked out of the kitchen, opened the cellar door, trotted down the steps to select a claret, returned with a bottle of Château Lynch-Bages Paulliac 1982, pulled the cork, sniffed it, and half-filled two bulbous wine glasses, which he set down alongside their still-half-full whisky tumblers.

"So, er, d'you want to talk about it?" Kenyon ventured.

"Jesus. Maybe. Look, I'm just so sorry about all this. That wasn't a typical Sunday night at Château Davis, honestly."

"Well, I was going to say, yeah. You seem, you know, so friendly and, well, you know, so balanced, but I guess your wife is maybe an alcoholic and your son is maybe coming to terms with being gay, right? Sorry to put it bluntly like that, but…"

Rex stared at Kenyon, then laughed. "Jesus. I s'pose so. I've only known about Danny's, er, likely sexuality for about twenty-four hours, but, funnily enough, I've never used that word about Jill. The A-word, I mean. But, yeah, I guess she may be. She's not often as bad as she was just now, but she's never actually completely sober after about 8.00pm."

"I think we can safely say she's an alcoholic then," Kenyon replied, and flashed Rex a benevolent smile. "And is it true, what she said, you know, about Danny cottaging on Harrow Road?"

"Oh, god, yeah, it is," Rex replied. "She eavesdropped one of his telephone conversations last night, and she heard him boasting about it to his, er, to Kimberly, his best friend. Please don't tell anyone though."

"She shouldn't have done that. And what about his black eyes?"

"No, she probably shouldn't. Football injury. Nothing to worry about." By rights Rex should have been distraught, he knew that. But in fact he was elated. He had Kenyon to himself, all ears, and, even better, the young man appeared to have forgotten that he was still naked from the waist up. "You're wise beyond your years, you know," Rex said.

"Thanks, and cheers," Kenyon replied, and they both necked their Scotches. Kenyon reached out, gave Rex's hand a squeeze, and, having done so, began gently to massage the older man's palm with his thumb. Rex did not respond, but neither did he withdraw his hand, which lay limp as Kenyon sturdily palpated it. Rex glanced upwards, briefly fearful that they could be overheard by either Jill or Danny. But the kitchen was part of a large extension that had been built onto the house, and above it there was nothing but a pitched skylighted roof and the stars. "Why did your parents call you Kenyon?" he asked finally.

"It means 'blond'," Kenyon replied, flicked his golden quiff with his free hand, and smiled.

Rex extricated his hand from Kenyon's grip, and smiled back.

"Look," Kenyon said, "if it helps, I mean if you think it would be useful at all, I could talk to Danny for you. The thing is, I'm gay, too, you see. Coming to terms with that side of life is tough at Danny's age, but you work through it all and then it's OK. It's more than OK actually." And he smiled again.

Rex said nothing for a while, then asked, "How old are you?"

"Twenty-four."

Rex sensed that he might perhaps be on the brink of a seismic experience. Here he was, his plump alcoholic wife and his troubled teenage son asleep or perhaps crying separately upstairs, and he neither wanted nor felt able to help either of them. Instead, here, sitting in front of him, was Kenyon, beautiful on the outside and it turned out maybe beautiful on the inside, too. Rex was feeling horny, yes, but also overwhelmed. He was aware that he was probably being foolish – he had known this young man for fewer than twelve hours – but he felt perhaps he already loved him. No, not quite loved, at least not yet; but he recognised that he had met someone who might become important to him, maybe even very important, someone whom he might be able to love with body, soul, heart and mind, and he had never felt that way about anyone before. He swallowed a mouthful of claret, and said, "This is a nice drop."

Kenyon beamed, raised his wine glass, clinked it against Rex's, and took a sip. "Yeah, it is," he agreed, then added, "but, anyway, it's up to you, obviously, but if you think it'd help for me to talk to Danny, I can. And, don't worry, I won't try to, you know, get up to any hanky-panky with him. I'm into older guys anyway."

Rex felt momentarily giddy, but steadied himself with another draft of claret. "Thanks. Look, first of all, I don't give a toss if you shag men or women, or even cats or dogs, for all I care. But, no, I'd prefer it if you don't talk to Danny. It's a very nice offer – honestly, thank you – but, no, I think that'd be a little premature. This is all still very raw, for all of us." The truth was that he wanted to keep Kenyon to himself.

Kenyon leant back in his chair. "No problem," he said, "the offer's there if you change your mind."

"Thanks. No, but what *would* help, I think, is if I could talk to you about Danny from time to time. You know, to help me help him. Would that be OK maybe? The odd pint, maybe the odd meal, so's you could tell me where I'm going wrong?"

"Sure, that'd be nice."

CHAPTER 8

CHINOS AND PANTS CRADLING HIS ANKLES

Jill awoke shortly after dawn. Rex was snoring. She had no recollection of how yesterday evening had ended, or when she had gone to bed. She had a dull ache in her gut, and she knew that too much gin was not the only cause of it. She recognised that anxiety was also a contributor. She began to muster to the front of her mind what events she could recall, so as to try to make of them a coherent narrative, and found that she could not; but she remembered that she had confronted Danny, and that their encounter had not gone well.

She wanted to wake Rex, so that he could fill in the gaps for her, but she was reluctant to do so, not only because it was 6.20am but also because she had a feeling that they had had a row. She switched on her bedside light, and saw that she still had on not only her knickers, tights and bra but also the dress she had been wearing yesterday, albeit now bunched up around her midriff. She stood up and, as she did so, she felt a sharp pain in her left hip. She rubbed it, looked down, hoicked down her tights and knickers, and saw a large purple-yellow bruise.

She walked gingerly into the en-suite bathroom, undressed, put everything she had been wearing into the dirty-clothes basket, and began to run the shower. She brushed her teeth, and, noticing in the mirror that around her neck still nestled the choker that she had been wearing yesterday, unfastened it and placed it next to the washbasin. She walked into the shower and stood still under the warm water for five minutes before starting her ablutions. When finally she began to coat her body in soapsuds, she took care around the area of her wounded hip, which was sensitive to both touch and articulation.

She dried herself, put on a clean nightie, and climbed back into bed. "Good morning, darling," she ventured.

The noise of the en-suite shower had awoken Rex, who had remained in bed and had not yet opened his eyes. "I wouldn't call it that," he replied.

There was a pause. "Was I blotto?" she asked.

"Pissed. Plastered. Sloshed. Paralytic. Fucking inebriated. Yes."

Jill considered. "Really? Did anything, you know, happen?"

"Oh, for fuck's sake. Yes. Surely you can't have forgotten everything?"

"No, no, of course not. I know I had a difficult conversation with Danny. About, you know, the situation."

"Difficult? That's one way of putting it." Rex rolled over to face his wife. "You told him you knew he'd been sucking dicks in public toilets, and you chose to tell him you knew about it in front of Nigel Jenkins' nephew."

"Who's Nigel Jenkins?"

"The chairman of my fucking tennis club."

"I couldn't have."

"You fucking did. And then you fell down the stairs in front of everyone."

Jill stared at the ceiling for some time. "What about Danny?" she asked finally.

"What about him? He fled. Scarpered to bed like a rat up a drainpipe. But you'd made him cry by then, you'll be pleased to hear."

There was another pause. "Obviously, I'm not remotely pleased to hear that," Jill mumbled.

"You need to stop drinking."

"We all like a drink."

"No, Jill. Not like you. You're out of control. You fucked up last night, big time. You need to get a grip. It was embarrassing. And Kenyon Jenkins saw it all. It'll be all over the club by lunchtime."

"Was he that gormless hunk who suddenly appeared at one point?"

"Yeah. No. He isn't gormless. And he didn't suddenly appear. He came to take photos of the 'Vette, for his photography MA, and I invited him because..." – Rex yawned as he planned his white lie – "… Nigel asked me to invite him, as a favour, so I did."

"I'd better speak to Danny. You know, to say sorry…" – she sat up – "… but perhaps it's all for the best, you know? At least we can all talk about things now that it's all out in the open."

"It's a snafu, is what it is."

"A what?"

"Snafu. Situation normal all fucked up. You going to work today?"

"Of course." She stood up, took off her nightie, switched on the main light, and began to get dressed. "Are you?"

"I'm going into the office a bit later, yeah. Working from home for the first couple of hours of the morning."

Rex knew that Kenyon would not tell his uncle about last night's events, and that news of Jill's drunken antics and Danny's sexual peccadilloes would not in fact therefore be all over the club by lunchtime. He and Kenyon had chatted until after midnight, sharing not one but nearly two bottles of Château Lynch-Bages, until, happy but wistful, Rex had reluctantly called Kenyon a minicab, pressed a fiver into his hand to cover the fare and then some, and sent him back to Gladstone Park Gardens, tipsy and topless. Still in bed, he watched his wife dressing, and thought about Kenyon's abs.

"OK," she said, now wearing a grey-checked coat and skirt, "I'll go downstairs, tidy up, wash up, which I'm sure you haven't done any of, then go to work. Danny'll be at home today, I think. They're all off school to do revision.

Try to make sure he does some. His A-levels begin in less than a month."

"I know that. Don't worry about the washing-up. Bridie's coming today, isn't she?"

"Yes, but she's a housekeeper, Rex, not a skivvy. Besides, I hate leaving everything all over the place for her."

"A housekeeper *is* a skivvy. That's the whole point of having one."

Jill tutted, shook her head, and went downstairs. About forty minutes later, Rex heard her mounting the stairs and walking along the corridor, passing their bedroom door, and stopping outside Danny's. She knocked. There was no reply. She knocked again, then, after again receiving no response, she leant against her son's bedroom door and said, "Danny, darling, sorry if I was a bit, er, squiffy last night. Love you." She then went back downstairs, where Rex heard her unlocking, opening, then closing the front door. He then showered, dressed, and went downstairs himself.

Jill had left a note: "Rex, Sorry about being so blotto last night. See you tonight. Don't show Danny this message. Love, Jill xxx". He folded it and slid it into the left front pocket of his chinos. He opened the front door, walked out onto the gravel, and saw Jill's Volvo still there – she had evidently thought better of driving to work – and his Corvette still parked in the far corner, its canvas top still stowed. It was a dry morning, thank goodness, but, even so, he jogged over to the 'Vette, anxious to verify that its exposed interior had not been rained on overnight, and was relieved to find that it had not been.

As he inspected its carpets and leather, he spotted a cerise short-sleeved shirt lying on the gravel a few yards away. He picked it up, ran it through his hands, sniffed its under-arms, and kissed it. He took it indoors and went up to his and Jill's bedroom. He kicked off his shoes, lay on their bed, pulled down his chinos and pants, and rucked them around his ankles. He wrapped Kenyon's shirt around his hardening cock, and began to stroke it through the cotton. He came in frenzied but silent convulsions, the fabric darkening as it stemmed the flow of his ejaculate. He stood up, shuffled in quick, tiny steps to the en-suite bathroom, his gait inhibited by chinos and pants still cradling his ankles, blotted a final droplet of sperm with the soiled shirt as it peeped out of the slit at the end of his dick, and dropped it into the dirty-clothes basket. He then pushed it to the bottom of the jumble within, pulled up his pants and chinos, went back downstairs, drove the BMW out of the garage onto the gravel, and reversed the Corvette into the space that the BMW had vacated.

He went to the kitchen, and found Danny there, wearing shell-suit bottoms and a T-shirt, craning his head over the sink so as to drink directly from the cold tap. "Coffee?" he asked.

"Tea, please," Danny replied.

"You OK, son?"

"Kinda."

Danny turned off the tap and stood upright. Rex looked at him. "Jesus," he exclaimed, chuckling. "You've got two pukka shiners there, boy. Good work, son." He let out a noisy belly laugh. "Your mother was out of order last night."

"Like I need you to tell me that, Dad."

"Yeah, well, just so's you know, I'm not angry with you. She may be, but I'm not going to lose my rag about this thing, er, you know, this homosexuality issue. It's something I've got no knowledge of, obviously, so I'm probably not the right person to talk to you about it, but, if it helps, yeah, I haven't got the hump. OK, I'm not exactly delirious about it, but, you know, as I say, I'm not cross about it either."

He handed Danny a cup of tea, and began to drink his coffee.

"Homosexuality," said Danny, and took a sip of his tea.

"Yeah, well, is that what it is?" asked Rex. "I mean, in your case, is that what you are? Queer? Gay, I mean?"

"It's just the word 'homosexuality'. I don't like it. I don't like 'queer' either. I think 'gay' is better."

"Well, that's what I asked you, son. Are you gay?"

"Maybe, Dad, yeah. Is it a problem?"

"Dunno. Might be, might not be. You tell me. As I say, I know bugger all about it. Sorry, no pun intended." Rex laughed.

Danny had always dreaded this day. He had occasionally daydreamed about coming out to Jill on some unspecified future date, supported by a loyal beloved sitting devotedly by his side, but the thought of Rex's reaction had always terrified him. And yet, instead of reading him the riot act, here was his father, making him tea and cracking chummy jokes about buggery. "Sorry, Dad," he said.

"'S'alright, son. But, yeah, what your mother said last night is true, even if she was pissed. Better steer clear of cottages in future. Illegal and dangerous."

"How d'you know they're called cottages, Dad?"

Rex hesitated. "Er, your mother told me. She listened at your door the other night when you were talking to Kimberly on the phone. That's how she knows all about it."

"Oh. Yeah, I guessed that. Dad, let's not talk about this again, OK? And please tell Mum not to, neither. I'm still a bloody good footballer, and I'll still beat you at tennis or snooker any day of the week." He shot his father a nervy smile.

"Any day of the week except Saturday," Rex corrected him, grinning. "If you recall, I beat you at snooker last time."

"Funny. That was a really jammy win. Anyway, you know what I mean. Because what I mean is, you know, none of this really matters. It ain't as if I'm, er, camp. I'll never embarrass you in front of your friends."

"Don't say 'ain't'. What does 'camp' mean?" asked Rex, anxious not to make the same mistake as he had made with "cottaging".

"Oh, you know, guys like, you know, Kenneth Williams."

"Oh, Jesus, son, no, you're nothing like that ridiculous old nancy. Topped himself, by the way. They covered it up, but that's what happened."

Danny took another sip of his tea. "So, Dad, OK, as I say, can we say nothing more about all this, please? For now, anyway? And could you please tell Mum to not say nothing about it neither? But thanks for being, you know, OK about it…" – he tried to smile – "… because I thought you might go mental."

"As I say, it's all Greek to me. Sorry, son, that wasn't s'posed to be an allusion to pederasty in ancient Greece…" – Rex laughed again – "… but, anyway, look, you need to do some revision. Try to put all this crap out of your mind and bury your head in your books. I've got to go to work. Shut the garage door, will you?" Rex put on his jacket, went outside, and drove off in his BMW. Danny followed him, and shut the garage door.

He went back indoors, picked up the hallway phone, and dialled Kimberly's number. She answered immediately. "Come round now, please," he said. "Get a cab. I'll pay the driver when you get here."

CHAPTER 9

An oleaginous gunk caked in a cracked and
brittle crust... and an inextricable caboodle

Jill had taken the tube to work, and had struggled through
the morning, nauseous and distracted. By midday she
had had enough, and had asked Bernard if he would be
prepared to mind the shop on his own for the afternoon
while she went home early. Mondays were always pretty
dead anyway. He had agreed.

She had hailed a black taxi on Upper Street, and had
spent the journey rehearsing what she would say to Danny
when she saw him. She was angry with herself, and had
decided not to drink at all this week.

Now, as she arrived, she was nervous. She let herself
in, and heard Danny's and Kimberly's voices. Annoyed
that he was obviously not revising, she was nonetheless

relieved that he was at home. She walked into the living room, to find the two of them sitting cross-legged on the floor, playing Monopoly. "Hi, darlings, getting on with your revision?" she asked, essaying a tone playful rather than censorious. "My goodness, your eyes are even worse today. Sorry, perhaps that was tactless of me. Do they hurt, darling?"

"No, Mum. I'm fine."

"Morning, or rather afternoon, Mrs Davis," said Kimberly, nervously. "We're going to do revision together this afternoon – look, I've brought my books with me – but we're playing a quick game of Monopoly first."

"So I see, dear. Are you OK, Danny, darling?"

"Yeah, I'm OK."

The truth was that, when Kimberly had arrived, a little more than three hours ago, Danny had hugged her tight and had cried on and off for forty minutes. In between great, heaving sobs he had told her about his mother's drunken inquisition of him yesterday evening, about her having blurted her accusation in unbearably explicit language, about the incongruously shirtless stranger having overheard everything, and about Rex's surprisingly sanguine reaction this morning. Monopoly had been Kimberly's idea, to try to cheer him up.

"Darling, can we talk?" said Jill.

"Mum, you said that yesterday. You told Kimberly to fuck off, and then you made a big scene. Can we not do that all over again, please?"

"I didn't tell Kimberly to eff off. I politely asked her to leave."

"Whatever. Look, Mum, Kimberly's staying. She's my best mate, and she's here to help me with my revision. After this, I mean." He gestured towards the board game between his friend and himself.

"OK, darling, fine. I had no intention of asking her to leave."

"Good."

"Shall I make us some tea?" asked Kimberly.

"No, don't," Danny replied, quickly. "Mum, you make the tea." He felt empowered to issue orders to his mother on account of his having been wronged by her yesterday. Jill disappeared into the kitchen.

"Oh, yeah, wow, there's something I forgot to tell you earlier," Kimberly whispered, shuffling on her haunches to Danny's side of the Monopoly board, so as to speak to him closer to his ear.

"What?" Danny replied.

"Well," she whispered, "when your mum asked me to go yesterday, as I walked out, there was this really good-looking guy, wearing next to nothing, just a really skimpy pair of shorts, that's all, and he was lying on your dad's car. On the old one, the red convertible. And your dad was taking photographs of him."

"What? Fucking hell, that's so weird. So, tell me again, what exactly was happening?"

"Shhh! Talk quieter. Your mum'll hear. That's all there is to it. I walked past quickly and quietly, and the guy didn't see me cos he was just lying on the car with his eyes shut, and your dad didn't see me cos he had a camera up against his face and he was taking photos the whole time. I thought it was really weird."

"Fuck. So weird. What did he look like?"

"Well, he was lying down, but I'd say he was tall. Blond hair, shaved at the sides and kinda messy but trendy on top, tanned, good-looking."

"That was Kenyon. He came round to take photos of Dad's Corvette. I never seen him before. Oh and my mum told him I'm gay for some unknown fucking reason."

"Why?"

"Oh, I dunno. Drunk. She actually told him I done cottaging."

"That's so wrong. Anyway, well, all I can tell you is, when I saw him and your dad, he wasn't the one taking the photos. Your dad was. And the other guy, the good-looking guy, was lying on the Corvette like a porno model. Really weird."

Jill re-entered the room, carrying a tray, and set down three teacups on the coffee table. She began the speech that she had rehearsed in the taxi. "Danny – and I don't mind if you overhear this, Kimberly – I want to apologise to you for being a bit squiffy last night. And for saying what I'd planned to say in a way other than how I'd planned to say it. But what I do want to make clear, now that I'm, er, not at all squiffy, is that the reason I said what I said is that I love you, darling. I only want the best for you. I'll always love you, whatever you are, whatever you do. But I don't want you to break the law, and I don't want you to contract, er, any diseases. And, by the way, that's obviously the main thing. I think you know what I mean. Did you wake up before your father went out this morning?"

"Yeah."

"And did you and he speak about, you know, all this?"

"A bit. He was OK actually."

"That's good. Look, I know he and I sometimes bark at each other like a couple of stray dogs, and I'm sorry about that, but we love each other very much and we love you very much. He finds this kind of thing, you know, gayness, if that's a word, very difficult to understand – more difficult than I do, I think – but he loves you and he only wants the best for you."

"OK, Mum, thanks, but can we drop this now, please? I get it."

There was a silence, which was eventually broken by Kimberly. "Mrs Davis, can I say something, please? Danny's my best friend. I love him, but not in a romantic way. We tell each other everything. So, OK, now you know about him. You know, the gay thing. Well, I'm gay, too. A lesbian."

Jill stared at the girl, and smiled. "Does your mother know, dear?"

"No, she don't," Danny interrupted, "so please don't tell her, nor her dad, neither."

"OK. Well, thank you for telling me, dear. That was very courageous of you. I won't tell your parents. But, in return, may I ask a favour of you? May I ask you to keep a sisterly eye on Danny, because, at your age, girls tend to be more mature than boys – sorry, Danny, but it's true – and I want you to make sure he doesn't do anything, you know, stupid, ever again. I quite understand that you tell each other everything, so I know you'd get to know whatever he gets up to, so please do me that favour."

"OK, Mum, that's it. No more talk about this, please," said Danny, and his wish was immediately granted when Bridie O'Shea chose that moment to let herself in.

Jill took her tea into the kitchen, began to make a chicken salad for herself, Danny and Kimberly, and checked the clock. It was 1.40pm. She switched on the radio just as *The Archers* was coming on. Danny and Kimberly returned to their Monopoly, and as they played they chatted effervescently about Jill, about Rex, and about Kenyon, of whom Danny said, "I wouldn't mind riding his bone, and I bet he's got a fucking massive one," just as Bridie was re-entering the living room. Perhaps Kimberly's howling cackle had prevented Danny's remark being overheard by the char; perhaps it had not. Perhaps Bridie, who was a fifty-something Catholic spinster from Strabane, Northern Ireland, and was in the habit of going to daily mass at the Church of the Sacred Heart in Quex Road, Kilburn, had not the worldly knowledge to understand what Danny had meant by "I wouldn't mind riding his bone"; perhaps she had. Either way, things like that suddenly did not seem to matter so much. Besides, all Bridie had said by way of a response was, "You want to put cold pineapple chunks on them eyes of yours, Danny, so you do."

A little later, after she had finished cleaning upstairs, Bridie carried the dirty-clothes baskets down to the kitchen, where Jill was still busying herself, *The Archers* having been a companionable accompaniment to the more creative kind of chores that she refused to delegate to a housekeeper. "Leave them, Bridie, please," Jill said. "I'm listening to the radio here, and the washing machine makes too much noise. There can't be much there anyway. But, since you've brought them down, I'll put a wash on once *Woman's Hour* is over."

"Right you are, Mrs Davis," Bridie replied, and began to mop the kitchen floor.

When *Woman's Hour* had come to an end, Jill opened the dirty-clothes baskets so as to load the washing machine. As she had expected, there was very little in them. Danny's contained only his dirty Ordell Arms football kit, which she herself had placed in it the day before. In the other basket she saw her dress, knickers, tights and bra from yesterday, and Rex's jeans, sweatshirt, pants and socks. She was just about to go upstairs to collect any rogue items that Danny, and perhaps even Rex, might have left irritatingly on a bedroom floor instead of putting into a dirty-clothes basket, when she spotted lying at the bottom of hers and Rex's a garment that she did not recognise. It was a cerise short-sleeved shirt, too big for Danny, and definitely not Rex's colour. She examined it, turning it over in her hands. Abruptly, she felt a coldness on her fingertips, an oleaginous gunk caked in a cracked and brittle crust. It was unmistakable. She held the shirt close to her nose, inhaled, and the salty-sugary-bleachy-mushroomy aroma confirmed her suspicions.

She placed her dress to one side, for dry cleaning later. She put Kenyon's shirt in the washing machine, together with her and Rex's underwear, his jeans and sweatshirt, and Danny's football kit, switched it on, and silently watched them all gradually entwine with one another until they had become an inextricable caboodle.

CHAPTER 10

A POLISHED TURD IF EVER THERE WAS ONE

Like Jill, Rex had found it difficult to focus at work today. His journey from Manor House Drive to Clerkenwell Green, where the RED offices were located, had taken him only half an hour, since he had set off as the rush hour had been coming to an end. En route he had tuned the radio to *Start the Week* on Radio 4, but he had concentrated on little of it, irritated with himself as he was for not having thought to give Kenyon his office phone number. When he had arrived, parking directly outside the building as usual and tossing his car keys to a reception desk clerk whose task it was to park his BMW in a nearby NCP, he had run up the two flights of stairs to his executive suite, had peremptorily greeted Ursula Hickox, his PA, and had tried to ring Kenyon three times in ten minutes, knowing that

Nigel would be at work; but thrice the phone had rung out without reply. He had tried again a couple of hours later, and Nigel's wife, Norma, had answered; Rex had rung off without speaking. Eventually, at about 3.00pm, he had driven home.

He arrived just as Bridie was leaving, and found Jill drinking tea on her own in the living room, watching TV. "Hi, Jill, you watching this?" he asked her. "I wanted to watch the snooker. It's the world championship."

"Don't I know it! It's quite interesting actually, a documentary about Hatfield House. Queen Elizabeth I grew up there, you know. But, no, feel free to watch the snooker. I missed the start of this and I'm not really paying it that much attention, to be honest."

Rex retuned the telly to BBC2. Terry Griffiths was playing Silvino Francisco, neither of them players whom he liked much, either for their style of play or for their looks. "Cheers. How's your head?" he asked.

"Much better, thanks. How's yours?" she replied.

"Fine. Why d'you ask? I didn't have a hangover."

"Well, I'm surprised to hear that."

"Why's that?"

"Well, when I came down this morning I was pleased to see you'd had a good, big helping of the lamb I made for us last night, and which Danny and I obviously didn't get to eat, but I was surprised you'd polished off two bottles of some of our very best claret on your own."

Rex hesitated. Had Jill not worked out that Kenyon had lingered after she had gone to bed? No, perhaps she had not, owing to alcoholic amnesia. He decided not to clarify things for her. "I didn't finish the second bottle, to be fair, but, yes, well, it'd been a weird and unwonderful evening and I wanted to calm my nerves. Nothing like a bit of Lynch-Bages to do that."

"I dare say. Tea?"

"Cheers, yes. Any phone messages?"

"No."

"Where's Danny?"

"In his bedroom, revising, with Kimberly. Rex, isn't it strange? Forty-eight hours ago, I'd have been half-wondering whether I should even allow them to be alone together in his bedroom, you know, but now I don't give it a second thought. In fact, I'd actually be rather pleased if they were having a bit of innocent slap 'n' tickle up there at this very moment, but of course they won't be. Actually, I was a bit uncharitable about her the other day. I was upset, I think, that's why. One really can't blame her for Danny's behaviour, and earlier today she was quite sweet. She thinks she's a lesbian, by the way."

"Really?"

"Yes. You couldn't make it up, could you? You and I are the only heterosexuals in this whole house. Well, I s'pose Bridie upped the het count until she left a few minutes ago, although I doubt if she's ever, you know…"

"… had sex with man, woman or beast," Rex offered.

"Really, Rex. I don't know why you have to bring 'beast' into it."

"Because it's an expression, and because it's funny."

Jill went into the kitchen and began making tea. She emptied the washing machine, hanging out its contents to dry in the scullery, but putting Kenyon's shirt to one side. Meanwhile, Rex slipped into the hallway, checked that the receiver was lying correctly on the telephone base, went upstairs to the landing, performed the same task there, and finally again in his study, then returned to the living room. "Rex," said Jill, appearing with a tray, "have you any idea whose this is?" She produced Kenyon's shirt, which was still damp, from under her arm.

"Show me," Rex replied. Jill handed it to him.

He examined it briefly, then passed it back. They both sat down. "I haven't the faintest idea," he said. "Why d'you ask?"

"Well, it's very odd actually. When I did a wash just now, I found it at the bottom of our dirty-clothes basket. How could it have got there?"

"I told you, I've got no idea."

"It's so peculiar, Rex. I've never seen it before. It's too big for Danny, and it isn't the kind of thing you'd buy, or I'd buy for you."

"Well, it's a mystery, Jill. But does it matter?"

"Well, yes, it does actually, because, when I found it, it was covered in…" – she grimaced – "… semen."

"What?"

"Semen. You know, sperm."

Rex guffawed. "Nonsense. It seems clean enough to me."

"Yes, because I've just washed it. Look, Rex, it must have something to do with Danny."

"Clearly," Rex replied. "It's got nothing to do with me – obviously – and it's biologically impossible for it to have anything to do with you, Kimberly or Bridie. But how d'you know it had spunk on it, anyway?"

Jill winced. "We don't make love all that often, Rex, but I know the sight and smell of spermatozoa well enough. I last did the washing very recently – Saturday it was, I think – and it wasn't in either of the dirty-clothes baskets then. So it must have appeared today or, maybe, yesterday. What time did you go to work this morning?"

"About 9.30am. Why?"

"Because, Rex, my fear is that, as soon as we'd both slung our hooks, Danny may have invited some frightful poofter to join him here, that's why, and this stinking shirt must belong to the debauched swine."

"He couldn't have. Kimberly was here, and Bridie, too," Rex replied.

"No, Rex. Bridie always arrives in the early afternoon. We don't know when Kimberly got here, and I wouldn't like to ask her. It'd seem odd if I were to do so, and anyway she'd almost certainly lie to protect Danny. So, yes, my point is that there may well have been plenty enough time for Danny to, er, do something with someone between 9.30am and when Kimberly arrived. D'you see what I mean?"

"Yes, but, I really think…"

Jill interrupted: "But, yes, maybe there wasn't anyone else involved, I agree. Maybe he used this shirt, whoever's it is, to wipe up after, you know, masturbation. To be honest, and I hope I'm not fooling myself here, that's what I suspect, and it's certainly what I hope. But what I find oddest of all, in that case, is that he put it in the dirty-clothes basket in our en-suite bathroom rather than the one in his own bedroom."

"I've got absolutely no idea why he'd do that," said Rex, "but, bloody hell, it's a really grotty thing for him to have done, and particularly to have made you have to deal with."

"Thank you for saying that, darling. Yes, it wasn't a very pleasant surprise. Would you speak to him about it, please, but nicely? Try to find out the truth of the matter. If he did it, er, on his own, if you see what I mean, I'm not really that bothered. He's a teenage boy; they do that sort of thing. But if he's had some ghastly queer in here with him, behind our backs, well, that's very different. So could you speak to him, please? Try to find out. Oh and talk to him about condoms. Maybe even buy him some. No, maybe don't. Oh, I don't know. It's so hard to know what to do. I mean, it's so hard to know what's *right* to do."

Rex raised an eyebrow. Jill went on: "I'd feel uncomfortable talking to him about such matters, especially after I confronted him a bit too doggedly when I was blotto last night. It'd be easier for you. It's wrong for a mother to have to talk to her eighteen-year-old son about condoms or even, you know, self-abuse. But, even apart from this shirt mystery, we've really got to lay down some ground rules. When he goes to university – assuming he knuckles down and passes his A-levels, which I'm not at all certain he will, by the way – to some extent he can do his own thing, within reason of course. But while he's under our roof, he's simply got to treat our house, and ourselves, with a bit of respect. So, as I say, please do speak to him."

"I certainly will." Rex knew that he would not. "Here, give it to me." Jill handed him Kenyon's shirt.

"Thank you, darling. Actually, Rex, over and above anything you say to him about this, er, incident, I really wish we knew someone whom we could get to talk to him about, you know, gayness."

"Who?"

"Well, that's just it. There isn't anyone. But if we knew anyone suitable, I think it'd be so helpful for him."

"For whom?"

"For Danny, of course. Who else?"

"No, of course."

"If only we knew a queer, a gay, I mean, close to his age but a bit older – a nice, responsible young man who'd already been at the difficult stage our son's at now and had worked through it all – well, as I say, I think it'd really help Danny if he could talk to a person like that."

Rex stood up and looked out of the window: the sunshine was sparkling prettily on his BMW. "But we don't know anyone like that, Jill, and we're unlikely ever to do so."

"I know. I wish we did though."

Rex turned, and watched a few minutes of the snooker. Griffiths was playing slowly, as usual, but well. Danny and Kimberly appeared. "Not snooker again," said Kimberly.

"Excuse me, all of you, I've got to make a phone call," said Rex, and he went upstairs to his study and closed the door. He dialled Nigel's number, which he had now memorised, and waited.

Nigel answered, for which eventuality Rex was ready. "Ah, good, you're in. It's Rex here, Rex Davis. I wondered if you fancied a game. It's a nice afternoon and I'd love one."

Nigel was more than somewhat surprised, but rallied quickly. Rex and he knew each other well enough, but were not mates, and, although they had sometimes played together when one of them had agreed to make up a four in which the other had already been involved, Rex had never telephoned him to suggest a bespoke game. "Well, yes, very well, that would be most agreeable," Nigel replied. "I was going to drive down to the club in a while anyway. Singles?"

"Er, no. You're too good for me. Doubles. Tell you what, I played with your nephew yesterday – can't remember his name but it was him and me against Terry Morrison and his lad – so if your nephew's up for it again we're bound to be able to find a fourth when we get there."

Rex heard the telephone receiver being placed on a table. "Kenyon, would you like to play tennis?" he could just hear Nigel shouting. After a pause, Nigel came back on the line. "He says he's too tired. Too knackered, actually, he said. The youth of today. But let's play anyway, you and I. I'm sure we'll find two willing victims to join us. I can be there in a little over half an hour."

"OK, see you soon," Rex replied. He replaced the receiver, and stared at the wall. He did not even like Nigel very much – an irritating fusspot in his mid-fifties, albeit still a fine player – and now he was going to have to play tennis with him for no good reason. No wonder Kenyon had not agreed to play with the soppy old fart.

Why had Nigel not shouted, "Kenyon, would you like to play tennis *with Rex and me*?" Rex was annoyed. His plan had been ill thought out. Surely his balls-up was fixable, though.

He hurried into his and Jill's bedroom, changed into his tennis togs, grabbed his racquet, and ran down the stairs. "Just popping out to the club for a game of tennis," he called as he skipped past the living room door, darted out of the house, slammed the door behind him, jumped into his BMW, and drove instead to Gladstone Park Gardens.

He was there within ten minutes. He could not remember what number the Jenkinses lived at, but he recalled from having been there for a rather dull drinks party in December that the house was a humdrum pebbledashed semi on the south side of the street. Moreover, Nigel had an immaculate blue Talbot Avenger, a polished turd if ever there was one, which would be easy to spot. In fact Rex recognised the house before he saw the car, which, when he noticed it stowed inside the small garage, whose door was open, served merely as useful confirmation. He parked his BMW on the street and rang the doorbell.

Nigel answered the door, still in civvies rather than tennis whites. "Oh," he exclaimed, "I, er, I…"

Rex walked past him into the house, and began to speak in a deliberately loud voice. "Didn't we say I was going to pick you up? Maybe I got the wrong end of the stick. No problem. Mind you, now I'm here, I may as well give you a lift, save you getting your car out of the garage. I'll wait here while you get changed. No problem, as I say."

Nigel looked perplexed and, raising his voice, said, "Very well, yes, thank you. Norma, would you be so kind as to make Rex a cup of tea while I change, please?"

But Rex was already on his way into the kitchen, where he found Norma and Kenyon, sitting at the table, chatting.

Kenyon's father, Brian, Nigel's younger brother, lived in Hong Kong, where he had been a senior officer in the Royal Hong Kong Police Force for the past thirty-odd years. Unlike many of his colleagues, he had escaped prosecution, owing to insufficient evidence, just over ten years ago, following the big clean-up that had been triggered by the Independent Commission Against Corruption of 1974, and he had more or less toed the line in recent years. But before that he had habitually overstepped the mark. As a result he had accumulated quite a lot of ill-gotten cash in the '60s and '70s, and had thereby become rather wealthy, although he had always been very cagey about it. When his wife Penelope, Kenyon's mother, had died of colon cancer in 1980, he had sent fifteen-year-old Kenyon back to England to live with Nigel and Norma. Nigel, a Latin teacher (although "schoolmaster" was the word he preferred) at the Cardinal Vaughan Memorial School in Holland Park, disliked and disapproved of his brother, and had been unhappy when Kenyon's move had first been mooted. But Norma – who had always liked Penelope and doted on Kenyon, had never been able to have children of her own, and had regretted that deprivation enormously – had insisted. She now loved Kenyon like the son she had never had, and even Nigel had become accustomed to the young man's presence in their lives, growing cautiously fond of him, although he remembered the Christmas Day five years ago, on which he had told them he was gay, as an embarrassing and disappointing one. Norma had not minded at all, had long suspected as much, and had ever since referred to Kenyon's Yuletide coming-out announcement as "the queen's speech".

"Hello, you two," said Rex, kissing Norma on both cheeks and shaking Kenyon's hand. "All well? I'm about to play tennis with Nigel. Fancy joining us, Kenyon?"

"Go on, Kenny," said Norma, "but don't forget to be home by 7.00pm if you can. Jason Donovan is on *Wogan*." She winked.

"That'll be easy enough. It's only just after 4.30pm now," said Rex. "So, are you up for it, Kenny, er, sorry, Kenyon?"

"Right now?"

"Yeah. Chop chop!"

"OK, sure," Kenyon replied, and ran up the stairs to get changed, passing Nigel, in immaculately starched whites and Frew McMillan-style white cap, on his way down.

"Kenny's playing after all, Nigel," Norma explained.

"Very well," Nigel replied. "Wait a moment, please, while I put the car away for the night."

Kenyon appeared, in blue shorts and a white T-shirt. "Bye, Mum," he said to Norma, and kissed her.

"Er, Norma isn't your mum, is she?" Rex asked when they were outside, watching Nigel struggling with the garage door.

"No, she's my auntie. Well, she's kind of my stepmum, too. I call her Mum actually. My real mum's dead. Oh, look at Nigel, he can't close the garage door, let's help him." Rex nodded. "Oh, and, by the way, I liked it when you called me Kenny just now."

Chapter 11

A MUDDLED CLUTTER OF SPORTING PARAPHERNALIA

"Well, he's in a hell of a rush," Jill had said as Rex had hurried out to play tennis. She had spoken the sentence aloud, but she had been addressing only herself, if anyone. Kimberly had also thought Rex's departure a bit sudden, although she had not alluded to it. Neither had Danny, who was now engrossed in the snooker.

Jill went into the kitchen to make more tea, returning with a tray carrying three cups and three plates on which she had arranged scones, clotted cream and strawberry jam. "I'm a bit peckish," she said. "You two waifs tuck in, too." They did.

After a while Danny stood up. "What's the time, Mum?"

"Five and twenty past four," Jill replied.

Kimberly frowned. "Mrs Davis, why do older people – sorry, you know what I mean, I mean people your age rather than our age – say 'five and twenty past' or 'five and twenty to'? Why not just say 'twenty-five past' or 'twenty-five to'?"

"That's an interesting question, dear. But it isn't only to do with telling the time, actually. Think of the nursery rhyme 'Sing a Song of Sixpence': there's a line in it that goes 'four and twenty blackbirds baked in a pie'. That used to be the convention in the eighteenth century, and before, I think. There's nothing actually wrong with saying 'four and twenty' or 'five and twenty' – it's arithmetically identical to 'twenty-four' or 'twenty-five' after all – and in fact we still use that rubric for numbers between thirteen and nineteen. Think about it: if you were to ask me my age, I'd say 'forty-one'. Well, I'd probably say 'thirty-nine' actually, but that's just my vanity. And yet if I were to ask you your age, you'd say 'eighteen'. But 'eighteen' is an elision of 'eight' and 'ten', isn't it? So what you're basically saying when you say 'eighteen' is 'eight-ten' or 'eight and ten', which is exactly the same construct as 'four and twenty' or 'five and twenty', whereas if numbers between thirteen and nineteen adhered to the conventional modern rubric you'd be teeneight."

"I'd never thought of it like that, but you're right," said Kimberly. "How d'you know all that?"

"There's nothing to *know*, exactly. It's just that I'm interested in history – and in language, too – so I've thought about things like that before. I didn't suddenly work it all out when you asked me just now."

"OK, well, enough of all that mumbo-jumbo. Is it four-thirty yet, Mum?" asked Danny, grinning.

"Not quite, darling, no. It's eight and twenty past four."

"Good. Well, I've got football practice. I'd better get ready."

"Where? Shall I pack your bag?" Jill asked him.

"Wormwood Scrubs Park. Don't worry about my bag, Mum. It's only practice. I'll go like this." He indicated his shell-suit bottoms and T-shirt with an ironic flourish.

"What about your black eyes, darling?"

"Mum, it's just practice. It ain't a proper match. And anyway I know I look like a badger…" – he smiled at Kimberly – "… but I can see perfect and the pain ain't too bad at all now." He went up to his bedroom in search of socks and trainers.

"I'd better get going, too," said Kimberly. "Thanks for the tea, Mrs Davis."

"I'll give you both a lift," said Jill, who then raised her voice, but chummily: "Oh and please don't keep saying 'ain't', darling."

Danny was downstairs again in a few moments, and they all got into Jill's Volvo, Danny in the front passenger seat so as to give her directions and Kimberly alone in the back. They drove along Manor House Drive, turned left onto Brondesbury Park, and left again onto Milverton Road, passing the tennis club. "Surprised we can't see Rex's car parked anywhere along here," Jill said. "Perhaps he walked."

"Unlikely," said Danny.

At the end of Milverton Road, Danny directed Jill to drive left onto All Souls Avenue, and then along Wrottesley

Road, at the end of which they turned right onto Harrow Road, on which the traffic was heavy, their progress correspondingly slow. After a few minutes Jill became aware that Danny, sitting on her left, was looking past her at someone or something on the right-hand side of the street. So she, too, looked to her right, idly interested in knowing who or what it was that was attracting her son's attention, and so it was that she found herself staring at a small, dilapidated, one-storey brick building, with a flat roof and two entrances. Above one was written "ladies" and above the other "gentlemen".

"Oh, god, Danny, that's the place, isn't it?" she said. He did not reply. "Heavens above, OK, look, I'll pick you up when your football practice is over. What time should I come and fetch you?"

"Look, Mum, I ain't going to go there. Please just relax. I'll make my own way home."

"How can I relax when I'm actually looking at the godforsaken hell hole in which you, er, did what you did just two days ago?"

"Danny's football practice is from 5.00pm to 7.30pm, Mrs Davis, so you can pick him up at, er, five and twenty to eight."

"Thank you, Kimberly," said Jill, and smiled at her via the rear-view mirror.

"Left here," said Danny.

As Jill turned the Volvo onto Scrubs Lane, passing the College Park, the pub that Rex had visited on Saturday afternoon, the traffic had become lighter, and they arrived at Wormwood Scrubs Park in good time.

"Thanks for the lift," said Danny, "bye." Kimberly could not tell whether his "bye" had been addressed to her, or was merely a continuation of his valediction for Jill, and she minded her unsurety. She wondered if he had been angered by her having provided details of the timings of his football practice, but she had done so because she had heard the panic in Jill's voice and had felt sorry for her. She transferred to the front passenger seat and, as she did so, she briefly stopped to watch Danny's back view as he headed off towards the pavilion.

Jill began to drive, nosing the Volvo north along Scrubs Lane, which was now quite full. "That was very kind of you, and quite brave, too," she said. "I've misjudged you. I don't mean I thought ill of you – well, I admit I was angry with you when I overheard Danny's half of your phone call on Saturday night, because it was obvious that whatever you were saying wasn't discouraging him from describing his experiences in that revolting *pissoir* in hideous detail – but you could obviously tell that I was shocked when I realised we were passing it just now, and that I was frightened that he might visit it again on his way home, so thank you for telling me what time his football training comes to an end. You're a good girl."

"That's OK, Mrs Davis."

"No, dear, it's more than OK. It's impressive. Thank you, honestly." They had now arrived at the end of Scrubs Lane, and were waiting at a red light, ready to turn right onto Harrow Road. When the light changed, Jill drove off, passing the cottage on the left, neither of them alluding to it this time, although Kimberly turned her head and looked at it as they went by.

Jill retraced their route, turning left onto Wrottesley Road, driving on along All Souls Avenue, on again onto Sidmouth Road, right onto Willesden Lane, and down the hill towards Kilburn High Road. "Your street is somewhere here, on the left, isn't it?" she said.

"No, on the right. Just go past the Prince – the Prince of Wales pub – and it's the first on the right. Tennyson Road. Then our house is about a hundred yards on the right."

Jill indicated right, turned onto Tennyson Road, drove on a bit, and parked where there was a space. Kimberly did not open the door, or get out. "Mrs Davis, can I ask you something?"

"Go ahead."

"Who was that guy yesterday? The guy Danny's dad was taking photos of with his old car?"

"Ah. That was the nephew of the chairman of Rex's tennis club. He's called Kenyon – although why anyone would give their son such an utterly idiotic name I have absolutely no idea. Apparently, he's training to be a photographer or something. But he was the one taking the photographs, not Rex. As a favour to the chairman of his tennis club, Rex let him come and photograph the Corvette. Why d'you ask? If I didn't know better, I'd think you were carrying a torch for him. I wouldn't blame you. He's quite a dish, although if he were a girl one would regard him as a bit of a blond bimbo."

Kimberly blushed. "Er, no. It's not that. No, it's just that, well, when I left, when you asked me to leave…"

"Yes, I'm sorry about that, I was upset and I'd had a bit too much gin, I think…"

"That's alright. No, as I was saying, when I left, as I walked past, it wasn't the guy who was taking the photos, it was Danny's dad. And what he was taking photos of was the guy, lying on the bonnet of the car, with his top off, wearing only these really skimpy shorts…" – Jill recoiled – "… I just thought you should know, that's all. Sorry, have I offended you, Mrs Davis?"

"No," Jill replied. "Thank you. Yes, thank you, again. But are you quite certain that it was Rex taking photos of Kenyon reclining on the Corvette, and not the other way around?"

"Absolutely, Mrs Davis, yes."

Jill shook her head, then shook it again. "Perhaps it would be best if you don't share that with anyone else," she said finally.

"Danny knows," Kimberly replied.

"I see. Look, Kimberly, I wasn't going to ask you this, but now I will. What time did you arrive at our house this morning? Think carefully and answer me honestly, please."

"Why?"

"Please just tell me."

"Well, I can tell you exactly, because Danny rang me and asked me to go round just as the Simon Bates show was starting on Radio 1. So that was 9.30am. He called me a minicab and it came more or less straight away. So I must have got to your house by about 9.45am."

"Thank you, dear…" – Jill leant across Kimberly to open the front passenger door – "… that's very good news."

"OK, if you say so, Mrs Davis," said Kimberly, and she jumped out and let herself into the Coleman family's home.

Jill did not move for five minutes. It was almost inconceivable that the girl had invented her bizarre story about Rex's and Kenyon's photoshoot, and yet, if it were true, it was inexplicable. Apart from anything else, Rex had had the Corvette photographed professionally not long ago, by a freelance automotive photographer who usually worked for *Car* magazine (not a RED title), and a framed print now hung glossy on his study wall. Moreover, Rex did not have a photographer's eye, by his own admission. Why, then, would he take photographs of the car now, and why especially would he want those photographs enhanced by the inclusion of a lolling piece of semi-clad beefcake? It made no sense. Anyway, there was sure to be an explanation, and she would ask Rex for it when an opportunity presented itself.

She started the car, looked over her left shoulder, let off the handbrake, then put the handbrake back on, and switched off the engine. Of course. The infamous cerise shirt must belong to Kenyon – it was obvious now – and, now that she thought about it, also, she recalled finding not only two Lynch-Bages bottles in the kitchen this morning but also two used whisky tumblers, two used wine glasses, two used plates and two used sets of cutlery. Rex must have had dinner with Kenyon in the kitchen after she and Danny had gone to bed, which had been very early, and Danny must have found the shirt in the morning, or during the night, somehow recognised it as Kenyon's, become aroused – after all, Kenyon was an attractive young man and he had been wearing next to nothing when Danny had met him – and, well, masturbated with it, or over it, or onto it, or into it, or something. It was an absurd thing for him to have done, clearly, but it was hardly the end of the world. She drove home.

When she arrived, she searched Danny's bedroom. She felt sneaky, disloyal even, but she had decided that she had no choice. She had to know more, if there was more to be known. She spent fifty minutes carefully inspecting everything she could see, rigorously putting it all back where she had found it as she did so. She made no discoveries; there were no incriminating diaries, letters, books, magazines, videotapes or anything else noteworthy or untoward. After she had finished, whereas she would usually have chided her son silently for the untidiness of his bedroom – football, tennis and snooker kit and accessories were strewn everywhere, heaped together along with a cricket bat, a badminton racquet, a baseball glove, a pair of swimming goggles, a skateboard, a dart, a Frisbee, a Bullworker – today she was buoyed and becalmed by the muddled clutter of sporting paraphernalia that she had spent the best part of an hour rooting through. She even left on the floor under the bed, undisturbed although not unexamined, a slightly grubby pair of underpants.

She went downstairs and into the kitchen. It was almost 6.20pm. She poured herself a glass of tonic, *sans* gin, and dropped two ice cubes into it. She opened a packet of Twiglets, tipped them into a bowl, put the bowl and the glass on a tray, and took it into the living room. She sat down, switched on the TV, and began watching the news. She leafed through the *Radio Times*. She saw that *Don't Wait Up* was on BBC1 at 8.00pm, followed by *Wildlife on One* at 8.30pm. She quite fancied watching both, although she realised that she might miss the beginning of the former while she was collecting Danny from his football practice, especially as she thought they might stop on the way home to pick up a Chinese takeaway. She wrote a note for Rex, and left it on the kitchen table: "Have gone to pick Danny up from football practice. Will be back by about 8.00pm with a Chinky for us all. Love, Jill xxx". She then set forth for Wormwood Scrubs Park, a little worried that she might not have remembered the way.

CHAPTER 12

AN ENRAPTURED LASCIVIOUSNESS

Rex had not enjoyed playing tennis as much as he had hoped and expected to, because Nigel had insisted on partnering him, having persuaded a chap called Dave Masters to partner Kenyon. "Oldsters versus youngsters," Nigel had trilled, clearly pleased with a quip that Rex thought not only feeble but also insulting. After all, he was thirty-seven, whereas Nigel must be fifty-five if he was a day; the so-called youngsters were twenty-four in Kenyon's case, Rex knew that, and probably about thirty in the case of Dave, in whom he had no interest other than as an object of envy, especially when he was aced by him and Kenyon congratulated him with a high five.

Moreover, Rex had not played well, getting very few of his first serves in and, at net, bungling a number of volleys that he should have put away, on one occasion losing Nigel's serve for him in so doing. Nigel had been annoyed, but had tried his courteous best to hide his irritation. He and Rex had lost six-four seven-five.

They repaired to the bar and, since it had just turned 6.00pm, Rex bought beers for them all. He was pleased when Dave gravitated towards Nigel, eager to discuss the arrangements for a forthcoming mixed doubles tournament, which meant that he had Kenyon more or less to himself. "I couldn't help laughing when you made all those balls-ups at net on poor old Nigel's serve," Kenyon said. "You played much better yesterday, to be honest, didn't you?"

"I did, yeah, I admit it," Rex replied, radiating an enraptured lasciviousness that casual bystanders might have mistaken for warm-hearted self-deprecation.

They chatted freely and chummily. "Hey, d'you fancy a bite to eat?" Rex said at one point, making sure that Nigel and Dave were not listening. "You know, to talk about your career, and stuff, and Danny, you know?"

"I'd love to, yes," Kenyon replied, "but I told Mum I'd watch *Wogan* with her."

Rex laughed. "That hardly seems like a three-line whip. Can't you video it? And, anyway, what was all that Jason Donovan business? And that winking business?"

"OK, well, since you ask, Mum thinks I should find a nice boy of my own age. She doesn't really like the fact that I tend to go for older men. I don't go for much older, by the way, but certainly older. She once told me that Jason Donovan would be a perfect boyfriend for me. He's twenty, I think. But I don't like that 'pretty boy' type, and he's obviously straight, and anyway it's all a silly fantasy of hers because he's a superstar and I'm just a horny gay boy living in a three-bedroom semi in Gladstone Park Gardens. Sorry, does that embarrass you?"

"Not at all, no."

"Good. It's just cos you and I chatted quite a bit about gay stuff last night, so I feel able to speak a bit more freely about it than, well, you know…" – he flashed Rex a big smile – "… but, look, the thing is, Mum's great, she's totally OK with me being gay and she's my best friend, so that's why I don't like letting her down. Mummy's boy, that's me."

"No problem. So why don't you phone her, ask her to video *Wogan*, and tell her you'll watch it with her when you get home, or tomorrow? And in the meantime I'll buy you dinner somewhere really nice. Deal?"

"Deal," Kenyon replied. "That'd be fab. I'll have to go home to shower and change, so I can tell her then. I might even get a chance to watch it before you and I go out. Do I have to wear a suit?"

Rex pondered. He had already scrutinised Kenyon almost naked at some length, and, although he ached with unalloyed ardour to inspect every inch of his body entirely unclothed, which aspiration he could feel was fast becoming a consuming obsession, he found himself suddenly captivated also by the prospect of seeing him in his best bib and tucker. "You should, yes, and a tie. Have you got a suit and tie?"

"Of course," Kenyon replied. "I scrub up pretty well, you know."

"OK, sorry," said Rex. "I'll book us somewhere nice. Shall I pick you up at 8.00pm? That way you can check out your future husband on *Wogan* before I whisk you away from him."

They both laughed. "You can whisk me away whenever you like," said Kenyon.

Rex bade Nigel a goodbye whose brevity startled him, ignored Dave, walked quickly to his car, and drove home. He went into the living room, saw Jill's note, and scribbled underneath her message one of his own: "Something's come up. Business dinner. Sorry. See you later. Don't wait up. R."

He then ran up the stairs, kicked off his tennis kit, showered, ran his beard-trimmer over his designer stubble and again over his pubic hair (albeit on a longer setting), brushed his teeth, flossed, splashed on some of his most expensive aftershave, and opened the wardrobe in which he kept his made-to-measure stuff. He selected a navy-blue herringbone Chester Barrie three-piece suit, a white regent-collared double-cuffed Egyptian-cotton shirt, an electric-blue micro-dot woven-silk tie, Victorian white-gold chain-link cufflinks that Jill had given him for Christmas a couple of years ago, black leather brogues, and a 1966 Rolex Steel Submariner with black bezel and dial. On his way downstairs he went into his study, opened his safe, and took out £500 in £50 notes and £200 in £20 notes, which wad he folded once and slipped into his left front pocket. He reached for his desk phone, lifted the receiver, rang Langan's Brasserie on speed dial, booked a table for two for 8.30pm, easy enough at short notice on a

Monday, ran downstairs, jumped into his BMW and drove to Gladstone Park Gardens, arriving at 7.57pm.

Kenyon was waiting outside, smoking, wearing a light grey suit, white shirt, dark grey tie and white sneakers. He walked over to the car, took one languid drag, dropped his cigarette butt on the pavement, stepped on it, and got in. "Do I look OK?" he asked Rex.

"Yeah, very smart. What's with the shoes?" asked Rex, engaging the BMW's dog-leg first gear, summoning quite a bit of throttle, dumping the clutch, and wheel-spinning away in a cloud of tyre smoke.

"Wow! This car's bloody quick," said Kenyon, grinning. "I told Mum and Nigel I was meeting some mates. Hope that's OK. They don't need to know I'm having dinner with you."

"That's fine, yeah. And the shoes?" Rex settled the car to a brisk but sensible 45mph.

"Ah, well, I often like to add a twist when I go formal. Sometimes I leave the tie off, but you said I should wear a tie, so I thought I'd put these on," he said, pointing a finger at his feet. "Are they OK? They're brand new."

"Yeah, of course, they're great. Glad you like the car. It's an '88 E28 M5. One of the last right-hookers made. The brand-new model, the E34, which is coming out soon, isn't as nice in my view. This one's very rare. They only made 187 right-hookers. It's got a 24-valve double-overhead-cam straight-six, basically the same unit as in the M1, which was a mid-engined supercar as you probably know…" – Kenyon did not – "… and it pumps out 286bhp which makes it pretty damn quick, as you say. It'll do nudging 160mph and it'll go from nought to sixty in six seconds dead. Grips and handles really well, too. Dog-leg five-speed 'box as you probably noticed..." – Kenyon had not – "... oh and we're going to Langan's. Have you been there before?"

"Fab. Of course not."

"You'll like it. Did you manage to catch *Wogan*?"

"I did actually, yeah."

"And did Norma manage to persuade you that you and Jason Donovan could live happily ever after?" Rex glanced at Kenyon, then smiled at him.

"She didn't, no."

They both chuckled. The journey consisted largely of one long run southbound along various iterations of the A5 to Marble Arch – Edgware Road, Cricklewood Broadway, Shoot-Up Hill, Kilburn High Road, Maida Vale and finally Edgware Road again – after which they passed Marble Arch and continued along Park Lane, turned left onto Piccadilly at Hyde Park Corner, and finally arrived at Stratton Street. Rex drove it all fast, sometimes very fast, touching 80mph as they passed the Dorchester, causing Kenyon to whoop happily. Rex parked outside Langan's front door, handed the doorman a £20 note, chucked him his car keys and said, "Park this old banger somewhere, will you, Mario?" and in they went.

They were shown to a good table, and Rex offered Kenyon the chair that afforded a view of the room. Rex was interested in only one view, that of Kenyon's face. "Is that Rula Lenska? And Dennis Waterman, too?" asked Kenyon.

"Probably," Rex replied without looking around to check. "They're in here a lot."

They ate and drank well. After an hour, by which time they had had two Blue Lagoons each and were coming to the end of the first of what would eventually be two bottles of good red Burgundy, they were beginning to feel pleasantly buzzed. "Why did you order Blue Lagoons?" Kenyon asked, lighting a cigarette and twisting his mouth so as to spew the smoke sideways, away from Rex's face.

"Oh, I like the colour, it's a '60s classic, and I prefer vodka cocktails to gin cocktails," Rex replied. He did not give Kenyon the more accurate explanation, which was that Jill had rented *The Blue Lagoon* on video not long ago, and had been bored by it, a reaction at odds with Rex's response, which had been an evening of intense arousal thanks to nineteen-year-old Christopher Atkins, who had spent almost the entire feature wearing nothing but a loin cloth.

Rex changed the subject: "May I ask you a personal question, Kenyon?"

"Go ahead."

"Why did you ask me to take photos of you lying on my Corvette? And why did you take your shirt off for them? And why did you want me to crop out the number plate?"

"Tell you later."

"Tell me now."

"No, later. Anyway, that wasn't a very personal question. You can ask me more personal questions than that if you like."

"Well, maybe I will."

"You can. Anyway, I'm going to ask you a personal question. Maybe I'm only being brave enough to ask it cos I'm already a bit pissed, but I'll ask it anyway."

"Be my guest."

"When's your birthday?"

"That's not a very personal question. December 14th. When's yours?"

"January 1st. It's a bit of a pain, yeah, cos everyone's got a hangover and no one wants to celebrate it with me, just in case you were going to ask."

"I wasn't going to ask, actually. So you were born on January 1st 1965, correct?"

"Correct. And this question is a little bit more personal: what year were you born?"

"Jesus. OK, 1951."

"So you're, er, thirty-seven. Fab. Anyway, that wasn't really the personal question I wanted to ask you. I wanted to ask you a far more personal question than that."

"OK. Go on."

"OK, well, sorry, but why are you still with your wife? OK, you'll probably tell me she's a nice person when she's sober, and I s'pose I didn't meet her when she was at her best, but you obviously look after yourself, whereas she's a bit fat, and she's a grouchy alcoholic whereas you're so nice and sorted, and, er, well, you don't seem to be very close to each other as far as I can tell, and, well, I just wondered, that's all."

Rex sipped some Burgundy, sighed, then began to speak: "OK, well, my life is obviously very different from yours. You're twenty-four. I'm thirty-seven. You're gay. I'm straight. You're single. I'm married. You don't have kids and I don't s'pose you ever will. I've got a son. You're footloose and fancy-free. I'm bound by what used to be called the ties of family and home…"

"You speak so nicely," said Kenyon, interrupting. "You present yourself as just this regular guy – you know, a businessman who likes cars and sport and all that – but actually you're spiritual and poetic."

Rex felt dizzy with an odd mix of desire and gratitude, but continued. "Thank you. You're quite wrong, but thank you. I *am* just this regular guy. Anyway, where was I? Oh yeah. Look, the fact is that Jill doesn't really like me. I don't say she hates me, although sometimes I really do believe she does, but she's cosmically bored by me and she thinks I'm a bit of a twat. And, if I'm honest, I'm cosmically bored by her and I think she's a bit of a frump. But she runs our houses well, she's been a brilliant mum to Danny, and I'm just not cut out for all that domestic stuff. OK, I love Danny – of course I do, he's my son – but it's only since he's been older that I've begun to know how to interact with him. And, by the way, more married men are like me than they'd ever admit, I promise you. Little kids are fucking boring. And, as you've probably worked out, I'm only nineteen years older than Danny, which means I got Jill up the duff when I was only eighteen. She was twenty-three. It was a one-night stand, literally. We got married because she got preggers. We had to. That was what the world was like in those days; well, England, anyway. We were never in love. In fact I resented her. I even resented Danny. They prevented me from going to university, which I'd been really looking forward to. And, even apart from uni, they cramped my style when all I wanted was to be out and about, sowing my wild oats. I used to marvel at how Jill would like nothing better than playing with Danny when he was all shit, snot and tears. OK, I loved him, even then I did, of course I did, but it was only later, when I could play football with him in the park, and watch sport with him on telly, and take him to Arsenal, and teach him to play tennis and snooker, all that kind of thing, that we became mates. And that's what we are now: mates."

"OK, I get that, I think. But that still doesn't explain why you stay with your wife. Lots of couples split up. Loads of my friends' parents have split up, and it doesn't seem to have done them any harm. Look, I was fifteen when my real mum died, we were living in Hong Kong cos my dad had a job in the Royal Hong Kong Police Force, and when she died he sent me to live with Norma and Nigel. I was OK. Life goes on."

"OK, look, you may not find this answer very impressive, but the fact is that I've got a big house in London, which you've been to, a flat in Montmartre, a villa in Umbria, a publishing company, three cars and a motorbike, and loads of watches and wine and investments and other shit, and, well, I like my life. I like having all that stuff. I like being able to come to places like this, and order good wine, and not have to worry how much it costs. OK, I could be richer, of course I could, lots of people are miles richer than I am, but I'm comfy, I've got my life how I want it, Jill doesn't bother me, and if I were to divorce her I'd be into a world of pain, she'd take half of everything I've got, or more than half probably, and I'd end up living in a one-bedroom flat on Stonebridge Park Estate, watching repeats of *Juliet Bravo* on my own every night, wanking over page three of *The Sun* before bedtime, and getting mugged whenever I went out."

"Where's Umbria?"

"Central Italy, bordering Tuscany to the south-east. It's beautiful. Jesus, that's a weird question to ask after everything I've just told you. You've heard of Tuscany, right?"

They both laughed. "Tuscany, yeah, I've heard of that, and Montmartre, too. It's in Paris, right?"

"Full marks."

"Phew! And would you really ever have a wank over page three of *The Sun*? Be honest."

"Well, that was just a manner of speaking. I was painting a picture of how dreary my life would be if I went through a divorce. Whereas, now, I can more or less do what I want. And Jill can more or less do what she wants, too. So that's why we're still together, and, if half the couples sitting opposite each other here this evening were to be a hundred percent honest about it, that's why they're still together, too. But tell me more about you. I didn't know your mum had died – well, not 'til you told me earlier and again just now – and I certainly didn't know your dad sent you back to England."

"Well, that's what happened. But I was OK. Mum and Nigel are great – Mum especially, Norma, I mean, but Nigel isn't a bad old stick – and I've had a good time back here in England. I studied fine art at Sussex, and it was great living in Brighton, and I learned a lot and sowed a lot of wild oats, to use your phrase, cos it's a very gay town as you may or may not know, and now I'm back living in London, and studying at Middlesex Poly, doing an MA in photography, which is my passion, and I've got lots of friends. My dad occasionally phones, but not often, maybe two or three times a year. It's OK though. Basically, he's just the guy who came inside my mum twenty-five years ago. I know that sounds hard-arsed, but it's true."

Rex wanted to reach out and hold Kenyon's hand, and he felt sure that the young man would welcome it, but he did not dare, not in the middle of Langan's, where he was well known to the waiting staff. Finally, he spoke. "That's not such a bad thing to say, Kenny. It's OK. I'll tell you about my dad one day. Anyway, you've got lots of friends, you say. Have you got a boyfriend?"

"No, I haven't, Rexy."

They finished their desserts. "D'you want a *digestif*?" Rex asked.

"After all that lovely food, I don't need a chocolate biscuit, thanks," Kenyon replied.

"No, I meant…"

"I know what you meant. I was joking."

"Oh, sorry."

"No problem. No, I don't want a *digestif*. But I do want to talk to you some more. I want to talk to you quite a lot more, in fact. Is there somewhere we can go, you know, to talk all night?"

"What d'you mean?"

Kenyon lit another cigarette. "OK, well, you're the older man, so usually it'd be up to you to take the lead. But you're straight, so that evens things up a bit. So, look, the fact is, which I'm sure you've worked out by now, I fancy you rotten. You're not only my type, but you're *exactly* my type. You're thirty-seven, you're good-looking, you're muscly, you've got designer stubble, which is a big turn-on for me, you're married, which makes things a bit weird but massively exciting, and you're kind and clever and witty. And, well, I may be wrong, although I don't think I am, but I think you quite like me, too."

Rex opened his mouth, but he could not find any words. "OK," Kenyon said, grinning, "I'll help you. I fancy you rotten, as I say. Specifically, I want to spend the next eight hours rolling around a big double bed with you. I want to lie on my back with my legs in the air while you pound my peachy arse with your big fat cock. I've even brought condoms, lube and poppers. I know I told you I was a mummy's boy, but, if you want me to be a daddy's boy, I can be that, too. Does that appeal? Any of it? At all?"

"It does," said Rex finally. "I'll get the bill."

PART 2

SATURDAY 20 MAY 1989

CHAPTER 13

A GRAVEL-CRUNCH DIMINUENDO

Jill walked into the living room. "You need to revise, Danny," she said.

"Yeah, I know, but it's the FA Cup Final. Everyone watches the FA Cup Final. It's the end of the football season, basically."

"I thought the football season was over already."

"Yeah, *my* football season is over already, but the professional football season is still going. Let me watch the FA Cup Final, Mum, please. I'll revise after it's finished, I promise. Please, please, please."

Jill stared at him, then smiled. "OK, darling," she replied. "When does it start?"

"In ten minutes. Kimberly's coming over to watch it with me – she's on her way – and we'll revise together afterwards. Then, after that, we'll be going for a drink-up in the Spotted Dog with a few of the others. Well, I won't have that much to drink, cos I never do really, but the others will. Please don't moan about it, Mum. I've already done quite a lot of revision today anyway." He had not.

Jill went back into the kitchen and began to make tea for them. She was irritated with Rex, who had flown to Paris the day before, called to an unavoidable series of business meetings apparently, and would be back on Tuesday evening. She was worried about Danny's A-level exams, which were imminent, and she felt that Rex should have declined his business trip, important or not, in order to help her keep their son's nose to the revision grindstone. She knew that Danny was not academically gifted, albeit not thick either, but the past month had been difficult for him – for all of them – and she was of the opinion that the concomitant anxiety must have distracted him from his school work. Nonetheless, this weekend aside, she had felt that recently Rex had been mostly if not invariably present and correct, less annoying than usual, and kind to Danny, whose sexuality had become something they all knew about but rarely now discussed, an April shower giving way to a blithe and balmy spring.

She returned with three cups of tea, which she put on the coffee table. "Who's playing, darling?"

"Liverpool and Everton."

The doorbell rang. Jill opened the door to Kimberly, who hugged her then walked into the living room, where she sat down next to Danny on the sofa. Kimberly's mother, Deirdre, had disappeared to her native Galway three weeks ago, to nurse an old and ailing maiden aunt there, leaving Kimberly in the "care" of her father, Joe, who had been born in Saint Helena but had sailed to London in the late '60s to work at the Unigate factory on Scrubs Lane, as had a couple of hundred other Saints, as the sons and daughters of that most remote of South Atlantic islands liked to call themselves. Since Unigate had moved out of London to the West Country, Joe Coleman had been unemployed, and far from saintly. He drank Carlsberg Special Brew from breakfast time onwards, chain-smoked untipped Player's Navy Cut, ate negligibly, bathed not at all, and rarely left the house. Jill had taken pity on Kimberly, alone as she was with a frail, slovenly, indolent drunkard, and had recently begun not only to like the girl but also to admire her honest stoicism. Accordingly, she had become a more or less daily visitor to 67 Manor House Drive, often staying the night, too.

Jill began to drink her tea, standing up, having not intended to watch the match, but found herself suddenly overwhelmed when Gerry Marsden, the Gerry of Gerry and the Pacemakers, began singing 'You'll Never Walk Alone' in the lead-up to kick-off. She sat down on an armchair, put down her teacup, and wept.

"Are you OK, Jill?" Kimberly asked.

"Yes, yes, darling. It's just that, well, Rex is from Liverpool, and it's only a few weeks since nearly a hundred Liverpool fans were crushed to death in Sheffield, isn't it? And now this famous Liverpool song, with all the fans joining in. Well, I find it very moving. I hope they win."

She wiped her eyes, but then the melancholy strains of 'Abide With Me' piped up, and she was off again. "Mum, shut up," said Danny, affectionately, and pecked her on the cheek. Kimberly walked over to Jill, perched on the arm of her chair, and took her hand.

*

Meanwhile, in Paris, Rex and Kenyon were in bed. They had flown from Heathrow to Charles de Gaulle the previous afternoon, had dined in splendour at Le Meurice on Rue de Rivoli, then had hurried by taxi to Rex's apartment on Rue des Abbesses, where they had fucked until dawn. Now, having slept until lunchtime and having fucked again on waking, they were chatting, Rex spooning Kenyon, his dick nestling in the cleft between his lover's buttocks, his right hand caressing his hair.

"This is beautiful," said Kenyon, wriggling his butt against Rex's groin.

"I know. It's wonderful. Thank you for being with me."

"Thank you for inviting me."

"You're welcome, sweetheart. D'you realise we've known each other for less than a month?"

"Yes, I know, but I can't even imagine what my life was like before I knew you."

"Same here. What d'you want to do today?"

"This."

They laughed. Kenyon went back to sleep. Rex continued to stroke his hair, then dozed off himself.

*

The Cup Final had gone to extra time, the score one-all at ninety minutes, and Danny, Kimberly and even Jill were watching it avidly. An Arsenal supporter like his father, Danny did not really mind which of these two scouse teams eventually came out on top, but he fancied John Barnes, and he had decided to root for Liverpool on that basis, a rationale of which Kimberly was aware but Jill was not.

Liverpool scored again. Everton equalised again. It was two-all. Then Barnes crossed, Ian Rush headed a third Liverpool goal, and that was it: three-two to Liverpool.

"Well, I'm delighted," said Jill as the final whistle blew. "Now, you two go and revise, OK?" Reluctantly, they complied. Jill put their teacups on a tray and took it into the kitchen, where she made herself a Lymeswold sandwich. She switched on the radio and tuned it to Radio 3, on which Peter Clayton was playing jazz requests. She looked at the clock. It had just gone 5.30pm. She began to wait for 6.00pm.

*

Rex awoke. He checked the time. It had just gone 6.30pm. Kenyon was still sleeping, but Rex was hard again, and horny. He took his cock in his hand and began to rub it against Kenyon's buttocks. "I'm asleep," said Kenyon, smiling, which smile Rex could not see.

"Not now you're not," Rex replied.

"OK, well, I'm knackered."

"Just relax. I'll do all the work. Anyway, how can you be knackered? You've been asleep all day."

"Sleeping's knackering."

"Bollocks."

They laughed again, and Kenyon squirmed around to face Rex, hugging him. They kissed. Rex reached for Kenyon's cock, and found it erect. "What's this then?" he said. "Knackered my arse."

"No, *my* arse, please," whispered Kenyon, and they made love again the way they always did.

*

Danny and Kimberly walked into the living room, where Jill was on her third gin 'n' tonic. It had just gone 8.00pm and she was watching a *Columbo* repeat. "We're off to the Spotted Dog," Danny announced. "We won't be late."

"OK, darlings, see you later. You can stay over if you like, Kimberly."

"Thanks, Jill. I will then if that's OK."

"Of course it's OK."

She heard them opening then closing the front door, listened to the gravel-crunch diminuendo as they walked away, then returned her attention to Peter Falk, Ray Milland and Messrs Gordon and Schweppe.

CHAPTER 14

A MAN FOR ALL SEASONS

Since their first night together, when they had fallen, drunk and horny, into the nearest hotel to Langan's they could find – the Washington on Curzon Street – Rex and Kenyon had seen each other almost every day. Rex had done a deal with the Holiday Inn Swiss Cottage, booking a suite indefinitely, and over the past month they had met there, mostly in the afternoons or early evenings but just occasionally staying overnight, as often as they could. Kenyon's term at Middlesex Poly had come to an end, and Rex had skipped work often, exercising his privilege as the boss so to do.

Their Paris trip was a relationship evolution, therefore: their first weekend away together. For both of them, despite the difference in their ages, it was an all-new experience. Kenyon had never yet had a beau with whom he had thought he was in love, and, a single special schoolboy crush aside, Kenyon was the first person whom Rex had ever felt romantic about as well as attracted to. They both had high hopes of their liaison. Rex relished the chicanery that their affair necessitated – got off on it actually – and was consequently keen to prolong its illicit status indefinitely, although he had not shared that aspiration with Kenyon, having correctly divined that the younger man yearned for a day when they would be able to be open about their relationship. Rex had told no one about Kenyon. Kenyon had told all his friends about Rex, and had confided in Norma, too, who had been nice to her nephew about the new man in his life despite having three serious concerns about him: that he was too old, that he was married, and that he was therefore incontrovertibly capable of living a lie. Nigel had not been informed.

Rex had had a shower, and was relaxing in the living room, wearing a bathrobe. He had turned the lights down low and had put on an Édith Piaf LP. Kenyon was now in the bathroom. "It's 7.30pm, Kenny," Rex shouted. "If we're going to have dinner, we should get our skates on."

"Keep your hair on, I won't be long," Kenyon replied, his voice made indistinct by the toothbrush in his mouth.

"My hair, or as much of it as I still have, is on, young man."

Kenyon emerged, naked, and sat on Rex's knee. Piaf was singing 'Padam Padam'. With every "padam", Kenyon bounced perkily, in time with the rhythmic crooning of France's most famous chanteuse. "You've still got plenty of hair, you silly sausage. OK, Rexy, I've got an idea. Let me cook dinner for us. We don't always have to go out to posh places. OK, I love them, of course I do, and last night was fab, but it costs you an arm and a leg. I'd like to cook for you tonight. Is there anywhere near here we can buy nice ingredients?"

"Sweetheart, we're in Paris. Of course there are places we can buy nice ingredients. Loads of places. Come on, get dressed, let's go down and I'll show you an amazingly nice *épicerie du terroir*. It closes at 8.00pm, though, so let's get going."

They went into the master bedroom and dressed. Rex's apartment was on the fifth floor of a mid-nineteenth-century building that had no lift, so they trotted down the stairs and out into the street. They walked briskly to the shop, and began to patrol the aisles together. "What are you planning to cook, Egon?" Rex asked.

"Boeuf bourguignon. Why d'you call me 'Egon'?"

"Egon Ronay. Doesn't matter. Boeuf bourguignon? Sweetheart, honestly, that'll take hours. I tell you what. I'd be delighted and honoured to sample your boeuf bourguignon another day, when we've got more time, but do the sums. By the time we get back to the apartment it'll be 8.30pm. It'll take you a good hour to prepare everything, and then two more hours to bake it. Boeuf bourguignon is a slow-cook dish. We won't be eating 'til midnight. No, let's just buy something to take away, good bread and good cheese and good red wine, and enjoy the evening together. Then maybe later we can walk up to Sacré-Coeur for a romantic midnight stroll."

He wondered whether he had hurt Kenyon's feelings, but he had not. "OK, yeah, I guess that's probably a bit more sensible," he replied.

"Good. You get the bread and cheese, and I'll get the wine," said Rex, and they set off in different directions around the bijou store. Kenyon chose Comté, Neufchâtel and Roquefort, a pat of butter, two baguettes, some saucisson sec, a bunch of grapes, two bottles of Perrier and a packet of Gauloises. Rex bought two bottles of Château Lafite Rothschild 1965, which cost him more than he would admit to Kenyon, even in France where wine was so much cheaper than in England, but he did not care. He chose it because 1965 was the year of Kenyon's birth, and he made sure that the young man did not notice the labels at the checkout. He planned to reveal the surprise as he uncorked the first bottle, and he was excited about it.

They heaved their purchases up the stairs, and entered the apartment, panting slightly. Rex selected another LP. "This is Jacques Brel, one of my francophone favourites. He's actually Belgian, not French, but same difference…" – Kenyon began to put the food out on plates – "… and, by the way, look what we're drinking." He held a bottle in front of Kenyon's face.

"Very nice, Rexy."

"Yes, it's a great wine, but check the year. I chose it cos of you." Kenyon peered at the bottle, stepped forward, and gave Rex a hug. Rex had hoped for a slightly more effusive reaction, but he was not crestfallen by it. He uncorked the first bottle carefully, decanted its contents, and poured out two glasses. They began to eat.

When they had polished off the first bottle, Rex immediately uncorked and decanted the second. They sat together on the sofa, Kenyon now naked, Rex fully clothed apart from his shoes, Kenyon's head resting on his chest. "Can I ask you a question, Rexy?"

"Ask me anything."

"This may sound a bit keen, but I promise you it isn't just the drink talking, even though I know I've had half a bottle of wine already, so, well, I want to ask you: d'you think, if we wanted to, if we *both* wanted to, I mean, we could one day live together?"

Rex sipped his claret, and looked down.

"What I mean is," Kenyon went on, "look, I think we both agree this has been a totally amazing month, yeah?"

"Absolutely."

"Well, so, you know, d'you think it might be possible?"

"Kenny, listen, I've told you before. I'd lose everything if I divorced Jill."

"Not everything."

"No, but half of everything, probably more than half. Besides, we don't have to make such big changes. Things are pretty much perfect as they are. We meet whenever we want, and we always will. Also, you're at uni. You'll need to focus on that again in the autumn term, and after that, in a couple of years, when you've got your MA, you can decide what you want to do and where you want to live and all that."

"Yeah, but you still won't want to divorce Jill, even then, and I don't understand why not, to be honest. You're gay, you're in love with me, I'm in love with you, you've only got one kid, and he isn't a kid any more, in fact, he's eighteen, and he's gay, too. I've offered to help him before, as you remember, because his age is a difficult one to be gay at, and I've been through all that not so long ago myself, and I came out the other side not so bad maybe, so wouldn't it be even better if I was always around, as your live-in lover, to help him understand that life for gay men can be normal and loving as well as exciting and horny? He'd be the luckiest gay boy in the world. And, look, Rexy, you've got three houses – to be precise you've got a big house in London, a villa in Umbria, which sounds massive, and this very nice apartment here in Paris. Give Jill one of them and keep two. Or give her two of them and keep one. Or sell them all and split the money. You and I could live together in a flat in London. We don't need a massive house. You'd be happier that way. So would I, obviously. So would Danny, too. And I bet even Jill would, in the end. After all, you don't really love her, and she doesn't really love you, and she'd still have Danny, and Danny'd still have her, and he'll be going to uni soon anyway, so he won't be living with either of you soon. And she'd get over losing you, you know she would. I'm sorry, but as you see I've kind of mapped it all out. I want it so much. At Langan's, over dinner, a month ago, you said you were 'bound by what used to be called the ties of family and home'. I remember your exact phrase. You're not, though, really, are you? That'd be true if I was a girl, and if you were straight, and if you loved your wife and enjoyed sex with her, and if your kids were small. None of that applies, though, does it? There, I've said it. Sorry."

"Sweetheart, you're so lovely. It warms my heart to think you've been plotting it all out like that. But let's not spoil tonight by talking about all this. Let's just enjoy the moment."

Kenyon lit a cigarette, exhaled a long stream of smoke, then play-bit Rex's arm.

"Ouch!" It had not hurt, but Rex had welcomed the boy's frolicsome reaction to his last remark, and now wanted to encourage his playfulness rather than allow a return to earnest inquisition. "That was painful, you little bugger!" he said, ruffling Kenyon's hair.

Kenyon looked up and smiled. "Why did your mum and dad call you Rex?" he asked.

"Eh? Where did that come from?"

"I've just always wondered and I've never asked."

"Well, OK, my mum chose Rex, after Rex Harrison, the actor, whom she adored, and my dad chose my middle name, which is Everton. He was – is – an Everton fan."

"Why don't you support Everton?"

Rex took a long sip of claret, and sighed. "Because my dad's a cunt," he said.

Kenyon smiled. "So's mine. Why's yours?"

"He often used to slag Arsenal – 'Boring boring Arsenal,' he used to say – so I started supporting them. Still do. No one supported Arsenal in Wallasey. It was either Liverpool or Everton. If I'd chosen Liverpool, my dad would've gone mad – definitely beaten me – but me choosing Arsenal just confused and annoyed him."

"Where's Wallasey?"

"The Wirral."

"What's the Wirral when it's at home?"

Rex chuckled, and kissed the top of Kenyon's head. "It's a peninsula. It includes Wallasey, where I'm from, Birkenhead, Bebington, Heswall, Hoylake, West Kirby and New Brighton. It's divided from Liverpool by the River Mersey."

"How come you don't speak with a scouse accent?"

"Because my parents were reasonably well off. Middle class, you could say, or perhaps lower middle class, if that's still a thing. Danny doesn't speak with a cockney accent, because we're middle class. Well, OK, he uses cockney-ish grammar sometimes and says 'ain't' for some unknown reason – I s'pose he thinks it makes him seem what youngsters these days call 'tasty' – but actually it just makes him seem a bit thick when actually he isn't. But his accent itself is actually pretty RP."

"RP?"

"Received pronunciation. Posh."

"Right. You didn't explain why your dad was a cunt."

"Is. Still is a cunt. Beat the shit out of me right from the start. Even when I was knee high to a grasshopper. Nasty to my mum, too. Mean. Snobbish. Racist. Sexist. Homophobic obviously. Just a cunt."

Neither of them spoke for a while. "You OK, Kenny?" said Rex after a while.

"Yeah. Why did your mum let him do that to you?"

"Oh, she was – is – a weak woman. Terrified of him. He hit her, too. He always thought she spoiled me, which she certainly didn't, by the way, and he was for ever scolding her for it. It was a very cold atmosphere in our house."

"Did they love you? Do they love you?"

Rex coughed. "Well, not so's you'd notice, no. No, in all honesty, no, they didn't, and don't. I've never talked about this before, to anyone."

"Not even to Jill?"

"Good lord, no."

"I envy Jill."

"Sweetheart, you have no need to envy Jill or anyone else. You already have more of me than Jill even knows exists."

"That's a lovely thing to say. My dad doesn't love me. My mum did, but my dad doesn't."

"Well, *I* love you…" – it was the first time Rex had said it and he was immediately pleased that he had – "… and you're the first person I've really loved, by the way, ever."

"You must love Danny."

"Yes, I love Danny, certainly, but as a son. In the sense that I meant it when I said 'I love you' just now, and I really did mean it, by the way, because it isn't just the drink talking in my case either, you're my first love."

"What? No one ever before, not ever?"

"No."

"Really? Seriously?"

"Well, maybe just one, but it was ages ago."

"Who?"

"You'll laugh."

"I won't. I asked because I want to know."

"OK, well, I've never told anyone this before either. In fact it's only very recently come flooding back to me, only since knowing you, in fact, my love. I guess I'd repressed it, stifled it, smothered it."

"Tell me, Rexy. Take your time. I'm just going to listen. I'm not going to say a word 'til you've told me."

"OK. Well, where to start? Er, OK, a couple of years ago Jill hired *A Man for All Seasons* from the video shop. As we watched it together, I found I could hardly stop crying. She kept asking me what was the matter, and the thing is I couldn't tell her because I didn't know. OK, it's a powerful film, a great film in fact, but honestly I was fighting back tears almost the whole way through. And, suddenly, only about two weeks ago, one night when I was lying awake alongside Jill, thinking about you and wishing I was with you, I remembered that I'd seen *A Man for All Seasons* many years before, when it first came out, when I was fourteen, maybe fifteen. I went to the cinema one afternoon during the school holidays, Christmas holidays, and watched a matinée. I went with my best friend, Christopher Harrow. He liked to be called Harry."

"Why?"

"Short for Harrow, of course. We were at school together, in the same year but in different streams, me in the top stream and him in the middle stream, but we'd bonded over football. Both of us were good players, in the first eleven of our year. I loved being his teammate, passing to him, being passed to by him, hugging him after he scored, the delicious feeling as I scored of knowing he'd hug me in a few seconds' time, all that stuff. I found showering with him after matches almost too exciting, although lovely all the same, but, anyway, such is the intoxicating cross that some teenage boys must always secretly and guiltily bear, or at least had to in those days.

It was thrilling but excruciating at the same time, and, such was my arousal, and my adoration, that I found it almost impossible to understand or even believe that it wasn't reciprocated. But it wasn't. Of course it wasn't. Harry was, and surely still is as far as I know, straight. OK, he liked me. He thought I was a good footballer and a nice lad. If we were laughing and joking in the showers after a match, chatting about this goal or that foul or whatever, he had no idea that inside I was on fire, my heart aflame, all my senses raised to the power of Harry, to use a mathematical metaphor. He saw me as a mate rather than someone with whom he might mate, in the sense that the term is used in the animal kingdom. In other words he was straight, as I say. But I, frightened, confused and ignorant teenager that I was, was gay, yet the only way I could achieve closeness to the object of my love, even an ersatz proximity that was so, so, so frustrating but still so, so, so much better than nothing, was to ape and embrace Harry's chummy, knockabout way of being with me, even though, even as my vocal cords were spewing empty cyphers across the showers like 'What a wanker that ref was, pass us the shampoo, Harry, mate,' my mind was saying, 'I love you, I adore you, be mine, my darling.' And, yes, coping cheerily with that dichotomy between what I was saying and what I was feeling gradually became habit-forming, and eventually evolved into the way I've lived my life these past twenty years, until a month ago, that is, when somehow you, sweetheart, reawakened in my heart what had been hibernating there throughout my adult life."

"Wow! That's so sad. What happened to you and Harry in the end?"

"Eventually, we drifted apart. He was dropped to the second eleven, and I remember hearing the news of his demotion like it was a death knell. I remember crying myself to sleep every night for a fortnight or more, longer probably. School was never the same for me after that."

"How old were you again?"

"I dunno. Maybe fourteen or fifteen. And because we'd always been in different classes, me in the top stream and him in the middle stream, as I say, we no longer spent any time with each other. None at all. It was agony for me. I used to see him in the distance during breaktimes, but, you know, kids are cliquey. He had his friends, the conduit of our alliance had been torn asunder – football – and, because of course I didn't mean to him what he meant to me, that was that. Slowly but inexorably, we became strangers. Jesus, I don't know why I'm saying all this now. I'm sorry. But it's all so vivid to me, and in a way still so raw."

"Did you ever say goodbye to each other?"

Rex found that he was having trouble controlling the timbre of his voice. He cleared his throat a couple of times. "Jesus. Sorry. Not really, no. A couple of years later, when we'd have been sixteen or seventeen, he shyly approached me on the bus on the way home from school one afternoon and said, 'Davis, there's a girl I like, and I want to go out with her this weekend, but she's got a friend, and she says her friend has to come too, so I need a pal to come with me to make it a double date. You're good-looking, so what d'you reckon?' I stared at him, momentarily torn, suddenly tremendously excited by his description of me but also enormously disappointed by the context in which it mattered to him, and quickly but politely refused. He replied, 'Oh, that's no problem, I just thought I'd ask,' and flashed me his beautiful smile. I don't think we ever spoke again. But in all these years, having never thought about him consciously even once, I realise I've never forgotten a single thing about him." Rex chuckled, wiped his eyes, which had begun to well up, and shot a cautious grin in Kenyon's direction.

"That's so sad, Rexy. Oh and, by the way, I love you, too." They hugged. "Come on, I've got to have a pee, come with me."

They went to the loo, Rex still clothed, Kenyon still naked, and pissed, the streams of their piss colliding, at first by mistake and then deliberately. "Let's always pee together from now on," said Kenyon.

They went back into the living room, and lolled together on the sofa. "You're still pretending actually, though, Rexy, aren't you? I mean, maybe you've admitted the truth to yourself now, at last, and to me, but no one else knows."

"No." His own coming-out plan was a subject that Rex was no more eager to discuss than whether or not he should divorce Jill. "So why was – is – your dad such a cunt, Kenny?"

"Just is. Bent copper. Doesn't love anyone apart from himself. Certainly doesn't love me. Never did. So, Rexy, going back to you, you say you've never loved anyone 'til now, apart from Harry and now me. Have you ever been loved, d'you think, by anyone, before now?"

"No, probably not. Have you?"

"That's so sad. Yes, my real mum loved me, and Norma, who's basically my mum now, she loves me, too."

"And me."

"And you, yeah."

"Kenny, can I ask you, and please tell me the truth because I've asked you before and you said you'd tell me later, which may as well be now, why did you want me to take photos of you lying on my Corvette that day, with your shirt off? And why did you ask me to crop out the number plate? What were those photographs for?"

"Did it turn you on?"

"Of course. I nearly came in my fucking pants. But that isn't why you asked me to do it, is it?"

Kenyon was silent. "I want to tell you the truth, because I don't want us to have secrets between us, but I'm scared you'll dump me if I tell you."

"I won't."

"How d'you know you won't? You don't know what I'm going to say yet."

"Kenny, sweetheart, I've done some bad things in my life. Not always my fault, but, yeah, some bad things. Everyone has. I won't be shocked by whatever you tell me. And, anyway, you're far too nice a person to have ever done anything really bad."

"You don't know that."

"I do. Tell me, Kenny."

"OK."

"Well, go on then."

"OK."

"Yes? I'm all ears. You can tell me. It's OK."

"OK, I'm an escort."

"You're a what?"

"An escort. Only part-time, to help pay for my studies, and buy my photographic equipment, which is bloody pricey, but, yeah, I've been escorting for about three years now. And those pics were to send to potential clients, cos I advertise in *Gay Times* and *Time Out*, in the 'Lonely Hearts' sections, and you have to send photos when someone contacts you."

"What exactly d'you mean by the word 'escort'? D'you mean you go out with women, or men, I don't know, for dinner and so on?"

"No, Rexy. Well, yeah, sometimes. But 'escort' is a euphemism. I don't like using the term 'rent boy', because I don't hang out on the Dilly, but, yeah, OK, I s'pose you could say I'm a part-time rent boy. What you do is you advertise in the 'Lonely Hearts' sections, as I say, but in your ad you say you like 'generous gentlemen', that's code, and it means that guys who are looking to pay for sex contact you, rather than guys who are looking for regular meets or relationships and so on." He sat up and began to cry.

Rex sat up, too, hugged him, and said, "Don't cry, little Kenny," a dozen or more times. They kissed. "Look," said Rex finally, "OK, I want you to stop doing that. Whatever it pays you, I can give you as an allowance. Stop it. Definitely, now, immediately, stop it. It's crazy and totally unnecessary. But if you think I'm going to dump you over it, no, absolutely not, never. In fact I think it shows courage and spirit. It must be scary and unpleasant. Is it?"

"Sometimes."

"How did you get into it, and why?"

Kenyon frowned. "I knew you'd ask that," he began. "Everyone asks that. But the truth is you don't just suddenly start. It's not like you wake up one day and say to yourself, 'I'm going to become an escort today.' No, what happened in my case, and I think this is pretty normal for most escorts actually, is that some fat, old, bald, ugly twat tries to chat you up in a gay bar, and you politely refuse him. Then, cos he's a bit drunk maybe, or a stubborn fucker, or both, he carries on asking you. You keep saying no. Then he says something like, 'What about if I give you £20?' You reply, 'Fuck off!' Then he says, 'What about £50?' You say, 'Go fuck yourself!' Then he says something like, 'What about £100 and all you have to do is let me suck your cock?' And then you think, *Well, why not? It'll be over in ten minutes, I won't even have to get undressed, and I'll have £100 in my back pocket for doing fuck all, basically*. So you say yes, and you go to his flat, and he sucks you off, and he gives you £120 actually cos he wants you to feel good about him, and then, well…"

"Go on," said Rex, determined to sound uncensorious.

"Well, you know, the next time some fat, old, bald, ugly twat tries to chat you up in a gay bar, and you politely refuse him, and he carries on asking you, you say, 'OK, I'll let you suck my cock for £120.' And the chances are he says yes, cos you're young and hot and he's drunk and horny.

And then it's a short hop to advertising in the 'Lonely Hearts' sections of *Gay Times* and *Time Out*, and after that I s'pose you could say you've become an escort. Except, Rex, d'you see how it kind of happens of its own accord? You don't ever set out to become an escort. Well, most guys don't, anyway. I certainly didn't. But the money is so easy, and, well, suddenly an escort is kind of what you've become. Or, rather, a part-time escort, cos I never bunk off lectures to see clients. I'm very disciplined about putting my studies first. Escorting just pays for everything."

"Why don't Nigel and Norma pay your student expenses? Or your dad?"

"I told you: my dad's a cunt. Norma and Nigel aren't that well-off. Nigel's a teacher. Norma doesn't work. They don't charge me for food or rent. And anyway they aren't my real parents, remember? I wouldn't like to ask them. And my course is an expensive one, cos cameras are expensive, tranny film is expensive, processing it is expensive, everything is expensive to do with photography."

"Tranny film?"

Kenyon laughed, and was glad to have a reason to do so. "Transparency, you silly sausage, not transexual. Transparency film. Kodachrome. Slides. You must've heard other snappers at RED talking about trannies, and art directors, too?"

"Yes, sorry. Look, Kenny, have you done escorting since we've been, you know, together?"

"Are we together?"

"We are, yes, obviously. Just because I'm married and we're not therefore official doesn't make us not together.

We're together in every sense of the word. We're as together as any couple I know. We're much more together than Jill and I have ever been. We're much more together than your parents or my parents ever were or are. We're together now, at this moment, I mean, aren't we? We're almost always together. So, yeah, we're together."

"I want us to be more together, to be always together."

"We're as close to always together as any couple I know. The only bit we don't do is argue about the washing-up and whose turn it is to sack the cleaner. Anyway, you didn't answer me. Have you been, er, prostituting yourself since we've been, er, you know, over the last month?"

"Don't use that word, please, Rex. Sorry, just please don't."

"OK, have you been, er, escorting since?"

"Not much, cos we've been together so much, but, yeah, I need the money."

"Don't you get a student grant?"

"My grant covers the basics, but it doesn't cover my cameras, my film, my processing, all that."

"Fuck."

"Are you upset, disappointed?"

"I'm upset, yes. Disappointed? Well, yes, that as well, but I don't think any less of you. I couldn't. I love you. But answer me this. Is it ever, you know, sexy, fun?"

"Honestly, no, it isn't. You learn to treat clients as a different species from regular tricks. You just don't think of them as sexual partners in any way. You just play a role. And, because you're playing a role, it doesn't even matter if they're really fat or really ugly. And, you know what's really odd, because you're playing a role, it doesn't even matter if they're really fit or really hot, either. You just don't think of them in that way. And, anyway, I'm a bottom, as you know, so I don't need to get a hard-on, and I never ever do with clients."

"You always do with me, even though I'm always the top."

"Exactly, Rexy. It's totally different. And, by the way, I haven't done anything with anyone except clients over the last month. No regular guys, I mean. No normal shags. Just you, which has been fantastic, and the odd client. And, before you ask, they always use condoms. I'm one hundred percent on that."

"OK, well, look, will you stop doing it right fucking now? If I give you an allowance, I mean?"

"I don't want an allowance off you."

"Why not? Look, I'm loaded. Well, not loaded, but extremely comfy. Let me, please. I'd be proud to give you an allowance. If you were my wife, girlfriend, partner, boyfriend, whatever, I'd give you an allowance. I give Jill a fucking allowance, after all."

Kenyon lit a cigarette, took a puff, then spoke quietly, slowly. "You say we're together, to use that word. So, er, am I your boyfriend?"

"If you want to be, sweetheart, yes." They kissed again.

"I do, Rexy. I want to be your boyfriend and I want you to be my boyfriend, OK?"

"Yes, that's what I want, too." Rex realised that he attached less importance to the adoption of this new word than did Kenyon, but he nonetheless saw no reason not to agree to it; doing so solved a problem and, besides, boyfriends they surely were.

"OK, I'll stop escorting. I'll stop now."

"Good, thank you, and, as I say, I'll give you an allowance. I'd be glad to, actually. Proud to."

Kenyon felt suddenly almost overwhelmingly happy, and he hugged Rex hard. As he hoped he had managed to explain, escorting had been a sideline that he had drifted into, inexorably rather than deliberately, and, although it was both easy and lucrative, it had always troubled him. The danger of his one day meeting a nutter who would murder him was not the source of his anxiety, although it was the reason why his few friends who knew about his secret occupation so often urged him to give it up. He always reassured them – and himself, too, perhaps – by explaining that he was extremely careful, always met new clients in public places, and would adjourn to flat or hotel room only when he felt completely confident that the man was in good faith. No, what he dreaded was Norma finding out. He was sure that she would forgive him – her love was the unconditional devotion of a mother for a son – but he knew that it would disappoint her bitterly, and he wanted her not only to love him but also to respect him; no, more than that, to admire him. He released Rex from his embrace, took another drag on his Gauloise, exhaled out of his nostrils so as not to blow smoke in his lover's face, and said, "Thank you, Rexy. I'll never escort again, I promise. So what are the terrible things you've done then?"

"Oh, nothing really."

"Thank you for being so wonderful about what I've just told you. It means a hell of a lot that you didn't judge me. But, yeah, you said a few minutes ago that you'd done some terrible things. What terrible things?"

"Oh, you know, a few dodgy business deals, that kind of thing."

Kenyon kissed Rex again, then spoke, his smoky lips still less than an inch from Rex's. "That wasn't what you meant when you said what you said, though, was it? Tell me what you meant, please."

Rex sighed and stood up. He paced around the room, then sat down next to Kenyon again, and held his hand. "Look, OK. So, er, oh, this is fucking difficult. Listen, Kenny, you're not going to like this. I thought I was going to keep this secret for ever more. Perhaps I still should. But I love you, I do, and this evening has been an evening of sweet but sad revelations, so, yeah, if you feel you can love me, warts and all, then I'll tell you. Can you?"

Kenyon looked apprehensive, fearful even. "You haven't killed someone, have you?"

"Of course not."

"Or raped someone? Or done something really terrible like that?"

"No, no, no."

"OK, tell me then."

"OK. Well, I've told you a story about myself which is personal and no one else knows but isn't really a secret *per se* – Harry, I mean – and you've trusted me with a big secret, so now I'll trust you with an even bigger secret in return, OK?"

"OK."

"Right. Well, obviously, you know that we, Jill and I, I mean, found out that Danny had been cottaging?"

"Obviously."

"Well, I'd been cottaging, too."

"Oh, is that all? We've all been cottaging. That's nothing."

"Wait. I'd been cottaging in the Harrow Road cottage on the same day as Danny had, that Saturday a month ago. I'd had a blowjob through a glory hole, and…"

"Yeah? Go on."

"Well, have you worked it out? It was a total accident."

"What was?"

"Well, for fuck's sake, I stuck my cock through the hole, and of course I couldn't see through to the other side, and it turned out that the guy, the boy, on the other side…"

"What? Rex, I don't know what you're on about."

"It turned out that it was Danny on the other side, and he sucked me off, and I came in his mouth, and he swallowed my cum. I found out as I walked out of the cottage into the street afterwards. I saw Danny walking away."

Kenyon stared at Rex, then dropped his head. Rex hugged him. "Can't be," Kenyon said.

"It was completely out of my control, obviously. I had absolutely no idea. But, even so, I felt so unbelievably fucking terrible. No one knows, by the way. Danny doesn't realise it was me, thank fuck."

"Oh my god."

"Are you shocked?"

"Of course I fucking am. You spunked in your own son's mouth, and you ask me if I'm shocked. Yes, Rex, I'm fucking shocked. In fact I wish I could go home right now."

"Oh, Kenny, I wish I'd never told you now. But, look, listen, I had no idea who was on the other side of the glory hole. You've understood that much, haven't you?"

"I've understood that my boyfriend, the man I'm in love with, came in his own son's mouth, who's under the age of consent for gay sex, by the way, and he doesn't think it's all that bad. That's what I've understood, Rex."

Kenyon stubbed out his cigarette, wrenched himself free of Rex's embrace, ran to the spare bedroom, and locked the door behind him.

CHAPTER 15

THE PROXIMITY OF TRAINLOADS
OF NORMAL PEOPLE

The Spotted Dog was on Willesden High Road – a street pullulating with pubs, some conventionally named, such as the Crown, others, such as the Case Is Altered, not – but the Spotted Dog was Danny's and Kimberly's favourite. On Saturday nights it was always busy, full of young people, many of them Irish and usually fun, and it was not the kind of place in which fights broke out, unlike the Case, as its invariably belligerent and sometimes psychotic adherents tended to call it for short.

Danny and Kimberly walked to the end of Manor House Drive, turned left onto Brondesbury Park, right onto Sidmouth Road, then left onto Willesden Lane, passing the Gateway supermarket and the Camerons Stiff estate agency on the left – "I hope I meet Cameron tonight and I hope he's still stiff," said Danny as they passed, a joke he made every time – crossed the road, and strolled on into Willesden High Road.

Abruptly, Danny stopped. "Kimberly, wait," he said.

"OK, why?" she replied.

He pointed to a car parked on a yellow line directly outside the Spotted Dog. "What?" she asked again. "Come on, let's go in."

"No, Kimberly. No, sorry. I've got to do this. I've been aching for it. Wait there, please."

"Aching for what?"

"That's Three-Eight's car," he said, walking up to the red Nissan Bluebird in front of them, and knocking on the glass of its nearside door.

"Where to?" said Three-Eight, leaning across to wind down the window that Danny had tapped, clearly touting for illegal unlicensed kerbside fares.

"Wherever you like," Danny replied.

"Silly boy. Where you want go?"

Danny opened the door, got in, and shut it again. "New Year's Eve, remember?" he said, unfastened the top button of his jeans and pulled down the zip, revealing a section of white Calvin Klein cotton.

Three-Eight said nothing, then nodded. "You got place?" he asked.

"No. Have you?"

"No."

"Can't we just do it in here, in the car, like we done before?"

"No, no, no. That was middle of night. Too dangerous now."

They both thought for a while. Danny toyed with the idea of trying to smuggle Three-Eight into 67 Manor House Drive, on the basis that Jill might well be getting pretty tipsy by now and therefore might not notice, but he quickly abandoned the idea: too tricky. He wondered whether he could ask Kimberly if he could take Three-Eight to her house – her dad would surely be comatose – but, no, that was also fraught with risk, as well as being not a little unfair on her.

"OK," said Three-Eight. "Finsbury Park. We there twenty minutes. Safe. We do what we want there."

"OK," said Danny, electrified with excitement. "Let me just tell my friend I'm going with you. Wait a sec." He hopped out, finding Kimberly on the pavement beside the car. "Kimberly, I'm sorry, this is Three-Eight. He's even sexier than I remember him and he wants to take me to his flat in Finsbury Park. I'm gagging for it. Sorry, I've got to go."

"Why? You don't *have* to go. You don't even know him. It's dangerous."

"It ain't."

"It is. Well, it might be…" – she peered into the car – "… and he doesn't look particularly sexy to me."

"He is. He's gorgeous. Anyway, how would you know? He wants to fuck me, like last time, and that's all I want, too. I'll see you tomorrow. You can still go to the pub – the others'll be in there already. Sorry. Look, I need to do this." He hugged her, jumped back into the car, and Three-Eight sped away.

Danny was febrile with lust, but also very shy, which Three-Eight was not. Danny tried to make conversation. "Busy tonight?"

"Maybe would been. Not now." He reached for his cab-to-base radio handset, held it to his mouth and depressed a button on its side. "Three-Eight POB to Finsbury Park," he said, which message was answered "Roger, Three-Eight" by the disembodied voice of the controller. He drove fast, blatting along Dartmouth Road, Shoot-Up Hill and Mill Lane without saying a further word. He reached over to the regular radio, switched it on, and cranked up the volume. Jason Donovan's 'Sealed with a Kiss' assailed them.

"How far is it from here?" Danny asked.

"No far."

They passed Whitestone Pond, after which Three-Eight floored it along Spaniards Road, the dead-straight avenue that links Hampstead and Highgate, bisecting the Heath as it does so. "No good there. Police sometimes," he said, cocking his head in Danny's direction, indicating wooded parkland on their left. Danny did not understand, but replied, "Yeah, I know."

They wiggled through the Spaniards Inn chicane, then powered on up Hampstead Lane, slowed for Highgate High Street, sped down Highgate Hill, and dived left onto Hornsey Lane. "Nearly there," said Three-Eight.

They swung right onto Hornsey Rise, left onto Ashley Road, and right onto Crouch Hill, which soon became Stroud Green Road. They turned left onto Woodstock Road, and parked. "Is this where you live?" Danny asked.

"No, I live Perivale," Three-Eight replied.

"Is that near here?"

"No, much miles from here, silly boy. Follow me."

They walked briskly towards then past Finsbury Park station, passing under a railway bridge. Three-Eight stopped, looked about him, then ducked through an open wrought-iron gate onto a narrow overgrown path. Danny hesitated. "Come," said Three-Eight. After a couple of seconds, Danny stepped after him.

It was a little after 9.00pm, and the sun had just set. It was not yet dark, but it was darkening. Three-Eight walked briskly, picking his and Danny's way along the path for a couple of hundred yards, passing lone figures, all male, either standing still or walking slowly, then he ducked off the path and began to push his way through thickets of small trees and dense bushes, courteously holding aloft low branches so that Danny could pass beneath them. After a couple of minutes they came to a wooded cul-de-sac, the far boundary a low brick wall topped by a tall wire fence, beyond which were railway lines.

"This place good," said Three-Eight. "We take off clothes." He removed everything except his socks, then put his trainers back on, now entirely naked apart from footwear. Danny did likewise. Three-Eight spread their clothes on the soil, which was slightly muddy, to make a makeshift bed, then pushed Danny to the ground, lying him on his back. He took from his right sock a small tube of KY Jelly, squeezed some of it onto two of his fingers, then applied it to the area of Danny's body that was now revealed, his legs splayed wide. They then did what Danny had been dreaming of repeating since New Year's Eve.

When they had both come – Three-Eight inside Danny, and Danny onto his tummy, by his own hand – they lay beside each other awhile, panting. Three-Eight lit a cigarette, but did not offer one to Danny. Danny did not smoke, but he would have accepted one of Three-Eight's Superkings if it had been offered. The trains were frequent, some faster and therefore louder than others, others stopping just yards from where they were lying, waiting at a signal for a platform to come clear; but they lay well below the level of the top of the wall, and were therefore out of sight. Nonetheless, Danny was excited by the proximity of trainloads of normal people on their way to pubs, curry houses and one another's houses – the usual Saturday night destinations – while he and Three-Eight sprawled naked and spent just a few paces away.

"What's your name?" Danny asked.

"Three-Eight," said Three-Eight.

"No, what's your real name?"

"Three-Eight is all. What your name?"

"Guess."

"How guess, silly boy? You call me Three-Eight. I call you 67 Manor House Drive."

"How d'you know where I live?"

"I drive you there New Year Eve, silly boy," said Three-Eight, and slapped Danny's thigh.

There was a silence, during which they became aware of another couple's presence in a neighbouring enclave, no more than half a dozen yards away. They listened and watched, although it was now almost dark and there was therefore not much to see, but it was clear that one of the men was black, the other white, and they were fucking.

"Why don't you ever use condoms?" Danny asked.

"I straight. No need condom. You boy. No AIDS in boy. AIDS only in old gay man. Come, we go." He stubbed out his cigarette against the bark of a nearby tree, stood up, and began to dress.

"Can't we do it all over again?" said Danny.

"No. We do again other day. I working Velite Radio Cars, Walm Lane, next Willesden Green station. You ring, tell controller you want cab to Finsbury Park, ask for Three-Eight. Is normal."

"OK, so we can do this again?"

Three-Eight stared at Danny, leaning his head close so that he could see him in the gloaming. "Yes. We do a lot from now. You call Velite. Ask for Three-Eight. We do a lot. Is good?"

"Is fucking super-good."

They put on their muddied clothes then walked back to the car. Three-Eight dropped Danny home at just before 11.00pm. As he drew up outside, still staring at the road ahead, he slid his left hand inside the back of Danny's Calvins, groped his arse a bit, rebuffed Danny's efforts to kiss him, then said, "Goodbye, 67 Manor House Drive."

"You can call me Six-Seven for short," said Danny.

Three-Eight smiled. "Goodbye, Six-Seven," he said.

"Goodbye, Three-Eight," Danny replied.

CHAPTER 16

THE THEOLOGICAL RUBRIC
BY WHICH SINS ARE CLASSIFIED

When Kenyon had locked himself into the spare bedroom in Rex's Paris apartment, Rex had stood outside the door for five minutes, trying to persuade Kenyon to open it. He had had no success. Indeed, Kenyon had made no reply, nor indeed any sound. Eventually, shaken and distressed, Rex had trudged back into the living room, had poured the remains of the second bottle of Château Lafite Rothschild 1965 down the kitchen sink, had taken a writing pad and fountain pen out of his bureau, and had begun to write.

My darling Kenny,

Even if you have decided to make good your threat to go home to London now, and presumably therefore to leave me for ever, which you must know my heart and soul ache for you not to do, then I hereby crave one last indulgence of you. It is this: please read this letter, in its entirety, with care and attention.

I love you. I said those three words to you this evening, and saying them made me feel wonderful. I said them because they were true, are true, and will always be true. I am thirty-seven, yet never before have I had occasion to say those three words and mean them. You are my first love. Yes, Harry was for me a schoolboy crush of absorbing intensity, and now that I have remembered him I will never again forget him, but he is a distant memory made accessible to me after all these years only by the revelatory power of my very real and abiding love for you. I want you to be my only love. I do not want to lose you. I believe you love me, too, even if you are angry with me now. I do not think you want to lose me.

In the month since I have known you, my life has changed. It has changed in ways I could never have predicted, and indeed did not know it was possible for it to change. I have become a man driven by love for another, whereas hitherto I have been stimulated by trivial things to do with money, houses, cars and status. I still enjoy those luxuries, I admit that, but the fact that I am feeling so wretchedly bereft now, as I write, without you by my side, underlines in the most transparent way imaginable how much more important you now are to me than anything or indeed anyone else.

Tonight we both told each other a secret. I will never reveal your secret to another soul. Even if you besmirch my name to all and sundry, damning me far and wide as an incestuous paedophile, which I think would be unfair as I plan to explain below, I will never betray your confidence. It will go with me to my grave. Also, although I was saddened and shocked by your revelation, it did not make me think any less of you, and I still do not. I not only love you, but I also respect and admire you. Of course I want you to stop escorting, whether or not you decide to end things between us, but I hope against hope that you will not leave me, and that you will therefore smile on the idea of my giving you an allowance so that you can live your life without financial pressure, and buy all the camera equipment you need to achieve the good MA that your talent and ambition so richly deserve.

I will say no more about escorting now, on the basis that, if we are to be together, it will have to end, and if we are not to be together, it will become none of my business. Either way, all I want is for you to be happy.

As regards my own admission, which I concede was more grievously shocking than was your own, I *am sorrier about it than you can possibly imagine. I am not a great husband to Jill – we married because we had to, as you know, as was the way of things in those days – and we have never loved each other. At best we are fond of each other, but that is all. I have been a decent father to Danny – not particularly attentive when he was tiny but increasingly so as he grew older – and I love him as a father loves his son. We enjoy each other's company, I am proud of his achievements, particularly his sporting achievements, and I have been uncritical of recent revelations about his sexuality. You may well say that that is the very least I could do, given that I share his proclivities and have indeed unwittingly engaged in a sexual act with him, and I would agree with you. Nonetheless, I have been not only uncritical but also supportive, difficult though that has been while Jill has been repeatedly and sometimes hysterically raising the subject of cottaging, an activity that I no longer want to discuss or indeed even think about in connection with anyone, least of all Danny.*

But, clearly, you and I must discuss it now, painful though that will be for both of us. Kenny, darling, please think carefully about what exactly I have done, before you decide to jettison the precious love that has developed between us. If guilt is gauged by not only the gravity of an act but also by the level of advertence and consent with which its perpetrator performed it – as indeed is the theological rubric by which sins are classified by the Church of England

and the Roman Catholic Church, I believe – then of what precisely am I guilty? Undoubtedly, my act was a grave one. It was incestuous and technically paedophilic, on the basis that the age of consent for sex between a male and a female in England is sixteen but between two males is twenty-one, but you must see that there was no advertence or consent involved. In other words, I did not know that Danny was on the other side of the cubicle wall – so there was no advertence – and neither did I therefore knowingly agree to perform a sexual act with him – so there was no consent. Moreover, I had been in that cottage hundreds of times over the past few years, and there was no earthly reason for me to suspect that Danny might also frequent it. Indeed, I had no idea that he was – is – gay.

In other words, what I did, which was and is of course deeply regrettable, was not my fault. I do not feel guilty, therefore, because the circumstances in which I did what I did specifically preclude my guilt. As I say, what I did was not of my wilful doing, simply because I did not know and indeed could not possibly know that Danny was or could be in the cubicle next door.

Let me ask you a question, my love: what would you have me do now? Think about your answer carefully, please. I love you and I value your kindness and wisdom. I have nearly finished this letter – I think – and I will shortly fold it up, place it in an envelope, seal it, and slide it under your *door. I will then try to get some sleep, which may or may not be possible. When we awake, I would like to sit down and discuss the matter with you, with no anger or pressure, but rather with thoughtfulness and tenderness, because the only person I want to consult about what I should do next is the only person I truly love on this earth: in other words you, my darling. I could write more, much more, about the nature of that love, which is immense and monumental, fierce and ardent, splendid and glorious, but I would rather whisper those words while I hold you in my arms.*

Open the door and I will do just that.
All my love, for ever,
Rexy xxxxx

Rex read his letter all the way through, made no changes to it, folded it, placed it in an envelope, sealed it, wrote "From R to K xxx" on it, and slid it under the spare bedroom's door. He then went to bed, and fell immediately into a deep sleep.

CHAPTER 17

A SORDID LITTLE TRYST
WITH A NAMELESS SHIT

When Kimberly had been left on her own on the pavement outside the Spotted Dog, Three-Eight having spirited Danny off to she knew not where in Finsbury Park, she had not gone into the pub but had instead walked straight back to 67 Manor House Drive. She had rung the doorbell, and Jill had been visibly startled to see her.

"What are you doing back so soon, darling? Where's Danny?" she had asked.

"I didn't fancy it. Is it OK if I watch telly with you instead?"

"Have you two had an argument?"

"No."

"Well, you left here only twenty minutes ago. Something odd must have happened for you to come back so soon, and on your own."

Kimberly did not reply.

"Is Danny in the pub now? He hasn't gone to that blasted lavatory again, has he?"

"No, no."

"Well, where is he then?"

Kimberly was beginning to regret having returned to the Davises' rather than to her own home, but her own home was now a place of loneliness and boredom in the absence of her mother, not sparkling company herself but a sight more agreeable than her father, depressive and dysfunctional as he was. She did not reply.

"Listen, Kimberly, I wasn't born yesterday. It makes no sense that you've come straight back here on your own no sooner than you and Danny left, both of you in good spirits and looking forward to a night out with your friends. Something must've happened. I'll get it out of you sooner or later, by god I will, so will you please stop messing about and simply tell me where my son is and what he's doing? If you don't, I'll call the police and report him as a missing person, and then you'll have to answer questions from a policeman as well as from me." Kimberly began to cry. "I'm sorry, dear. I know you're going through a lot at the moment, and you know you're always welcome in this house. But that support goes both ways. Now, where's Danny?"

"With Three-Eight."

"What on earth are you talking about? What does that mean?"

"With a minicab driver."

"He's in a minicab, you mean? Going where? Why?"

"Finsbury Park."

"Why?"

"Well, er, it's a friend of his. They bumped into each other as we were going into the pub, and Danny went with him to Finsbury Park."

"Why? Who's this friend? You mean the minicab driver is his friend? I've never heard of a minicab driver friend of Danny's. Whatever next?"

"No, I s'pose not. I don't know his name. Danny calls him Three-Eight."

"Listen, young lady. Start again, tell me everything, including all the background info I obviously don't know and you obviously do, or I'll lose my temper with you."

So Kimberly explained everything, eventually warming to her task, pleased to have an adult so attentive to her, realising as she went on that Jill was not about to interrupt her, or lose patience with her, but was instead going to hear her out, with interest and absorption, until she had finished her account. Eventually, after ten minutes, she had.

"Thank you, dear. D'you know if there are other such men whom Danny makes a habit of seeing?"

"No, there aren't, Jill, honestly." Jill realised that the girl was speaking the truth.

"Damn fool son of mine. Would you like a cup of tea? Or something stronger? I don't want to get you squiffy, but I'm having another gin 'n' tonic."

"A gin 'n' tonic would be very nice actually, Jill, thank you, yes."

"No, I'm not offering you a gin 'n' tonic. I'm not your father. You can have a glass of white wine 'n' soda." Jill repaired to the kitchen, while Kimberly reflected on the extreme unlikelihood of her vague and torpid father doing anything as civilised as offering her a gin 'n' tonic. Indeed the absurdity of such a suggestion, and the extent that the bleakness of her own situation exceeded the gravity of the Davises' comparatively trivial problems, suddenly struck her as risible, literally, and she began to laugh, quietly but uncontrollably. She was still giggling when Jill returned. "What are you sniggering about?" Jill asked her.

"Nothing, sorry."

"For heaven's sake, am I the only person in this house with the brains they were born with?"

Kimberly did not reply, but the inclusion of herself in Jill's rhetorical question, listed as a "person in this house", pleased her immoderately, which reaction she noticed in herself, and caused her to begin to cry again.

"Oh, pull yourself together, girl. Here, take this." Jill passed Kimberly a glass of white Le Piat d'Or cut with Schweppes soda, and took a decent-sized sip of gin 'n' tonic herself. But Kimberly found that she could not pull herself together, nor anything like it, and she began to sob unrestrainedly. She cried for a long time, and, by the time she had finished, Jill was sitting next to her, gently rocking her, saying "There there" repeatedly, as though she were soothing a teething baby rather than trying to becalm a morose teenager.

It was at that point that Danny let himself in. "You two OK?" he asked.

"What does it look like? Why are your clothes covered in mud?" Jill replied.

"Well, it looks like you ain't OK. That's why I asked, obviously. Kimberly, you OK?"

"Yes, sorry, I'm just upset, that's all. You know why. My dad, my mum, all that."

Jill intervened: "Yes, but that's not all, darling, and don't say 'ain't', by the way. You know how upset she is, with her mum away and her dad in the state he's in, and yet you deserted her to take yourself off with a queer minicab driver."

"Why did you tell my mum about that, Kimberly?"

"Don't blame your friend, darling. She tried extremely hard not to tell me. But I pressed her until she had no choice. She's been a lot more loyal to you this evening than you've been to her."

Danny sat down. "Oh, god, I can't stand this," he said. "Why does my life have to be everyone else's business? Why does everyone have to treat everything I do as a major crisis? So I got off with a minicab driver. It ain't the end of the world. Dad was having sex when he was my age. I'm the proof. You can't say that was a bad thing unless you say I should never have been born. Is that what you're saying, Mum?"

"That's a *reductio ad absurdum* argument, darling, and a very silly one at that."

"Well, obviously, I ain't got a clue what that means. Speak English, please, Mum."

Jill sighed. "It's rather different, darling, isn't it? Your father and I got together when he was your age, yes, that's true, and some people did indeed think he was a bit too young to get married, especially to a woman nearly five years his senior, but nearly twenty years later we're still married, happily married in fact, and we've made a lovely home for ourselves and for you, in which you live the life of Riley I might add. Are you seriously trying to convince Kimberly and me that this sordid little tryst between you and a minicab driver whose name you don't even know is comparable to your parents' first date?"

"Why does it have to be described as a sordid little tryst, whatever that means? If he was a girl, you wouldn't call it that. That's just prejudice, Mum. Think about it, honestly. You're only saying that cos I'm gay."

"Nonsense."

"It ain't nonsense."

"Well, OK, of course I wish you weren't gay. But the reason I wish you weren't gay is that your, er, gayness repeatedly triggers this kind of awful situation. Because if this chap of yours were a girl, you wouldn't have suddenly deserted your best friend to go off to a hell hole in east London, or wherever you went, to have sex. Because that's what you did, obviously, isn't it?"

"How d'you know I wouldn't? Young people are different now, Mum. If I had a girlfriend, I'd probably be shagging her. There's no difference."

"There is. How old is this nameless shit anyway?"

"You see, there you go again. Why does he have to be referred to as a nameless shit? If I'd started going out with a girl, even if I called her by a nickname, you wouldn't immediately refer to her as a nameless shit. And why is it always me that gets the third degree? Why is it OK for Dad to take nudie photos of a guy lying on his Corvette? Why's that so bloody normal?"

Kimberly stood up. "Listen, sorry, can I say something? You're both right. You're both wrong, too, but you're both right as well. Danny, it's normal that your mum's going to take her time to get used to this stuff. You can't expect her to just be happy with everything immediately. And, yes, it *is* different to what your mum's used to that you and Three-Eight meet only to do, you know, what you do. But, Jill, you have to understand that Danny's gay. He just is. It isn't a phase. He's totally gay, and he always will be. And he's got to find his way in life, as you did, and as I'd like to if my life wasn't so shit." She began to sob again. Jill began comforting her afresh, cradling her gently, and no one spoke.

Finally, Jill said, slowly and quietly, "Thank you for saying all that, Kimberly. That was very mature of you. Now, Danny, I'm asking you nicely, how old is your friend and what's his name?"

"I dunno."

"How can you not know his name?"

"Because I call him Three-Eight and he calls me Six-Seven."

Jill toyed with the idea of pointing out the inadequacy of her son's explanation, but decided against it. "And did you use condoms?" she asked instead.

Danny answered with a quick and easy lie: "Of course we did, Mum. D'you think I'm crazy?"

"Good. Well, not good, but better than if you hadn't. And how old is he?"

"Twenty-one," said Danny, lopping a good eight to ten years off the age Three-Eight looked, at a guess.

"And the mud, darling?"

"Fell over."

"A likely story," said Jill. "OK, let's all go to bed."

CHAPTER 18

Rex awoke early, reached across the bed to where his lover should be, but found then saw only his absence. As he assimilated the first few seconds of the day, he brought to mind an instant précis of everything that had happened the previous evening. He stood up and, still wearing the pants and T-shirt that he would have hornily discarded had Kenyon gone to bed with him rather than elsewhere, he went to the loo, then quietly padded around the apartment in search of Kenyon or evidence of traces left by him. He found none. Gently, silently in fact, he tried the spare bedroom door; it was still locked.

Rex was relieved. His worst fear had been that he would awake to find that Kenyon had done a moonlight flit. Clearly, he had not. In his mind's eye he replayed the angry young man's escape to the spare bedroom, and was gratified to recall that he had been naked: even in his horrified misery, he had been aroused by Kenyon's fleeing back view, his lean buttock muscles rippling athletically as he bolted for the door.

So Kenyon was unclothed, was accordingly unready to skedaddle in a hurry, would surely soon need a piss, and would therefore appear before too long. Rex brushed his teeth, washed his face, pulled on the jeans he had been wearing the evening before, and sat down on the sofa in the living room. He looked at his watch; it was 8.40am; he would wait as long as it took.

What, precisely, did he want, or expect, from this relationship, if it were to survive its current crisis? Did he want the two of them to be boyfriends, the new word that Kenyon had embraced so delightedly, if briefly, the evening before? Did he want them to be together, in the sense of the domestic cosiness that Kenyon had described in such endearing detail? He realised that he could not tell. On the one hand he knew, understood with a burning certitude in fact, that he wanted their affair to continue. OK, if Kenyon ended it, well, Rex's life would go on. Yes, of course it would. But it would not be the same, never again, not only because he would have lost the only person he had ever truly loved – cherished with adult might rather than adored with childish zeal – but also because life *sans* Kenyon would be empty, pointless, inane even. The things that had been so important to him for the past ten opulent years – money, houses, cars, status – mattered to him still, but the realisation that he might have to choose between them and Kenyon had now changed everything. In and of themselves, as the furniture of his internal world, they had shrunk in significance. He suddenly now thought of them as hygiene factors, like the phone, the telly, efficient heating, and hot and cold water summonable by the twisting of a tap. Desirable or exciting they were not, or not so much at least.

If Kenyon had forgiven him, that forgiveness lubricated by sleep, sobriety or indeed the receipt of a careful and loving letter, would their relationship have changed? Again, Rex did not know. Despite being closer to forty than thirty, and in spite of having been married for more than half his life, he was a romantic neophyte. How had he ever allowed himself to become so breezily inured to co-existing with Jill, his leisure time spent tolerating her put-downs, playing sport with his friends or his son, and occasionally slinking off to have quick, skanky, anonymous sex with strangers in public toilets? How was it possible that he had allowed that state to become his *mode de vie*? It beggared belief. And, now, if Kenyon were to reject him, he would be left with only the put-downs and the sport. It was inconceivable – unthinkable – that he would once again be able to put up with the furtive isolation of intermittent cottaging as a replacement for making love with Kenyon every day and, in time perhaps, every night, too. And he did not think it would be possible for him, let alone tempting or enjoyable, to fuck Jill ever again.

And there was more. He had now told Kenyon his secret. Kenyon therefore knew that he had committed a crime unspeakable – a felony so monstrous, so sickening, so vile that, if detected and prosecuted, would not only land him in gaol but would also shatter his reputation, with everyone, for ever; yes, shatter, and yes, with everyone, and yes, for ever. He pondered those three absolutes as he made himself a cup of coffee. Kenyon would *have* to forgive him.

He switched on the radio and began to channel surf, stopping only when he discovered music of sufficient cacophony that, volume pumped up, it would unquestionably awake even a tired and emotional twenty-four-year-old. So it was that, not ten minutes later, a naked Kenyon entered the living room as the tuneless lyrics of the French post-punk band Les Thugs were being howled across the apartment. "Will you switch this fucking shit off, please?" he said.

"Of course," Rex replied, and did so. "Have you read my letter?"

Kenyon did not reply immediately, but went into the master bedroom, put on a pair of pants and a T-shirt, returned, then muttered, "I have."

"And?"

"And what?"

"Sweetheart, what d'you mean, 'And what'? I wrote you an important letter. It took me a long time to write. I put my heart and soul into it. I love you. I want you. My letter was my bid for you. Did it work?"

Kenyon said nothing for a while. The truth was that he felt confused. He reckoned to be worldly-wise to gay mores, cannier by far than Rex in that regard, and he minded having been caught on the hop by his lover's revelation. He understood that Rex had done what he had done not by design but by accident, but still it shocked him. It was incest with a minor, for fuck's sake. It was an atrocious thing to have done, and the fact that Rex had not intended to do it did not erase the fact that it had occurred. Moreover, it was a very far cry from the image of Rex that he was growing not only to love but also to depend on, that of an older man, wise, kind, constant and loyal. But there was more to it even than all that. He had not slept well and, ruminating and fretting during the night, he had realised that he was both jealous and envious: jealous of Rex and envious of Danny. What Rex and Danny had done felt to him like an infidelity, and an extremely weird one at that. "Why didn't you tell me about you and Danny?" he said finally.

"There isn't a 'me and Danny'."

"You know what I mean. Why didn't you tell me what happened in the Harrow Road cottage?"

"Kenny, listen. I did. I have. That's exactly what's just caused all this trouble. Perhaps I shouldn't have told you, but I did, because I wanted us to have no secrets between us. You told me a secret about yourself, and I responded by telling you a secret about myself in return. But, look, we've known each other for less than a month. When was I s'posed to tell you? Never? Immediately? Cast your mind back to our wonderful evening at Langan's, which turned out to be our first date. As we'd sat down at our table, and as you'd asked me, 'Is that Rula Lenska?', which you did if you remember, I s'pose you reckon I should've replied, 'Yes. Oh and, by the way, I spunked in my teenage son's mouth the other day. Hope you don't mind.'"

"Don't be ridiculous."

"OK, fair enough, but you take my point. What happened between Danny and me was outside my control, not my fault…"

"Yeah, yeah, yeah, I read all your intellectual posturing about advertence and consent and all that shit."

"It isn't shit, Kenny. OK, I'm sorry if I have a habit of intellectualising disagreements. Once a journalist, always a journalist."

"A journalist? Is that what you call it? You used to write about cement."

"I was proud to be the news editor of *Global Cement Review* in 1972, which was that august publication's undisputed zenith, by the way, yes," Rex replied, essaying what he hoped Kenyon might take for a self-deprecating smile.

Kenyon saw it and ignored it. "Make me a cup of coffee, will you?" he said instead.

Rex busied himself with the task, glad that Kenyon had asked him to do it rather than do it himself, then said, "Kenny, look. What I meant was, there would've been no right time to tell you about Danny's and my mix-up in the cottage. Maybe I should've never told you. Maybe I should've waited 'til our golden wedding anniversary, by which time you'd be a spry seventy-four and I'd be suppurating in a puddle of my own piss. Maybe I should've told you on the occasion of the wondrous arrival of our first-born son…"

"Fuck off, Rex. Stop taking the piss. Can't you see I'm upset?"

"OK, well, I'm allowed to be upset, too, aren't I? I'm thirty-seven, not ninety-seven. I'm older than you, but I'm not Methuselah. I'm made of flesh and blood, too, you know. I've had a sleepless night…" – he had not – "… and I've been sitting here on tenterhooks, waiting for hour upon hour to find out if the person I love more than anyone else on god's good earth suddenly hates me or not, and that's not a nice situation to be in. OK, a bad thing happened in a public toilet, totally outside my control, and I feel terrible about it. There's nothing I can do about it though. I've told one person about it – you – because you're my boyfriend and I love you and I trust you. I told you after knowing you for less than a month. Why is the biggest issue the fact that I didn't tell you earlier? What was the optimal date on which I should've told you? If not in response to your Rula Lenska enquiry on our first date, then when exactly? Maybe a week later, over cream tea at the Holiday Inn Swiss Cottage? You know, 'Strawberry jam or raspberry jam, darling? Oh, silly me, it slipped my mind to tell you that my son sucked my dick the other day'? Or as we were checking in at Heathrow on Friday? You know, 'Kenny, here are your tickets. Oh and I can't wait to come in your mouth when we get to Paris, like I did with…'?"

"Rex!"

Kenyon had bellowed the syllable at the very top of his voice. A silence followed. Finally, it was Rex who spoke. "Kenny, as I said in my letter, I'm not in a nice situation, and I want you – need you in fact – to support me through it. Why? Because we're boyfriends, partners, a team. I'd do the same for you, whatever you'd done, without a second's hesitation. And the not nice situation I'm in isn't my fault. I'm not a saint, but I'm not a bad man either. What's done is done. I wish more than almost anything else that it could be undone, but it can't be. So, since I did it entirely by accident, and since Danny knows nothing about it, I want us to move on from it now. I've told you about it, which is as it should be, because you and I should have no secrets from each other, but it nonetheless remains a secret: a secret between you and me, just like the fact that you've sold sex. Two secrets to be kept secret, for ever, by two men who love each other. So tell me now, yes or no, is this angry stand-off going to continue for ever, so that our beautiful relationship is brought to an end, or are we going to hug each other as tight as two strong men can, right now, and agree to move on from what I unwittingly did, for both our sakes and for Danny's sake, too? And, once we've done that, are we going to begin planning our life together? Which is it to be? Here's your coffee."

Kenyon made no sound for a whole minute, sipped some coffee, lit a Gauloise, took a couple of puffs, then smiled and said, "Methuselah was older than ninety-seven, Rexy, wasn't he?"

"He was, sweetheart, yes, a lot older."

CHAPTER 19

AN EPHEMERAL POSITION ON
THE PERIPHERY OF HIS INTERNAL WORLD

As Rex opened the front door and let himself into 67 Manor House Drive, he was greeted by the jaunty strains of 'Barwick Green', a '20s maypole dance that he had always hated. It was not the melody he disliked, *per se*, but rather the fact that it was the theme tune of *The Archers*, which for some unknown reason Jill loved. He looked at his watch. It was 7.05pm. She must be in the kitchen, cooking dinner.

"Hello, dear," he shouted.

Jill walked out of the kitchen and into the hallway. "Good. You're back. Not before time. I've got a lot of news to share with you. It never rains but it pours."

"Yes, so you said on the phone."

"Danny and Kimberly are upstairs revising. I'm cooking dinner for us all. Come into the kitchen with me so I can fill you in while I listen to *The Archers*."

"How can you cook dinner, listen to *The Archers* and fill me in, all at the same time? Anyway, you know I detest *The Archers*."

"I'm a woman. I just can." She smiled coquettishly and walked back into the kitchen.

Rex had been home for less than a minute, and already he was being assailed by what he now recognised as the absurdity of his home life. He had spent five days and four nights in Paris, separated from Kenyon only by his self-imposed spare-room exile on the Saturday night, and, although that evening and the Sunday morning that had followed it had been difficult, stressful and sad, they had talked their way back into a state of happy and exuberant intimacy and had celebrated that hard-won *rapprochement* by making love with more passion, if not necessarily more athleticism, than ever they had before. After they had both come, they had continued kissing for hours. The rest of Sunday, Monday and Tuesday had also been blissful – loving, sexy, fun and funny – and saying goodbye in the taxi that they had just shared from Heathrow had been excitingly upsetting for both of them. Kenyon had cried, and so, as the cabbie had pulled up outside Nigel's and Norma's house, and Kenyon had hugged him tight and had whispered, "I love you and I always will," had Rex. But their separation would be bearable, because it would be brief: they had already arranged to meet at the Holiday Inn Swiss Cottage for lunch and sex tomorrow.

And now here was Jill, in a chummier mood than her usual grumps that would have assuaged Rex's dull feeling of uneasy duplicity, being comely and wifely, when wifeliness and comeliness were no longer currencies of any value to him. She could not know that, of course, but nonetheless the incongruity of what she offered and what he wanted, and now had from someone else, jolted and unsettled him. It was a tragedy, is what it was, and yet he felt irritated by her as much as sorry for her.

He followed her into the kitchen. She handed him a vodka 'n' tonic. "Cheers," she said. "How was your trip?"

"It was fine, dear, fine."

"Why are you calling me 'dear'? You've never called me 'dear' in your life before, and now you've called me 'dear' twice in a single minute. You've always called me 'love' and I've always called you 'darling'. I call some people 'dear' sometimes, young girls and old women mainly, but never you, and you never do. So why suddenly 'dear' now?"

"Oh, for god's sake, I don't know. I'm knackered. I've been working like a dog in Paris. I've only just got home. Give me a break, please." He almost shouted the "please".

"Well, I'm giving you a drink and a nice welcome-home dinner. That's what I'm giving you. But all you want me to give you is a break. I see. OK, have it your own way. Go and unpack. Let's hope you're in a better mood by dinnertime."

Rex plonked his vodka 'n' tonic onto the kitchen counter, spilling a little of it, walked out into the hallway, hung up his jacket, and carried his suitcase and briefcase upstairs. He put the latter in his study, having taken it to Paris solely as business-trip camouflage for the purpose of fooling Jill, then walked on into his and Jill's bedroom to unpack his suitcase, rehanging two unworn business suits (camouflage again) in his wardrobe and chucking everything else in his and Jill's dirty-clothes basket. Although he knew he was being unfair, he felt affronted by Jill's presumptuousness. How dare she henpeck him when she occupied such an ephemeral position on the periphery of his internal world? How dare she chide him for calling her "dear"? How dare she address him in the imperative mood – "go and unpack" – without so much as a qualifying prefix such as "please" or even "OK then"? Who the fuck did she think she was?

He knew the answer to that question: she was his wife. But what was that, really? He suddenly thought of Kenyon's description of his father, delivered with a luminous smile at Langan's a month ago: "Basically, he's just the guy who came inside my mum twenty-five years ago." Abruptly, Rex spoke aloud: "Basically, Jill's just the girl I came inside nineteen years ago."

He went downstairs, walked into the living room, switched on the telly, and sat down on the sofa. A Western was showing. It appeared to be nearing its denouement. He watched it listlessly at first, then, recognising the actor Audie Murphy and realising that he had seen it before, with more interest.

Jill brought him his vodka 'n' tonic, which she had topped up after he had spilled some of it. He took a sip. "Better mood now?" she asked him.

"There was nothing wrong with my mood. I was knackered, that's all. Still am. And I hate *The Archers*. Thanks for the vodka 'n' tonic."

"You're welcome. I don't want to have an argument straight away, Rex, but your manner just now was totally uncalled for. You know, shouting at me, deliberately spilling the drink I'd made you, then storming off without so much as a by your leave. I've had a difficult few days with Danny, especially on Saturday, as I hinted on the phone, and I want to tell you about it properly before he and Kimberly join us for dinner."

"I'm watching this."

"What?"

"This."

"What is it?"

"It's a film. *Forty Guns to Apache Pass*. It's good."

They both stared at the screen, on which could be seen two military men, Audie Murphy one of them, his arm in a sling. "Good work, Captain. For once I'm glad you disobeyed orders," said the other, older, man. "So am I, sir. The boy made the difference," Audie Murphy replied. Jill walked over and switched off the telly.

"I was watching that, Jill," said Rex.

"We need to talk, Rex," she replied.

"The boy made the difference," he whispered.

"What?" said Jill.

"I said, 'The boy made the difference.'"

Jill tutted. "Sometimes I think you're stark staring mad. Anyway, about Danny, it may interest you to know that he's having a fling with an Indian minicab driver."

"I'm pleased for him."

"What?"

"I said, 'I'm pleased for him.' If he's having a fling with someone who makes him happy – a minicab driver, a butcher, a baker, a candlestick maker, from India, China or Timbuk-fucking-tu – then good for him. I'm not going to regard everything Danny does as a calamity any more. He's gay. Gay guys have flings with other gay guys. Some of them are Indian. Some of them drive minicabs. Get over it."

"Sometimes I think I don't know you at all, Rex Davis."

"I think there's a lot of truth in that. Sometimes I think I don't know you at all, either. The boy made the difference."

He walked over and switched the telly back on. *Forty Guns to Apache Pass* had ended and *Business Matters* was just beginning. "I quite like this presenter, Andrew Neil," he said, flopping onto the sofa. "He's the editor of *The Sunday Times*, you know."

"I know," Jill replied, staring at her husband. "Are you OK?"

"Never better, dear. The boy made the difference."

"Hi, Dad," said Danny, entering the living room, Kimberly alongside him.

Rex stood up, walked over, and hugged his son. He then embraced Kimberly and kissed her twice on each cheek. "I've just been in Paris. That's how French people greet each other, you know," he said.

"Yes, we know," she replied. "Everyone knows."

"And so they should. Yes indeedy, so they should. So, son, tell me about this Indian minicab driver of yours. Is he a nice guy? Is he hot? When can we meet him?"

Danny looked at Kimberly, then at Jill, then back at Rex, giggled momentarily, then composed himself. "He's OK," he replied.

"Good, good. OK is good. And does he make you happy, son?"

"Rex, are you off your rocker? Why are you encouraging our son like this? He's eighteen. He's below the age of consent. OK, I know young people do things earlier these days, but your whole manner is totally bizarre this evening. What in god's name's got into you?"

"Good question, dear. A very good question indeed, yes, if I may say so. But, anyway, you say young people do things earlier these days, by which I take it you mean young people have sex earlier these days, but earlier than whom? Not earlier than me, for instance, as simple arithmetic will prove. Thirty-seven years, which is my age, minus eighteen years, which is Danny's age, minus nine months in utero, equals Danny conceived by a boy exactly his age now. Yours truly. I wasn't below the age of consent, because you, dear, were female. Danny's only below the age of consent because his Indian minicab driver is male. The law's an ass. How old's your chap, son, and what's his name?"

"Er, about twenty-one, I think, and he ain't Indian, by the way."

"And his name, son? And don't say 'ain't.'"

"He's from Sri Lanka," Kimberly interjected. "He's a Tamil. His name is very long, probably, possibly. Danny calls him Three-Eight."

"Then Three-Eight it shall be. Congratulations, son. May I propose a toast? To Three-Eight. This calls for bubbles." Rex bounded out of the living room, ran along the hallway to the cellar door, opened it, skipped down the steps, and re-emerged less than a minute later with a bottle of Dom Perignon 1971. "There we are. Perfect. The year of your birth, Danny boy. Now, if you'll all excuse me for a moment, I'm going to have a quick shit. Son, please open this and pour out four glasses. We're all very pleased for you. Jill, dish up. I won't be long." He walked out of the room and into the downstairs loo.

When he returned, he found the living room empty. He went into the kitchen, where Danny was struggling with the Dom Perignon, and Jill and Kimberly were whispering to each other as they put shepherd's pie onto four plates. "Let me help you with that," Rex said, whipping the bottle out of Danny's hands, opening it with speedy aplomb, and pouring four glasses into the flutes the boy had readied. "I prefer coupes for vintage champers myself, son, but flutes will suffice. Help me carry them into the living room, will you? Ah, shepherd's pie. Or is it cottage pie? Oh no, bad word, cottage. No cottage pie in this house therefore. Far too gay. Must be shepherd's pie. But it looks very tasty. You've done us proud as usual, dear."

They walked into the living room, Rex leading the way, Danny, Kimberly and Jill in pursuit. They sat down, and the women put plates in front of all four of them. "To Three-Eight!" shouted Rex, surprisingly loudly, then added, "Make sure we all clink glasses. That's six clinks in all, OK?"

"Why six?" asked Danny.

"Does it matter, Danny?" asked Jill, tetchily.

"Well, son, thanks for asking. It's quite simple really. In order for us all to clink, each of us would have to clink once with the other three. So we'd each have to clink three times. There are four of us, so that's four times three clinks, which is twelve clinks. But that would count my clink with you as two clinks, and Jill's clink with Kimberly as two clinks, and so on, whereas obviously each pair of us has to clink only once. So you divide twelve by two, and you get six."

"Fascinating, Rex," said Jill. "*Bon appétit.*"

"*Mais oui! Bon appétit!*" Rex replied, making an effort to pronounce the words *en français*. "That's yer actual French, as Julian and Sandy used to say. D'you young things know who Julian and Sandy are? Or were? Jules and Sand? No, thought not. They were on *Round the Horne*. They were gay. Queers we used to call them in those days. Benders. Poufs. Pansies. Nancy boys. Shirt lifters. Pillow biters. Bum bandits. Fudge packers. Shit stabbers. Uphill gardeners. Odd term, that last one, I always thought. Hugh Paddick and Kenneth Williams. Kenny Williams. Kenny. Not *the* Kenny, of course, but *a* Kenny. You remember *Round the Horne*, don't you, dear?"

No one replied.

"Well, if no one else wants to say anything, I'll carry on. *Round the Horne* was a total hoot, a BBC radio comedy programme massively popular in the '60s, starring the eponymous Kenneth Horne – another Kenny but also not *the* Kenny of course – and co-starring Kenny Williams, Hugh Paddick, Bill Pertwee and Betty Marsden. Anyway, I can see you're all bored stiff by my *Round the Horne* witterings, so I'll move on. Ah yes. Now, that was a very good film I was just watching: *Forty Guns to Apache Pass*, starring Audie Murphy. I doubt if you young things have heard of Audie Murphy any more than you've heard of *Round the Horne*. Interesting man. Very humble origins. Texas white trash, you could say. His father fucked off when he was a baby, then his mother died when he was still a kid. So he had to cut school and become a cotton picker so as to provide for his little brothers and sisters. He did that throughout the rest of his childhood. Then, when war broke out, World War II, I mean, he faked his papers to fool the US Army into thinking he was old enough to enlist, joined up, and went off to France to fight Hitler. And guess what: he became a brilliant soldier, and won every single military combat award that the US Army can possibly bestow. Every single one. And after the war he became an actor. He was a very handsome man, and he appeared mostly in Westerns. He died in his forties, killed in a plane crash. And he said just now in *Forty Guns to Apache Pass*, before you so rudely switched it off just as it was reaching its climax, dear, 'The boy made the difference,' by which he meant a boy played by the actor Michael Burns, so blond and so handsome, who was about twenty when *Forty Guns to Apache Pass* was made, but is now a history professor at some American university or other, as it happens. Yeah, the boy made the difference. And so say all of us."

"Have you quite finished, Rex?" said Jill.

"Finished what? Finished that anecdote? Yeah, probably. Finished speaking for ever? No, I doubt it. But why don't you tell us something interesting, dear? Or one of you two? Danny, tell us more about Three-Eight. Or, Kimberly, I gather you're a lesbian. D'you have a girlfriend?"

"Dad, you're being weird and embarrassing."

"Sorry, son. I'll pull myself together. There, I won't say another word."

Rex was not quite sure why he had embarked on such an eccentric oratorical performance, and had not planned it, but the truth was that he had enjoyed it. He felt he could not remember what normal family life was like any more, nor how to behave within a conventional family unit. It was all so boring. Was he coming out? He had not intended to, but perhaps, in his way, yes, he was. Maybe. He glanced at Jill. She had an odd look on her face, sinister even. She leant towards him. "The boy made the difference, you keep saying. What boy? What difference?"

"Another very good question, dear. Sadly, we can't ask poor old Audie, because he's dead, deceased, departed, passed away, no longer with us, six feet under, pushing up the daisies, brown bleedin' bread."

"I'm not asking Audie. I'm asking you, Rex. What boy? What difference? Is it the same boy you took photographs of half-naked on your Corvette a few weeks ago, by any chance?"

Rex looked startled. "Oh yes, Rex," Jill went on, glowering now. "You may not have thought you were seen, but seen you were. You took photographs of Kenyon Jenkins lying half-naked on your Corvette. Why did you do that? Since you appear to be so keen for everything to be out in the open, perhaps you could share your answer with all of us. I'm sure we'd all be fascinated to know."

Rex paused, then spoke quietly: "He asked me to. He wanted the photos for his own purposes. I was glad to take them for him."

Jill stared at her husband, laughed bitterly, then said, "'Curiouser and curiouser,' cried Alice. For his own purposes, eh? What purposes might they have been, pray? And, while you're working out a credible answer to that, why was your BMW not parked outside the tennis club, where you said you'd gone, when I passed it on my way to drop Danny at Wormwood Scrubs Park a few weeks ago, for football practice?"

"It was."

"No, it wasn't. When we passed the club, your BMW wasn't there."

Rex thought for a few seconds, then replied truthfully. "Ah, well, that would've been because I'd arranged to play tennis with Nigel, and I went to pick him up from his house beforehand. You must've passed the club while I was on my way to pick him up."

Jill smirked. "Children, in case you don't know, Nigel is the chairman of Rex's tennis club, a man whom Rex has often described as the most boring man in all of Christendom. Odd that he should suddenly be so keen to play tennis with him, and even to ferry him about at his beck and call, isn't it? But perhaps not quite so odd when you realise that Nigel's surname is Jenkins, and he's Kenyon Jenkins' uncle, and Kenyon Jenkins lives at his house, and of course Kenyon Jenkins is the boy whom my husband here makes a habit of taking nudie photos of, as you so eloquently put it the other day, Danny."

There was a silence, a long and pregnant one. Finally, Jill spoke again, slowly and icily. "I think the boy made the difference, as you've said about a thousand times this evening, Rex. The boy Kenyon. The half-naked boy. The nudie boy. Yes, that boy. That boy, the boy I now realise you've been referring to when you've said '*the* Kenny' a couple of times this evening, has made a very big difference to you, hasn't he, Rex?"

There was another silence, equally pregnant and equally long. "If he were to join us now," said Rex, at last, "which would be very nice in many ways, and if I were to propose a toast, there'd be nine clinks all told. It'd be ten, if all five of us clinked, but you wouldn't clink with Kenny, Jill, so there'd be one less."

"Fewer, not less," said Jill.

CHAPTER 20

THE MOST NORMAL THING IN THE WORLD

It was mid-morning by the time Danny awoke on Wednesday. He showered and put on a shell-suit, then padded downstairs in his bare feet. "Mum? Dad?" he shouted. There was no reply; clearly, they had both gone to work. He walked back upstairs and knocked on the door of one of the spare bedrooms, the one that Kimberly had recently appropriated.

"Yeah?" came a muffled reply from within.

"Wake up, get up, come on," he said. He heard sounds of mobilisation. "Come on," he said again. "I'll make tea. Come down and chat."

He trotted downstairs again, walked into the kitchen, and began busying himself with a kettle and a packet of PG Tips. Shortly, Kimberly joined him, in pyjamas.

"Wow! Wasn't my dad weird last night?" Danny ventured, handing her a mug.

"Totally."

"What the fuck was he on about? Was he just trying to wind Mum up, d'you reckon?"

"Dunno. Maybe more than that. But, when it suddenly started getting really ugly, you know, when your mum started hinting that he was gay and all that, he just suddenly went off to bed on his own, didn't he? And then your mum just hit the gin 'n' tonics, so, yeah, I dunno."

"D'you think she was seriously hinting that he's gay? Really?"

"Yes, obviously. Didn't you?"

"I dunno."

"No, Danny, definitely, honestly, she really was. All that stuff about, you know, 'The nudie boy has made a very big difference to you' and all that. Yes, absolutely, certainly. And, by the way, I reckon he really *is* gay."

"Why?"

"Because he kept saying, 'The boy made the difference' in that really kind of weirdly significant way, because he described some actor as 'so blond and so handsome', because of all the right-on stuff he kept saying about gay people, because he just openly asked you if Three-Eight was hot like it was the most normal thing in the world, because he called Kenyon 'Kenny', who's also so blond and so handsome, by the way, all that stuff. Oh and don't forget I actually saw him taking photos of Kenyon that day. That looked really gay…" – she smiled at her friend – "… but would it freak you out if your dad turned out to be gay?"

"How *can* my dad be gay? He's married. He's got a kid. Me."

"Well, Rock Hudson was married. A lot of gay guys got married in those days. It wasn't like now."

"To be honest, if he *is* gay, it'd kind of annoy me. Why does he have to copy me?"

"I really don't think he's copying you, Danny." She laughed. "Anyway the person I feel sorry for in all this is your mum. I mean, she was finding it hard enough to cope with you being gay – and I know she doesn't always say the right thing but she really is trying, honestly – but for her husband to turn out to be gay as well would be, you know, well, it's going to be bloody hard on her, isn't it? And it's not like he was being very nice about it, either. He was almost kind of rubbing her nose in it, wasn't he?"

Danny sipped his tea. "Rock Hudson," he mumbled finally. "Dad always used to be really shitty about him, when he was on the news all the time a few years ago, when he was dying of AIDS, I mean. Dad kept talking about AIDS standing for 'arsehole-injected death sentence'. Dad *can't* be gay. He must just be friends with Kenyon. Anyway, how do we even know Kenyon's gay? He probably ain't. He's probably got tons of girlfriends. There must be *some* straight people in the world."

"Look, Danny, last night when you were ballsing-up opening that bottle of champagne, and I was helping your mum dish up, she told me something interesting. She said she'd seen your dad's latest credit card receipts, and he's been spending loads of money in the Holiday Inn Swiss

Cottage almost every day. Why would he be doing that? Let's go there for lunch today and see if we can spot him."

"What? Spy on my old man, you mean?"

"Yes, exactly. Why not? It'd be fun. And if he isn't there, it doesn't matter. It's only an eight and a thirty-one."

"I ain't taking buses. No way. OK, let's do it. But, listen, Kimberly, what time's it now?"

She looked at the clock on the kitchen wall. "Quarter past eleven."

"OK. Right. Don't be arsey about this, but I've got a plan, too. I'm going to call Three-Eight, and he can drive us there, but I can spend a bit of time with him here first, OK? I've never had sex with him in a bed. It'll be brilliant. Oh and don't tell my mum. I know you tell her everything these days, for some unknown reason."

"I *don't…*" – Kimberly's response was shrill – "… but, yes, I feel sorry for your mum and she's been really nice to me since my mum's been in Ireland. But, OK, I won't tell."

Danny dialled Velite Radio Cars' number on the hallway phone. He was nervous, but he need not have been, because the transaction turned out to be far easier and more straightforward than he had imagined. "Morning, Velite," a brusque cockney female voice replied, pronouncing it "mornvleet" owing to endless repetition and consequent truncation of a numberlessly reiterated sobriquet.

"Can I have a car to Finsbury Park, please? Oh and can I request Three-Eight, if that's OK?"

"One moment, love. [Then, quieter:] Three-Eight, Three-Eight. [Pause.] You on the plot? [Pause.] Roger, Three-Eight.

[Then, louder:] Yeah, he's available. Address, please, love."
Danny told her. "Right you are, love. [Then, quieter:] You
want 67 Manor House Drive, Three-Eight. [Pause.] Roger
rog. [Then, louder:] OK, love, he's on his way to you now."

Danny replaced the receiver and stood still for a
moment in the hallway. "He's on his way, so stay in the
kitchen, will you," he shouted through to Kimberly, "until
we're upstairs anyway, OK?" She grunted agreement. He
felt a bit sorry for her, but he could not be bothered with
that now. Five minutes later there was a knock at the front
door. Danny opened it to see Three-Eight wearing jeans
and a cap-sleeved T-shirt that showed off his lean but
sinewy biceps and triceps, standing next to his car, which
was parked on the gravel, its engine still running.

"Come in," said Danny.

"We go Finsbury Park?" said Three-Eight.

"No. I say that on phone to make look normal. We
do here. House empty," Danny replied, simultaneously
noticing and wondering why he was aping Three-Eight's
tenseless and article-free English.

"No, no, no."

"Yes, yes, yes. No one here all day. Come on." Three-
Eight hesitated, then opened his car's door, took a tube of
KY Jelly from the centre console, switched off the ignition,
removed the keys, and locked all the doors. He then
walked across the threshold into the Davises' home.

Danny led him upstairs and into his bedroom, and
shut the door. He essayed a snog, but Three-Eight refused
it. "No kiss, only fuck," he said. They got naked in silence,
undressing mechanically but rapidly, barely looking at

each other. Danny lay on his back and raised his legs into the air. Three-Eight lodged a brawny shoulder in the crook of the exposed underside of each of Danny's knees, and bore down upon him. He lubed his dick and Danny's arse, then eased his way in. Danny tensed, then slowly relaxed. It was so much better here. Beds were ideal for sex – comfy and supportive whereas car seats were awkward and parkland lairs muddy – and he clasped his legs around Three-Eight's back and drew him towards and farther into him. The curtains were still drawn from last night, but the light in the room was on, and for the first time he could see Three-Eight's sex-face, frowning and urgent as he built up his rhythm, slowed, accelerated, slowed again, and accelerated again. Finally, after about fifteen minutes, his mouth opened, his nostrils flared, his eyes widened, he gasped a few times, then he stopped. "Stay in," Danny hissed, "I want you still inside me when I come."

"OK, little Six-Seven," Three-Eight replied, caressing Danny's nipples as he remained in position, and watching with detached interest while the boy sorted himself out. As Danny completed his task, Three-Eight chuckled affectionately. They then disengaged and lay side by side. Three-Eight shut his eyes, and began to breathe heavily. Soon he was asleep. Gingerly, Danny propped himself up to inspect his lover. He had never had a chance to do so before. His body was beautiful – the colour of demerara sugar, slim but strong, hairless except for a thick but neatly trimmed jet-black pubic bush, a faint trail leading up to his navel, and a light down in each armpit. "I love you, Three-

Eight," he whispered, so quietly that he was absolutely sure he could not be heard. He then lay down and rested his head on Three-Eight's chest.

Three-Eight stirred, then awoke with a start. They both sat up. "That was wonderful," said Danny, consciously now vowing to speak in proper sentences, complete with tenses and articles.

"Was good," Three-Eight replied.

"Now let's do it all over again."

"Next time. I go now."

"No. OK, so, look, can you take me to Swiss Cottage now? I was going to call a cab anyway but I may as well ask you."

"You pay?"

Danny hesitated. "Er, yeah, of course."

"OK, we go."

They put on the clothes that they had so hurriedly discarded, and went downstairs. Kimberly had showered and dressed, in her usual trainers, ripped jeans and crop top, and Three-Eight recoiled when he saw her, but Danny quickly said, "Don't worry, she's OK," and he looked less shell-shocked after that. They drove to Swiss Cottage in total silence, however, Danny in the front beside Three-Eight and Kimberly in the back. As they pulled up outside the Holiday Inn, Danny said, "That was so great. See you again soon."

"Fiver," Three-Eight replied. He rewarded Danny with a vapid smile as the note was handed over.

Danny and Kimberly walked into the hotel, and made for the large, airy, ground-floor restaurant. "No way should that journey be a fiver," she said. "Three-fifty more like." Danny knew she was right, but he was saved the pain of having to answer because, straight away, they saw Rex and Kenyon sitting beside each other on one side of a table set for four. As they approached, it was clear that his father and his companion had not seen them. They walked nearer. "Hi, Dad," said Danny, as they arrived table-side.

"Oh, Jesus, hi, son," Rex replied. "What are you doing here?"

"I'm about to have lunch with my friend. What are you doing here?"

"Same."

They stared at each other for a few seconds, but said no more. "Why don't you join us?" offered Kenyon, finally. "I've met you before, Danny, although in a not very nice way, as you may remember, and you must be Kimberly. I'm Kenyon."

"Yes, we know," Kimberly replied.

"Sit down," said Rex. "Join us."

Danny was feeling bewildered. He realised that he did not know where he stood with Three-Eight, and, although he understood that the strength of his feelings for his lover might be intensified by novelty, inexperience and youth, and was probably not requited therefore, nonetheless his ardour burned fierce. Moreover, he was still reeling from Three-Eight's mercenary one-word reply to his warm but understated *au revoir*: "Fiver." It had hurt him, and it hurt him still. Perhaps Three-Eight had been disconcerted then tongue-tied by Kimberly's presence? Danny did not know. He did know, however, that he had been upset when Three-Eight had said, "No kiss, only fuck." He did not understand, and indeed could not now fathom, try as he might, why a man who was so gloriously eager to come in his arse would draw the line at a modest kiss. He felt he knew nothing, and had no one to ask. Neither had he forgotten that, the last time he and Three-Eight had met, the Finsbury Park time, his beloved had casually described himself as straight, as though it were a trait incidental to what he did with his dick, like being left-handed or vegetarian. What did it mean? What could it possibly mean, when clearly he was not straight at all? And, even more confusingly, Danny now realised that he rather liked Kenyon. In fact he thought him stunning and sexy. And here Kenyon was, smiling and welcoming him. "Danny, you sit next to me, darling," he said, pulling back a chair, "and, Kimberly, you sit opposite Danny, next to Rexy."

"Look," said Rex. "Kenyon and I haven't ordered yet. We were going to have the buffet, it's very good here, but, before we do, because we've all now been thrust together by happenstance in this rather extraordinary way, I think I should say a few words by way of explanation. It's very awkward, not least because I haven't had a proper talk with your mother yet, Danny, other than that rather dysfunctional conversation over dinner yesterday evening, for which I apologise. So, yes, Kenyon here and I have been having a few meals and drinks and so on recently. We get on very well. I think you'll get on very well with him, too, in time, Danny."

"What your dad's trying to say is that he and I are in love with each other," said Kenyon.

Danny looked at his father. "That ain't very fair on Mum, is it?"

"Bloody hell, thanks a bunch, Kenny," said Rex. "Jesus, OK, look, I know what you mean, son. I'm sorry. It's a difficult situation. That's why I'm going to go and see her straight after this. OK, let's get our grub."

They walked to the buffet. Kimberly began constructing a small, elegant and healthy-looking salad, while Rex made a beeline for the carvery. Kenyon and Danny explored the various sections together. As they scanned the array of available dishes – all-day breakfast, cold meats, fish, veg, soup, fruit, dessert and so on – Kenyon put his left hand on Danny's right shoulder and said, "I guess this is a bit hard for you. But your dad loves you a lot, you know. He talks about you and worries about you. And, yeah, I guess it's a surprise for you to find out he's gay, but on the other hand I s'pose it's also easier for you to understand, because you're gay yourself. This is bound to be a tricky time, for your mum, of course, probably most of all, but she'll be fine after a while. And you and I can be mates, I hope. Honestly, I'm sure it's all going to be OK in the end."

"No, it's all fucked up," Danny replied. "I don't blame you. You're OK. You ain't done nothing wrong. But my dad's behaving like a cunt. Sorry, but it's true."

"OK, well, we can't discuss this now, darling, can we? We've got to go back to the others…" – he pointed to their table, where Rex and Kimberly were sitting in front of full but untouched plates, neither looking at, nor talking to, each other – "… so why don't you and I have a proper chat afterwards, while your mum and dad are having their big discussion?"

"What about Kimberly?" Danny asked.

"I think she can make herself scarce just this once," Kenyon replied, beamed, and gave Danny's shoulder another squeeze.

CHAPTER 21

LONG, LOVELY, ATTRACTIVE, BEAUTIFUL HAIR

Rex had found lunch distinctly uncomfortable. He had wanted to ask Danny what the fuck he was doing eating in a hotel nearly three miles from home on a crucial A-level exam revision day, and specifically the one hotel in all of north London in which he and Kenyon had secretly made their temporary love nest, but he had felt unable to, not least because he had not pushed his son's study regimen as hard as he should have done in recent weeks, or perhaps ever, and suddenly to do so today would have been transparently disingenuous. Nonetheless, he had been irritated and suspicious. After all, if Danny and Kimberly had fancied a café lunch rather than something humdrum and home-made, to liven up their day perhaps, they could have strolled to Walm Lane, specifically the section of it near Willesden Green station, where there were plenty of decent places to eat, many of them as nice as, and cheaper than, the Holiday Inn Swiss Cottage. Moreover, bumping into Danny and Kimberly had scuppered his and Kenyon's usual weekday routine, which was lunch followed by sex. The transition from eating to fucking would have been socially unmanageable. How could he have finessed it? "OK, kids, I'll call you two a cab now, after which Kenny and I will go upstairs for our usual fuck"? No, clearly not. Moreover, the fact that Danny and Kimberly – bloody Kimberly, why did she have to horn in on everything these days? – were now aware that he and Kenyon were an item meant that bringing Jill up to speed had suddenly become an urgent priority. He did not want to wait until this evening, when it would be difficult for them to be alone together and she would be knocking back the gin 'n' tonics nineteen to the dozen. So, having finished his roast beef, new potatoes, carrots and peas, he stood up and said, "OK, I'm off. You three stay here as long as you like. Danny, here's some money." He peeled off two £20 notes from a wad in his trousers pocket and chucked them onto the table in front of his son. "Pay for lunch and your cab home and keep the change. Bye, all."

He fired up his BMW, headed straight for Camden Passage, and parked in the NCP on nearby Upper Street. He felt he needed a bit of Dutch courage before facing Jill, so he went looking for a pub. He spotted one on Bromfield Road, a side street near the car park, and went in. He ordered a double Scotch 'n' soda. As he was sipping it, and people-watching, it slowly dawned on him that all the other drinkers were male. He was in a gay pub. He suddenly felt besieged. He loved Kenyon, and he adored the way they had been gay together so far – their love, their sex, their good times, all of it virile yet discreet – but he was damn sure he did not want to sign up as a professional '80s gay man in the way that these charlies clearly had, with their camp ways, and their calling one another "she" and "her", and their clucking over Judy Garland, Barbra Streisand and Donna Summer. Besides, surely, being gay was about being male – and loving, and indeed fucking, other males. What the hell had women got to do with it? Why "she" and "her"? Why lionise female pop stars instead of male celebrities whom gay men might actually want to fuck, or have a wank over? Why Donna Summer, Barbra Streisand and Judy Garland and not Michael J Fox, Robert Redford and Tab Hunter, in other words? It was all so unmanly. And why had Kenyon insisted on calling Danny "darling" over lunch, like an over-protective mother keeping tabs on her little daughter? It was demeaning of both of them, yet Danny had clearly liked it. Rex called Kenyon "sweetheart" – and, yes, occasionally "darling", too – but those were special appellations reserved for the one man whose place in his heart was unique. Danny was "son". Every other man was "mate". Rex felt he knew nothing.

The barman approached him. "D'you want me to top you up, ducky? Oops, let me rephrase that."

"No, mate, I fucking don't," said Rex, got up, and walked to the door. He struggled with it, pushing it hard and repeatedly to no effect before realising that it opened inwards, and heard titters behind him. "Ooh, hark at her," cooed the barman as Rex made good his getaway. As he stomped off, he looked over his shoulder and clocked the pub's name: King Edward VI. How odd it was – how ridiculous in fact – that an establishment whose *raison d'être* was surely to provide a safe haven in which adult men could get drunk together then go home to fuck one another's brains out should be called after a boy who had been crowned at nine and was dead by fifteen. As he crossed Upper Street, still liverish, he figured that the pub must have been named long before it was ever gay, but still. He spotted a William Hill, strolled in, staked £100 at seven to one on a four-year-old mare called Caspian Mist to win the Chichester Festival Theatre Handicap at Goodwood, watched Pat Eddery ride her to fourth, chucked his betting slip on the floor, and walked to Jill's shop.

He found it empty of customers. Jill, too, was nowhere to be seen, but an effete-looking man in his late middle age was sitting on a Victorian high-backed Windsor chair in the corner, reading an old clothbound copy of *The Tenant of Wildfell Hall*.

"Is my wife around? Sorry, Rex Davis," said Rex, extending a hand. "You must be, er, Bernard Culpepper?"

"How d'you do, Mr Davis," Bernard replied. "I don't believe we've ever met. How nice to make your acquaintance at last."

"Yeah, lovely. Is she around?"

"Well, I actually think she may be spending a penny, not to put too fine a point on it. Will you wait?"

"Will I wait for my wife to finish pissing, having driven here for the sole purpose of seeing her? Yes, I think so."

"Quite."

Rex strolled around the shop, while Bernard returned to Anne Brontë. He picked up a large drinking glass and turned it upside-down, examining it from all angles.

"Rex!" Jill shouted. "What on earth are you doing here? Be careful with that."

"I'm not going to break it, love, don't worry. It's rather nice. What is it?"

"It's a rummer."

"A what?"

"A rummer, mid-Victorian, twelve fluid ounces, lens-cut, knopped stem, polished pontil."

"It must be seven inches tall."

"Probably."

"Who'd ever want to drink that much rum?"

"It's from a seventeenth-century Dutch word, *römer*, which means a glass for drinking toasts out of. It's got nothing to do with rum."

"Interesting. You know your stuff. How much is it?"

"Of course I know my stuff. Rex, stop it. Why are you here?"

He put the rummer back in its place and turned to face his wife. "I'm sorry about last night. I was out of order. I behaved badly. I apologise."

"Yes, well, thank you. You were appalling. What got into you?"

"I think you know."

She looked at her watch. It was 2.55pm. "Bernard, could you give us a minute, please? Actually, I think I'm going to close early. It's dead quiet this afternoon anyway. You can go home if you like."

"Oh, no, I'm quite content here."

"Bernard, mate, take a hint, will you? She wants you to fuck off."

"Rex, please! I'm so sorry about my husband, Bernard. He's taken leave of his senses recently. But, yes, please go home now, OK? I'll see you tomorrow."

Bernard stood up, looked Rex up and down haughtily, then walked out of the shop. Jill followed him out, said, "Bye then, see you tomorrow, as I say," turned around the open/closed sign, and locked the door. "Now, Rex, OK, d'you want a cup of tea?"

"Thanks, yes." He sat down where Bernard had been sitting, and picked up *The Tenant of Wildfell Hall*, in which Bernard had left a sterling silver bookmark incorporating a small glazed photo frame, into which had been inserted a sepia portrait of a woman in perhaps her late thirties. Jill handed him a teacup and sat down on a nineteenth-century oak settle. "What's this, love?" Rex asked her.

"What's what?"

"This."

"It's Bernard's bookmark. Leave it alone. Don't lose his place. That's his mother, his late mother."

"It's rather nice, too."

"Yes, Rex, it is. Put it back. Don't lose his place. Now, why are you here?" She took a sip of Earl Grey.

"Well, look, this isn't easy. I was hinting at something yesterday evening, and it didn't come out right." He paused. "I guess you could say *I* didn't come out right."

"What were you – are you – trying to say?"

"Surely you know."

"Perhaps I do, perhaps I don't."

"I think you do."

"Try me."

"Jesus, this isn't easy."

"Look, all day long I've been thinking about practically nothing other than the asinine stunts you performed yesterday evening, and I can only assume they were part of some very peculiar and rather sick joke. I found you extremely irritating last night, as you probably noticed, as did Danny and Kimberly, I might add, but I'm determined not to lose my temper with you again now. Just tell me what you've come here to tell me, will you?"

"Well…" He could not find the right words. He looked about him, but the stern if pretty antiques that surrounded him offered no inspiration. He stared at Jill.

Finally, it was she who spoke. "OK, I'll do it for you. Were you – are you – trying to tell me that you think you may be a homosexual?"

"I s'pose so, yes."

"Absolute nonsense. Pathetic. Aping our silly son, at your age. Ridiculous. Of course you're not."

Rex took a deep breath. "I am, Jill. I'm not aping Danny, obviously I'm not. But I can't carry on like this any more. I love you, honestly I do. I respect you. I admire you. I think you're a brilliant person, a great wife, a wonderful mother, clever and kind. But you deserve better than me, you really do, because, yes, I think I've found, recently, that I'm attracted to, you know, men."

"My god. You've been running around after that blond boy bimbo you paraded half-naked through our house a few weeks ago, haven't you?"

"Yeah, we've been seeing something of each other. He isn't a bimbo."

"He most certainly is. 'Seeing something of each other', you say? What does that mean?"

"Well, you know…"

"Rex, OK, since you don't even appear to be able to *talk* straight any more, I'll have to be the grown-up and ask you a direct question: have you or have you not been having sex with that young man?"

Again, Rex could not speak. He looked at Jill, and smiled hesitantly, although he could easily have cried instead. Finally, he found a voice. "I'm sorry, I really am, but we've reached the end of the road, Jill, that's what's happened. The answer to your question is yes, but really that's only part of the problem. The rest of the problem – the most of it, I think – is that you and I don't love each other any more. Perhaps we once did, perhaps we never *really* did, I don't know. I genuinely don't know. We got married because we had to, like people did back then, and we haven't made a complete Horlicks of it, we really haven't. You'll always be massively important to me, the mother of my son, the person I've spent all my adult life with, and, as I say, I respect and admire you enormously. We made a nice home for Danny, and he's turned out well…"

"Has he? I love him more than anyone or anything else in the world, but he's allowed himself to be led astray recently. I've been trying to get him back on the straight and narrow over the past few weeks, you know I have, but you haven't been much help, to be honest. You never were, really. There's more to bringing up children than playing sport with them. Let me put it this way: I hope and pray that this idiotic behaviour of his is just a phase. He's such a fool to himself, and he'll regret it bitterly. I mean, instead of revising for his crucial A-level exams, he just mopes about the house daydreaming about making the beast with two backs with an Indian minicab driver, for heaven's sake. But, if it does indeed end up being just a phase, and if at some point in the future we can say with confidence the words you just said – 'he's turned out well' – it'll be no thanks to you."

"Three-Eight is Sri Lankan, not Indian. What d'you mean, it'll be no thanks to me?"

She snorted. "Three-Eight. Three-bloody-Eight. Ludicrous. What a lot of nonsense. Couple of silly queers, my husband and my son."

"I didn't make Danny queer. Gay, I mean."

"Didn't you? Really, Rex? Are you sure about that? Because I'm damn sure I didn't."

"No one did, Jill. No one made Danny gay. No one made me gay. No one made Kenny or Three-Eight gay, either."

"I refuse to refer to Danny's loathsome cabbie as Three-Eight, because, even apart from the gay issue, it depresses and infuriates me to think that our son has fallen for a person who won't even tell him his name, and it annoys me that you don't seem to regard that cowardly failing of human kindness as a problem. And, while we're on the subject of names, Kenyon is barely more sensible. But, more to the point, why d'you think I want to hear about either of them, ever? Please shut up about those two home-wreckers, Rex."

"OK, Jill, for the moment I will, but they both exist and they both matter…" – he frowned – "… but, no, actually, since we're sitting in an antiques shop, and since you're s'posed to be interested in history, you should know that the name Kenyon first appeared in English records as long ago as the fourteenth century. It's a perfectly respectable name. It means 'blond'."

She snorted again. "Well, that figures. Blond. I might have guessed. And I s'pose the name Three-Eight appears in the Domesday Book, does it?"

Rex sighed. "OK, let's just talk about Danny and me then. No one ever makes, or can make, anyone gay. I know that now. I don't know why some people are gay. I don't think anyone does. Neither Danny nor I are remotely poufy, which makes it a bit trickier for you – or for anyone – to understand, I s'pose, but then not every gay guy is like, well, like Bernard. Straight people tend to think all gay guys are screamers, because the screamers are the ones they can spot a mile off and can duly identify as gay. But the gay guys who aren't screamers they can't identify, and therefore they assume they're straight. Guys like me, Danny, Kenny."

"I'd spot Kenyon a mile off."

"Jill, I know this is hard, but I want us to be nice to each other now if we can. I'm sorry I wasn't nicer to you over the last twenty-odd years. Perhaps you're even a bit sorry you weren't nicer to me. If you want a divorce, obviously, I'll understand. There's no easy way to say any of this, but I'm trying to be, well, straight with you, if that's not the wrong word to use.

I'm sorry if some of this is coming out a bit clumsy. It's all so hard to talk about, especially as you and I haven't really made a habit of discussing, you know, feelings, much. But, look, we don't really love each other any more, not like a man and wife should, we haven't had sex for weeks, I'm seeing someone else, who just happens not to be a woman, our son is about to leave home and go to uni, and we've done OK. We've done our bit. I shouldn't have stopped you seeing that black guy all those years ago. That was wrong of me."

"I'll thank you to leave my solitary indiscretion out of this, Rex, if you don't mind. Oh, I just can't believe this is happening to me. Why me? It's unusual enough to have to cope with having a queer son, but a queer husband, too? It's too cruel, honestly." She began to cry. "Aren't you even going to comfort me?"

Rex stood up and shuffled over to her, then sat down beside her on the settle. She inclined her head towards him, and he received it, allowing her to rest it on his chest. He began to stroke her hair. She continued to sob, quietly but unremittingly. Rex felt he was the wrong person to be consoling her, but he realised that she had no one else who could do it, not only not here and not now, but not anywhere. "You've got lovely hair, Jill, my love," he said. "Long, lovely, attractive, beautiful hair. You always did have. You're a very handsome woman, you really are." She began to cry more noisily.

"Jill?"

"Yes?"

"I bumped into Danny and Kimberly at lunch today. To be precise, Kenny and I bumped into them."

"Why? Where?"

"At the Holiday Inn Swiss Cottage. It was rather awkward. D'you know why they chose to have lunch there, out of all the millions of other places there are to eat in London?"

"Maybe."

"Yeah, I thought so. Never mind."

There was a pause.

"Shall we go home, Rex?"

"Yeah. I've got my car here. Have you got yours here?"

"Yes, it's in the NCP, where I always park it."

"Yeah, mine's there, too. We'll have to drive separately."

So Jill stood up, pulled herself together, let them both out of the shop, switched off the lights, set the alarm, and locked up. Together, but without speaking, they hurried across Upper Street to the car park. Rex walked Jill to her Volvo, and watched her manoeuvre her way out of her parking space and drive out. As she straightened up the steering wheel, she momentarily let go of it with her left hand, to give him a little wave. He waved back, but she had driven on a way by then, and she did not see his reciprocation. He then walked to his BMW, which was on the floor above.

On his way home he overtook her on the Marylebone flyover. As he did so, he studied her face in his rear-view mirror. She had not noticed his car passing hers. She was crying.

CHAPTER 22

A MILLION AND ONE QUESTIONS ABOUT THREE-EIGHT

After Rex had left the Holiday Inn, the lunch table conversation, which had been tricky while he had been there, flowed even less well, if anything. Kimberly found she had nothing to say, and Danny and Kenyon found they had nothing to say that they were prepared for her to hear. Eventually, once they had all finished eating, Kenyon lit a cigarette and took the initiative. "Kimberly, listen. Danny and I are going to go to a pub and have a little chat. We've got a lot to say to each other, as you can imagine. No offence, but it's kind of private. I really hope I'm going to get to know you better soon, but, now, sorry, I think it's best if Danny and I have a bit of time on our own, OK? So, Danny, if you could give Kimberly one of the £20 notes your dad gave you, so that she can get a taxi home, that'd be great."

"I don't need a taxi. I'll get a thirty-one and an eight. I'll go home and see my dad for a bit. I might be around later, Danny, OK?"

"OK."

She stood up, hugging Danny and ignoring Kenyon, and walked out of the restaurant, across the foyer, and into the street.

"Does she live with you now?" Kenyon asked Danny.

"Kinda, yeah. Not permanently, but for the moment. Her dad's a pisshead and her mum's in Ireland, and she's an only child like me, so her home life's a bit shit. He's a *real* pisshead, by the way. Not just like my mum – you know, a few gin 'n' tonics every night – but drinking in bed from first thing in the morning, never eating, never washing, all that. She's my best friend, and she and my mum get on well. They never before, but they do now. She really loves my mum actually, I think. She's a bit clingy, but she's OK. What pub d'you want to go to?"

"Oh, I don't think we need go to a pub, darling."

"But you said…"

"Yeah, I know what I said. That was to get rid of Kimberly. Sorry to be blunt, but it's true. No, we've got a suite here, your dad and me. Come on up and let's chill out a bit, and maybe order some champagne on room service. Might that be fun?"

Danny was not at all sure what to make of Kenyon's offer, but he was absolutely sure he was going to accept it. He liked being around Kenyon. He was not only sexy but also nice, entirely confounding Danny's presumption that he would think him a twat. He also appeared to be kind and wise, and he realised that here at last was a gay man whom he could ask the million and one questions about Three-Eight that he so burned to have answered. "Yeah, that'd be fun," he replied.

Kenyon asked for the bill, charged lunch to the room, and guided Danny towards the lifts. "A few extra quid in your back pocket now that I've put lunch on the room rather than using the cash Rexy gave you, eh, darling?" he said, and patted Danny's left buttock with his right hand as he did so. Danny liked that.

Kenyon opened the door to his and Rex's suite, flopped onto the bed, lit another cigarette, and ordered room service champagne on the bedside telephone. Danny switched on the telly – *Knots Landing* was on BBC1 – and sat down on a sofa on the other side of the room. "I quite fancy Ben in this," he said, "do you?"

"Which one's Ben?" Kenyon replied.

"I'll show you. Wait. He's a bit old, but he's really good-looking." They watched in silence for about a minute, at the end of which Danny shouted "Him!" as a slick-looking black-haired actor appeared on the screen. "He's called Douglas Sheehan."

"How d'you know that?"

"I just do. Well, I fancy him, that's why."

"Yeah, he's not bad. He's my type actually. How old is he? Thirty-five? Forty? I go for that age. Well, I guess you know that. What's your type?"

Danny pondered. "Well, I ain't really got a type. Guys bigger than me, I s'pose. Not massive guys, but taller and musclier. I've been seeing a guy, from Sri Lanka, and he's gorgeous and sexy, but…"

"Yeah?"

"No, nothing."

"Tell me."

There was a knock at the door. Kenyon answered it. A waiter wheeled in a trolley on which stood an opened bottle of champagne in an ice bucket, two flutes alongside. Kenyon gave him a pound coin, showed him out, hung the "Do not disturb" sign on the outside of the door, and closed and locked it. He poured himself and Danny a flute each, clinked glasses, said, "Bottoms up," took a swig, and let himself tumble back onto the bed. "Actually, just before you and Kimberly turned up, Rexy was telling me about your Sri Lankan. You told everyone about him over dinner yesterday evening, right?"

"No, my mum told my dad about him actually. But, yeah, Dad asked me about him afterwards. D'you always call my dad Rexy? It sounds weird. But, actually, yeah, Dad was quite nice about him, about my, er, my guy."

"Well, why wouldn't he be? Anyway, what did you want to tell me about him? Or ask me about him? Yeah, I always call him Rexy, and he always calls me Kenny. It's no odder than Danny, if you think about it. I assume your full name is Daniel, right?"

"Yeah," Danny replied, sipped a bit of champagne, then embarked on his saga. He told Kenyon all about all three meetings he had had with Three-Eight – the fuck in the car, the fuck in the park and the fuck in his bed this very morning – and he was touched that Kenyon listened attentively, rarely interrupting, only doing so to ask friendly, clever, relevant questions. When Danny had finished, Kenyon refilled their glasses, lay back on the bed, and said, "Look, Danny, to be honest with you, I know quite a lot about that type. He won't tell you his name. He won't kiss you. He says he's straight but he's happy to fuck you. There's no foreplay. Don't ever even dream of trying to touch *his* arse. Honestly, to be blunt, there's no love."

Danny looked forlorn. "Well, he called me 'little Six-Seven' this morning."

"Yes, that was quite nice, I'll give him that. But wouldn't you have preferred him to call you 'little Danny'?"

"Maybe, but that's our secret code. I'm Six-Seven and he's Three-Eight. I explained that already."

"It's *his* secret code, not yours. You think it's charming because you're infatuated with him. It's only natural that you want to see the best in him all the time. He hasn't told you his name because he doesn't want you to know anything about him. He's probably married."

"No way!"

"Well, obviously, I don't know that. But I wouldn't be surprised. My boyfriend's married, after all. How old is he?"

"About thirty, I reckon."

"OK. Anyway, there's no reason for you not to carry on seeing him, but just don't expect wedding bells, OK? You give him exactly what he wants, which is a willing arse with no strings attached. And, sorry to say this, you're obviously not his only regular squeeze. You know that, right?"

"Well, I don't *know* that, do I?"

"OK, darling. Let me put it another way. D'you think he was a virgin the day he suddenly decided to fuck you in his car, using a tube of KY Jelly that he just happened to have handy? And d'you think, when he took you to Finsbury Park, and led you in darkness straight to a concealed place where you could fuck without being seen or interrupted, that it was the first time he'd done that? Really? No, exactly, I thought not. Anyway, there's one thing you didn't mention, which I want to ask you about, and I'm hoping your answer is going to be the right one. Does he use condoms?"

Danny hesitated. "Er…"

"He doesn't, does he? Darling, we *always* need to use condoms, especially guys like you and me. Bottoms, I mean. It's so much riskier for us than it is for the tops."

"Why?"

"Well, use your common sense. The AIDS virus is carried in the sperm. So, when the penis goes into the anus, it injects the sperm. But, before the sperm is injected, tiny tears have almost always been made in the lining of the anus as a result of the penis thrusting in and out, and those tiny tears bleed a little, and, as the sperm shoots out of the end of the penis, the penis rubs it into those tiny tears, and it carries on rubbing it in as it carries on going backwards and forwards, rubbing and rubbing and rubbing the sperm into the tiny tears as it goes. So, unfortunately, the process of fucking is perfectly designed for getting sperm from the fucker into the bloodstream of the fuckee. D'you see?"

"How d'you know all this?"

"I'm gay, that's how I know all this. All gay guys have to know this stuff these days."

"So d'you always use condoms then?"

"Yes, always, absolutely always, without fail, even with your dad. Well, I only ever have sex with your dad now anyway, no one else, but even so, yes, always."

"Three-Eight said there ain't no need for condoms with us cos he's straight and I'm a boy, so neither of us could have AIDS. Only old gay men have AIDS, he says."

"Well, first of all, since when has Three-Eight been a world expert on the subject of the transmission of infectious diseases – he's a minicab driver for fuck's sake – and, second, does that really sound likely to be true? Think about it: only old gay men have AIDS? No, no, no. It's *almost* true to say that only silly boys who get fucked up the arse without asking their partners to wear condoms have AIDS. OK, I'm not trying to scare you, but this stuff's got to be said. On the plus side, though, you're far more at risk if you've had multiple partners. You haven't, have you?"

"Well, I've sucked loads of dicks."

"Yeah, I know…" – Kenyon shuddered – "… but how many guys have you had unprotected anal intercourse with? That means how many guys have fucked you up the arse without a condom?"

"Just Three-Eight."

"OK, that's good. Well, it's not good, but it's much better than if you'd had tons. So, from now on, Danny, always use condoms, OK? Always, always, always. Here, I've got some here." He opened the drawer in the bedside table on "his" side of the bed and gave Danny two three-packs of Durex Fetherlite. "There, take those, and, if you're too shy to buy them in future, ask me again and I'll always make sure you've got some, OK?"

"Thanks."

"You're welcome. Now, darling, I'm sorry, but you're going to have to have an HIV test."

"Shit."

"HIV leads to AIDS, OK? That's why you have to have an HIV test. You knew that HIV leads to AIDS, right?"

"Yeah."

"So, yeah, it's a bit shit, cos you can't have a test for three months yet. HIV takes three months to incubate, so you need to get tested exactly three months from today, or any time after that. If you get tested before that, then if today's unsafe fuck has infected you, it won't show up. D'you understand?"

"Yeah, but why d'you think Three-Eight's got AIDS?"

"I don't. That's not how it works. Why d'you wear a seatbelt in a car?"

"Yeah."

"No, not 'yeah'. I asked you a question. Why d'you wear a seatbelt in a car?"

"Cos it's the law."

"Yes, that's one reason, but the other reason, the main reason, is that if you have an accident it'll save your life. When you put your seatbelt on you aren't *expecting* to have an accident, but you put it on just in case you do have one. Just in case you do, d'you understand? So, in the same way, you've got to make guys wear condoms when they're fucking you, just in case they're HIV-positive. Because they may not know they're HIV-positive, because they may not have been tested, or, even if they do know, they may not tell you. For fuck's sake. Sorry. Your dad should've told you all this. I'm fucking annoyed with him, to be honest."

Danny was having a lot less fun with Kenyon than he had hoped to be having, not that he had been at all clear what Kenyon had been planning when they had gone up to the room, but he felt cared for all the same, and that was nice. The truth was that he had been hoping Kenyon would jump him right here and right now. But, although Kenyon's earlier caresses and squeezes had turned him on, especially the pat on the bum, it had slowly dawned on him that his father's boyfriend had never envisaged having sex with him as even the remotest possibility. "How d'you know when a guy fancies you, and when he's just your mate?" he asked Kenyon suddenly.

"I dunno," Kenyon replied. "What an odd question. You just know. I guess it's the same as for straight people. You just get a feeling when guys fancy you. Why d'you ask?"

"No reason."

Kenyon smiled. "Look, Danny, I'm not an idiot. Maybe I've worked out that you like me a bit, and maybe in a silly way I kind of responded to that – you know, the odd bit of very innocent touching – but I can tell you now that you and I are never going to have sex. I'm your dad's boyfriend, I fancy older guys, and anyway you and I are both bottoms. You're a cute lad, and you're loads of guys' type, but you're not mine. But the main reason is that your father is my boyfriend, so you're off limits. OK, I could never see you as a son, cos you're only six years younger than me, but maybe more like a little brother. Is that OK?"

Danny nodded. He was rather excited about being Kenyon's little brother. "Good," said Kenyon. "Now, going back to Three-Eight, it's up to you if you carry on with him or not – obviously, cos it can't be up to anyone else – but I want you to promise me that you're going to make him wear a condom next time, and every time after that, OK? D'you promise me?"

"Yeah, OK."

"I'm serious, darling. It's important. You do know AIDS is fatal, don't you?"

"Yeah."

"OK, let's change the subject. D'you still go cottaging?"

Danny brightened. "Yeah, I do. Why?"

"No real reason. Only obviously I was there when your mum was a bit drunk and she blurted out what you'd done in the Harrow Road cottage that day. That must have been embarrassing, eh?"

"Yeah, it was really shit."

"Yeah. Anyway, what's the biggest cock you've ever sucked through a glory hole?"

"I dunno. Why?"

"Cos it's interesting, that's why. Seven inches? Eight? Nine?"

"Dunno. Maybe nine? Black guys are bigger. There are quite a lot of them in the Harrow Road cottage."

"D'you still go there now?"

"Yeah, a lot, to be honest. Why d'you want to know? Is it an AIDS thing again? I don't swallow no more. I used to but I don't now. When I feel they're about to come, I take it out of my mouth and just wank them off onto my face. I prefer that anyway."

"Do you indeed, you dirty little bastard?"

"Yeah." Danny smiled, suddenly feeling more in control, more Kenyon's equal, less a boy struggling in a man's world.

"So, darling, are you OK with me being with your dad?"

"Yeah, I s'pose so. I feel a bit sorry for Mum, that's all. And, also, Dad was a bit dishonest when he found out I was gay, a month or so ago, telling me stuff like 'I've got no knowledge of gays' and all that kind of shit."

"It's understandable that you should feel sorry for your mum. But that sorry feeling is useful, because she's going to need you. Be there for her. My mum died when I was fifteen, and I miss her every day. My dad was – is – useless. Yours is lovely, but he's obviously been hiding his gay side for years, so he's not anyone's idea of a conventional father, is he?"

"I know what you mean."

"No, that's right. So, one last question: can we be mates, you and me?"

"Definitely."

"You're a good kid, Danny. Come on, let's go home. We'll share a cab. Not Three-Eight, if you don't mind. A black taxi. I'll drop you off on my way. Come on, give us a hug, OK?"

"OK."

CHAPTER 23

SOMETHING LIKE SORROWFUL
IF TETCHY ACCEPTANCE

When Jill arrived home, it was almost 5.00pm. Rex's BMW was already parked on the gravel, and she pulled up her Volvo alongside it. As she let herself into the house, she found Rex and Danny in the living room, sitting next to each other on the sofa, watching *Robbie, a Ripe Old Age*, on which Fyfe Robertson, after whom this BBC2 series had been named, was interviewing Charles Forte on the subject of his hotel and catering business. "You beat me home, I see?" she said.

"Yeah," they said in unison.

"I meant your father," she replied. "We left the shop simultaneously."

"Oh, right," said Danny.

"Well, I know how to cut my way through London's rush-hour traffic," said Rex.

"We both know you drive like a total loony," said Danny, rolling his eyes. "This guy's really old and boring." He pointed at Fyfe Robertson.

"Well, actually, son, he's dead, not really old. This must be a repeat. And he's not at all boring, actually. He was born in poverty, one of six children. His father was a Scottish miner, but he became one of the most successful reporters in broadcasting history."

"How d'you know all this stuff, Dad?"

"Well, like everyone, I only know what I know. But I read a lot and I like rags-to-riches true stories. I like it when people make something of themselves, despite humble origins. That's why I like Audie Murphy, the actor who starred in that Western I was telling you all about yesterday evening. Or, rather, liked, not like, cos he's dead, too." He did not add that he regarded himself as an example of such an elevation, but he thought it. OK, his father had not been poor; in fact he had been, and remained, moderately well-to-do, but Rex was worth at least ten times as much, maybe twenty, and that pleased him.

"Where's Kimberly, Danny? Go and revise," said Jill.

"I'll revise in a minute, Mum. She'll be here in a bit."

"Go on, the programme you were watching has ended now…" – it had – "… so go and revise now before you become engrossed in something else. Rex, back me up, please."

"Danny, your mother's right. Go and revise."

Danny trudged upstairs. Jill went into the kitchen, made tea for herself and Rex, and brought both cups back into the living room, handing him his.

"Thanks, love," he said, attempting an encouraging smile.

"Apart from anything else, Rex, you're such a *bore*," she replied.

"Eh?"

"Why d'you have to parade your general knowledge the whole damn time? It's as though you think life is one long game of Trivial Pursuit. D'you really think any of us wants to know the life story of Fyfe Robertson? Or Audie Murphy? You don't converse, Rex, you broadcast, and it's incredibly, incredibly, incredibly boring."

He looked at her, said nothing, then essayed another kindly grin. She shook her head, then said, "Have you always been homosexual, d'you think? Since the very beginning, I mean?"

"Jill, I really don't know," he replied, surprised to find himself happier to discuss his sexuality again than defend her sudden Trivial Pursuit jibe. "I've spent a lot of time thinking about it recently. When we first met – when I was eighteen, I mean – I was pleased to snog girls, even have a bit of slap 'n' tickle with them, and, in your case, which was my first time, as you know, to actually have sex with a girl. Well, with a woman, because you were twenty-three. But I was a horny young lad, like all young lads are, and, although we had sex satisfactorily enough, and it was fun, somewhere deep in my heart – or deep in my dick, I don't know where, truth be told – I was aware that it was men and boys who got me going, not women and girls. But I s'pose I was in denial. In those days so many men and boys like me were. It was 1970, remember."

They fell silent, both of them simultaneously but independently traversing memory lane. Jill, privately noticing that she was finding Rex's revelations increasingly bearable, her shock in her shop steadily being replaced in her home by something like sorrowful if tetchy acceptance, was nonetheless bewildered by her nineteen-year failure to decrypt her husband's long-encrypted sexuality. Had she always secretly known, she wondered? Had she been in denial throughout her marriage? No, she really did not think so. She had had sex with four men before Rex, and one afterwards, but Rex had initially been as randy as any of them, although by no means as unbridled as Jaden, the personal trainer whose bravura love-making had briefly thrilled her thirteen years ago. Rex's initial randiness had quickly subsided, however, replaced by Saturday-night sex whose rhythm and remit soon varied not one jot. But, even so, she had not suspected it. She had assumed that sexual diminuendo was the stuff of married life, like it or lump it. Nonetheless, he had lied to her for nineteen years, and she did not yet know whether she would find that betrayal possible ever fully to forgive.

"Look, love, being gay was pretty scary in 1970," Rex resumed. "Sex between men had been legalised only three years before – the Wolfenden Report only gained royal assent in July 1967 – and society hadn't yet responded to the change in the law. If anything, there'd been a backlash. In fact, gay men were more vilified and indeed more prosecuted in the years after 1967 than they'd been immediately before. The only thing that had been legalised was sex between two consenting adult men in private, you see? If there were three men, or even if the sex took place between two men in a house in which other people were present in other rooms, or in a hotel, that was still illegal, because the law didn't classify it as private. And the police were very assiduous about spying on, arresting and charging any poor buggers who breached those conditions. So all gay men were in a more or less permanent state of shitting themselves back then. And because I wasn't camp, because I was good at sport, and because girls tended to fancy me right enough, I realised I could pass as straight, so I did. Life was easier that way. Then, when you and I had to get married, well, I had the perfect cover. And the years just rolled by, I got used to my life, I made a success of my work, then suddenly I met Kenny and everything changed. Sorry, but it's true. It's best to be honest, now, at long last, isn't it?"

"I think it is, Rex, yes, although you can spare me the history lesson. Trivial Pursuit again. So did you never have hanky-panky with any men before Kenyon then? Never? Not even once?"

"No, never."

Rex wondered why he had lied, but the lie had come out almost without his being aware of it. Lying about sex had become so very habit-forming. He would have to get over that, in time, but not now, not today, and perhaps not ever with Jill. She need not know that he had been messing about in cottages throughout their marriage, since before she had met him in fact. Besides, for other reasons, of course, cottaging was a subject that he had recently become reluctant to discuss with her in any detail, and that would never change, especially not now that she knew he was gay.

"Why not, Rex? Weren't you keen to try it?" She realised, even as she spoke, that she did not really want Rex to provide the answer to the question as she had framed it. No, she had asked it as a means of trying to tease more information out of him. The truth was that she did not believe Kenyon was the first man with whom Rex had ever had sex.

He realised that he would have to expand and deepen his lie. "Well, in a way, yes, but you and I had sex from time to time, and I had the odd wank of course, and I'd just got so used to switching that side of my life off. I guess that's why it was so electrifying when Kenny switched it on after so long."

Jill felt a lump forming in her throat, but she was determined not to cry again. She had long been dully aware that Rex and she did not perhaps love each other as passionately as a man and wife ideally should, and she knew that that had been the case for years, maybe always, but she had accepted their life for what it was – respectable, opulent, envied – and she took pleasure in cooking, telly, her antiques shop and of course their adored son. Even so, she was proud of Rex, and fond of him, too, despite his many irritating failings, and his choice of the word "electrifying" to describe his falling for Kenyon had smarted.

"D'you love him?" she asked.

Rex looked at the floor. "I think I do, Jill, yes."

That hurt, too, but again she rallied. "It's so strange, Rex. Today we've had two conversations that anyone would expect to have been extremely difficult – one in the shop and one now – but in actual fact they haven't been so very hard, have they? OK, I've just called you a bore, and you were a bit hesitant at first, in the shop, I mean, but I think that was because you thought it would be decorous to your cuckquean to appear to be reluctant to divulge the details of your infidelity. But, when you finally started saying what you wanted to say, it was easy enough, wasn't it? It flowed, in fact. OK, I was a bit derisive initially, and again just now, but here we are, having a better, more candid and more sincere conversation with each other than we've had for years. And, for the most part, we're being civil with each other, too, even though some of what you're saying to me is inevitably upsetting. Odd, isn't it?"

"I s'pose it is, yes. I guess trying to keep something afloat when it's holed below the waterline – either a ship or a marriage – is always exhausting, and always difficult, and always causes friction among those who are doing the bailing out."

Jill wondered why Rex had not said something nice, and specific, about her plucky reaction to his declaration of love for Kenyon, especially as she had admitted to being upset by it. She stared at him. "We'll have to get a solicitor each, Rex, you know that, don't you?" she said.

"Yes. Don't call yourself a cuckquean, by the way. Doesn't that mean a woman who willingly allows her husband to take other lovers? Oh, and, obviously, you can have the house. This house, I mean."

"I thought 'cuckquean' was just the female version of 'cuckold'. I'll look it up later. Anyway, as I say, we'll both have to take legal advice. Let's let our respective solicitors beat each other up, if needs be, so that hopefully we can remain civil with each other, for Danny's sake if nothing else. But, yes, obviously, I'll keep this house, be in no doubt of that. It's your actions that'll have triggered a divorce, so you should be the one to get a new place. Besides, this house is Danny's home, and it'll continue to be his base, his home in fact, while he's at uni, and perhaps afterwards for a while, too. So it makes sense for it to continue to be mine rather than yours and Kenyon's. So, yes. I assume you and Kenyon are planning to live together?"

"We are, I think, yes. We'll probably get a flat somewhere not too far away. Jill, I think you'll like him, once you've got over the shock of all this, I really do. He's lovely. He really isn't the blond boy bimbo you always cast him as. OK, yes, he's blond, and of course he's strikingly handsome and tall and slim and muscular and all that, but he's also kind and clever. He's taught me a lot. And Danny was telling me just now that, after lunch, they had a chat after I'd left to go to see you and Kimberly had gone home, and Kenny was apparently being very helpful and supportive about his relationship with Three-Eight."

"Rex, it's much too early for you to be trying to promote Kenyon to me as a future chum. Why can't you see that? But, anyway, that aside, I don't know if it's good news or bad that he's been advising Danny about his Indian cabbie. Do we actually want Danny to be encouraged to continue with that association?"

"Well, neither of us has ever met Three-Eight, which I have no problem calling him, by the way. I think it's rather a sweet name. Oh and he's Sri Lankan, not Indian. But, anyway, whether we or anyone else encourage or discourage Danny's relationship with Three-Eight, it'll either carry on or it won't. That's what happens. That's how it works. That's what life's like. I know that now."

There was a pause.

"Rex?"

"Yeah?"

"You know you said earlier, you kind of asked me, whether it was a coincidence that Danny and Kimberly had gone to lunch at the Holiday Inn Swiss Cottage today?"

"Oh, yeah, but don't worry about that now. I've worked it out. You must've gone into my study, seen all my credit card receipts, and told Danny about them."

"Yes. Well, no, actually. I told Kimberly about them and she must've told Danny."

"OK, love. Look, that kind of thing really doesn't matter any more, does it?"

"No, just as it really doesn't matter any more that you didn't actually have any business meetings in Paris over the past few days but were instead enjoying a romantic weekend with Kenyon. That isn't s'posed to sound sarcastic, by the way. I really do mean it really doesn't matter any more."

"Well, actually, it was both business and pleasure. I had a few business meetings…" – he had not – "… but I admit I took Kenny with me to make the trip more fun."

"Alright, Rex, if you say so. And, another thing, why were you so furiously censorious about Danny's, er, cottaging when I first told you about it? You called it 'repulsive' and 'stomach-churning'. You even called him a 'filthy little shit'. I distinctly remember you using all those words."

Rex paused. "Well, it was stomach-churning, repulsive and filthy. It is. The fact that I'm gay doesn't make Danny having sex in toilets suddenly respectable."

"I s'pose. And why were you so vituperative about Rock Hudson when he died of AIDS? Why have you always been so, you know, anti-gay?"

"Oh, I dunno, Jill. I was a closet case."

"A what?"

"A closet case. I was closeted, hidden, hiding, in denial."

"I see." She shook her head. "OK, there's one last thing I want to ask you. I had a good look around your study, as it happens, and one of the things I found there, under some papers in a drawer, was that cerise short-sleeved shirt from a few weeks ago. I'd assumed Danny had, er, soiled it, and you went along with that theory when I asked you about it at the time, but I later worked out that it was Kenyon's shirt and now of course I realise that in fact it must've been you who, er, used it in that way. It was, wasn't it?"

"Good lord, no."

"Rex, it must've been. I found it in our dirty-clothes basket, not Danny's. I'm not going to be angry, or upset, but I just want to know, because I don't want to think it was Danny if it wasn't. So please be honest. Was it you? It was, wasn't it?"

"It was, Jill, yes, sorry."

She laughed, which surprised her, paused, snorted, paused again, then replied, "You really are an unutterable cretin, Rex Davis, aren't you?"

PART 3

SATURDAY 14 DECEMBER 1991

CHAPTER 24

SPECKS OF SILVER-WHITE RIME

Rex awoke early, and, as was his habit on days on which Kenyon was not working, he heaved himself out of bed quietly so as to allow his boyfriend to sleep on for a bit. He put on a light blue shell-suit, had a piss in the main bathroom rather than in his and Kenyon's en suite, so as not to disturb him, and walked downstairs into their large L-shaped living room cum kitchen diner. He gathered up the remains of last night's dinner – a Marks & Spencer ready meal – and took the two plates into the kitchen, where he scraped the residue into the bin and washed up. He boiled a kettle and made himself coffee – Douwe Egberts real rather than the Maxwell House instant that had been the staple at Manor House Drive. Kenyon never ate in the morning, and would not therefore breakfast today, whereas in the early years of their marriage Jill had often cooked Rex and herself omelettes, sausages and bacon on Saturdays. So Rex shook a bit of Alpen No Added Sugar into a bowl, chucked a few raspberries into the mix, added semi-skimmed milk, and spooned the assemblage rapidly into his mouth, standing up at the kitchen counter as he did so.

He looked at his watch. It was 7.50am. He switched on the radio and tuned it to Radio 4. Fr Oliver McTernan, the parish priest of St Francis of Assisi Roman Catholic Church in Pottery Lane, Notting Hill, was halfway through his 'Thought for the Day', but Rex paid him scant attention. Instead he looked out of the window into Haverstock Hill, on whose expansive asphalt and wide pavements the winter sun had not quite risen. It was darkish still, but brightening, and freezing fog had caused specks of silver-white rime to cling prettily to the bare upper branches of the trees. He continued to sip his coffee, and watched a squirrel darting about on the frosty roof of his brand-new jet-black Porsche 911 Turbo.

"Happy birthday, Rexy!" said Kenyon, walking naked towards him, carrying two packages wrapped in pink paper, each of them tied with a white ribbon, one larger than the other.

"Oh, you're up early," Rex replied. "That's so sweet of you, thank you, sweetheart."

"Open them then!"

Rex carefully removed the wrapping from the larger package. "Ah, a bottle," he said as the paper came away, "but, wow, not just any bottle. That's superb, absolutely superb."

"I hope you like it, darling. Have you spotted the vintage?"

Rex read the label aloud: "Château Cheval Blanc St Emilion Héritiers Fourcaud-Laussac 1951. The year of my birth. Thank you, sweetheart, thank you so much." They kissed.

"I hope it actually tastes nice. Will it, d'you think?" Kenyon asked.

"I'm sure it'll be gorgeous, yes. But it must've cost you a fortune."

"It did. I saved up. Open the other one."

"I'm so spoiled."

"Well, it *is* your fortieth, darling."

Rex began to open the other package, which was small and cubic. "Is it a watch?" he asked.

"Aw, how did you guess? It is, yes," said Kenyon, "but it's a bit special, too, a bit personal, I mean, like the wine. I really hope you like it."

Rex held the now unwrapped box, which was slightly tattered, then opened it and revealed a large chronograph. "Ah, it's a Breitling," he said. "That's fantastic."

"Yes, but it's a 1951 Breitling, Rexy. So I've got you two prezzies from the year of your birth."

"That's so incredibly kind of you, sweetheart…" – they kissed again as Rex turned the watch over in his hands – "… and it's superb. I love the patina, and the words on the back: 'Waterproof, Antimagnetic, Shock-protected, Swiss'. Wonderful."

"The man in the shop told me to tell you that Breitlings only began to be made in significant numbers in the '60s, so this watch is actually quite rare. He also says it's in superb condition."

"I can see that, yes. Oh, it's fantastic. Stainless steel in the post-war years was a little primitive, not to put too fine a point on it, so you often find acid pitting on watches of this era, but this one doesn't have any at all. It's been really well looked after. I'm thrilled."

"Fab," said Kenyon, "and now can I have my prezzy?" He placed Rex's right hand on his own left buttock; Rex chuckled, let his fingers wander towards the young man's anus, and found it sticky to the touch. "I've douched and lubed already," said Kenyon, "so get that stupid shell-suit off you and get busy with my arse. You look like Jimmy bloody Savile in it anyway."

"I don't, do I?"

"You fucking do." They laughed, Rex raised a playful hand as if in readiness to strike, and Kenyon bolted to their bedroom; Rex lumbered after him.

For two years they had lived together in their plush three-bedroom three-bathroom flat, which consisted of the upper two floors of what the estate agent had described as "an imposing and prestigious mid-Victorian terrace, ideally situated for the many fashionable shops and cafés of Belsize Park, the plentiful Underground and bus connections, and the green open spaces of Hampstead Heath". Rex had bought it outright for £225,000, which was slightly but not much more than he had trousered when he had sold his villa in Umbria, for which he felt he had no need now that family holidays of the type that he, Jill and Danny used to take would be a thing of the past. Their erstwhile home on Manor House Drive had become Jill's, and he had not sold the Montmartre apartment, which was still his. The divorce had not been turbulent, smoothed as it had been by Rex's being able to bestow upon Jill a generous alimony plus a decent monthly allowance in respect of Danny's maintenance, despite his being, at twenty and no longer in full-time education, not of a status that strictly warranted its payment. Nonetheless, he had not started working.

By contrast, having successfully completed his MA, Kenyon had become a freelance photographer, as had always been his plan. Most, if not all, of his work came from RED, Rex having awarded him a retained freelance contract. If that act of naked nepotism had annoyed RED's art directors at first, Kenyon's charm and talent had gradually assuaged their irritation. He was pleasant to rub along with, he had a good eye, and he worked fast. Herb Ritts he was not, but he was what most of them called "a pretty decent snapper".

Rex rolled off his lover and onto his back. Kenyon lit a cigarette, and began to blow smoke rings towards the chandelier above their bed. "You're on Danny duty today, you know that, don't you?" he said.

"Yup," Rex replied. "He wanted to see me on my fortieth, so I thought I'd better. To be honest, I wanted to anyway. I haven't seen him since Sunday. You know how busy work's been this week."

"Yeah. I don't really know what a fortieth is s'posed to be like – life begins at forty, they say, don't they? – but, what with the Danny situation, I guess yours is going to be a bit different."

"It will be, sadly, sweetheart, yes. Put it this way: I'm certainly not going to use the phrase 'Life begins at forty' in front of him."

"No, I s'pose not."

"But we can still have fun later, when I'm back, I mean. Let's have a nice dinner, just you and me. I don't fancy anything elaborate, and I don't want to see loads of your boozy mates afterwards if that's OK."

"OK, that's fine, so let's just stroll down to the Shahbhag. Then we can have a couple of drinks in the William IV afterwards if we fancy it. If Rich and Paolo are in there, that'll be OK, won't it? I've got work tomorrow anyway."

"Have you? On a Sunday?"

"Yeah, I've got a shoot."

"Oh, OK. Which one's the Shahbhag? Is it the one on Rosslyn Hill that Michael Foot sometimes goes in?"

"It is, yeah. I'll book."

"OK, yeah, fine."

Rex stood up, walked across their bedroom, and looked out of the window. It was 9.30am, and Haverstock Hill was busier now. The traffic was still light, but a few keen shoppers were milling around, despite the cold. Kenyon studied Rex's naked back view. "You look well hot for forty," he said, and giggled.

"Thanks, sweetheart," Rex replied, wiggled his bum at Kenyon ironically, then felt rueful about behaving so childishly when Danny was in the situation he was in.

CHAPTER 25

A LITTLE TARTAN SKIRTY THING

Rex opened the door of his Porsche, lowered himself into the driver's seat, fired it up, and drove south down Haverstock Hill. As usual, the radio was tuned to Radio 4. *Any Questions* had just begun. The guests were four MPs: Menzies Campbell, Edwina Currie, Gerald Kaufman and, to his consternation, Enoch Powell. He recognised that the latter was an intelligent man – perhaps even brilliant – but the fact that he was also one of his loathed father's heroes made him a figure detestable in Rex's eyes. Besides, he was an easy man to hate.

Rex retuned to Capital, on which was playing the current number one single, George Michael's and Elton John's 'Don't Let the Sun Go Down on Me', which had a fortnight ago been the subject of a fierce row when

Kenyon had observed that, if the word "sun" were spelled with an "o" rather than a "u", the song's title would be rendered a suitable maxim by which Rex would have done well to abide thirty-two months ago. Kenyon had said it had been a joke, which claim Rex had countered with, "Well, it was a fucking shit joke in that case, you stupid little twat," possibly the nastiest thing he had ever said to his lover. The lingering and rancorous aftermath of their quarrel had ruined a whole week, and relations between them had returned to their playful and sexy equilibrium only last weekend. Rex retuned the radio to LBC, and learned that the BBC's legendary cricket commentator John Arlott had just died. He switched off the radio.

He was now on Albany Street, heading south, not far from his destination. He turned left then right onto Osnaburgh Street, crossed the Euston Road, and drove on again into Great Portland Street. At the junction with Mortimer Street he turned left, and began to look for a parking space, which, it being a Saturday, he found in a side street easily enough. He climbed up out of the low-slung driver's seat, locked the door, and began striding fast against the cold. It was a short walk, which he interrupted by stopping at a corner shop to buy a Caramac and a Lilt, Danny's favourite choc 'n' pop combo. He then marched on towards the Middlesex Hospital, passed through its grand and porticoed entrance, and walked upstairs to the Broderip Ward, which had been opened four years ago, by Princess Diana, in a fanfare of publicity. Rex had often reflected recently that Jill, Danny and he had watched the

TV coverage of the opening in what he now regarded as a guileless daze, not realising then that a hospital ward going by the peculiar name "Broderip" would ever be of any significance, relevance or utility to any of them.

"Hi, Rex," said Margaret Dickson, the Broderip staff nurse whom Danny liked best. She was beaming, which Rex thought game but inappropriate. "I believe it's your birthday," she went on.

"Er, yeah, that's right, it is."

"Yeah, Danny told me."

"How is he?"

"You haven't seen him since last weekend, right?"

"That's right, yeah."

"Well, first of all, as I've told you before, he's such a lovely lad. But he's obviously still upset about his loss of vision, which was the result of his CMV, or cytomegalovirus retinitis, which was what actually caused him to be admitted last month, and which we couldn't do much about, as you know. But he's been playing the CDs you bought him – I don't think I've ever seen so many CDs in a ward in my whole life – and that's been great. The area around his bed and his CD player has become a bit of a party zone, with the guys dancing to his CDs in the evenings. They've been really sweet with him, actually. The Queen CDs have been particularly popular, what with Freddie Mercury having died only about three weeks ago."

"The guys? What guys?"

"Oh, the other patients, I mean, those of them who are fit enough to dance. Danny's made some good friends here already."

"Of course, sorry, yes. Can I see him now, please?"

"Sure. He's very drowsy so far today though."

The Broderip Ward had just twelve beds. Rex found it a jarringly jolly place, the courage of the patients magnificently impressive, the devotion shown by their partners, family and friends sometimes touching in the extreme. There was a lot of hand-holding, hugging and indeed even some sedate love-making, which the staff covertly facilitated by drawing blinds around the beds as required. Some of the men entertained a large number of visitors, their mums, dads, brothers and sisters mixing chummily with even their campest chums, and Rex had often felt socially inept around such patients, finding it difficult to chime with the vibe. The second-youngest on the ward, Danny had only five regular visitors – Rex, Kenyon, Jill, Kimberly and Liam, his London Lighthouse home support volunteer or "buddy" – whose serial attendance Kenyon had recently organised into a quintuple rota so that there would rarely have to be a visitor-free day. The teenager in the bed next to Danny's, who was Belsen-thin, never seemed to have any visitors at all.

Rex walked closer to Danny's bed, stopped, then looked at him. He was lying on his back, wearing only a mini-kilt, his torso emaciated, his legs and face, but not his arms or chest, pock-marked with raised red, purple, brown and black lesions, the result of Kaposi's sarcoma, which Rex had learned to refer to as KS. He knew that his son's back was similarly afflicted, but it was not visible now. Danny lay perfectly still, staring at the ceiling with almost sightless but not quite tearless eyes. "Hi, son," said Rex.

Danny took a moment to hear the greeting, or to register it, Rex could not be sure which, then slowly turned his face towards his father. The movement took some effort, and the motion was slow at first, then suddenly rapid as his weakened neck muscles failed to arrest it in the normal way; his head then lay sidelong, therefore, unnaturally so. He murmured indistinctly, his lips pressed against the pillow. Rex reached down and gently straightened him, stroking his brow as he did so. He was not able to control his tears, and was momentarily gratified that Danny was unable to see them. He then immediately cursed himself for having felt relief so ignoble.

"How are you today, in yourself, I mean, son?" he asked.

The reply came slow and soft. "I'm spiritually OK. Happy birthday."

"Thanks, son." Rex was surprised by "spiritually". It was not a very Danny word. But then nothing was as it had been before, nor would it ever be again.

"Sorry I never got you a present, Daddy. Kenyon was here yesterday. He told me he got you, er, I can't remember, er, a clock and, er, something…"

"A watch and a bottle of wine, yes. Very nice, too. Mum'll be here tomorrow." Rex tried to smile. "Daddy" had also been a surprise.

Danny fell asleep. Rex put the Caramac and the Lilt on his bedside table.

Margaret approached. "He's been sleeping quite a lot today, as I say, and yesterday too actually, but that's OK, that's normal."

"I see."

"He's been up and down lately. Mostly like this, but sometimes suddenly more alert. He's great on those days – fun and chatty and so uncomplaining and playing his CDs far too loud…" – she beamed again – "… but his KS is painful, it must be, it always is when it's widespread like his is, but you'd never know it. We're hoping he's going to get a bit better, so that he can even go home maybe. That would be a great thing. But, if that happens, he'd probably have to go to your place, not his mum's, and you or your partner would have to learn to give him his meds, including the intravenous ones, every day, to preserve his vision, er, well, what vision he still has anyway. That's very important. I don't think his mum would be able to do that. It's great when she visits, he loves it, but, well, to be honest, she's often, you know…"

"Yes, I know, she's often the worse for drink, yes. She's finding all this harder than any of us, I think."

"Yes, well, that's understandable. Her visits are great, as I say, but she shouldn't be in charge of meds if he goes home. You and your partner would have to do that. He's a very switched-on guy, isn't he?"

"Kenny? Kenyon you mean? Yeah, he is."

In fact, Rex had found Kenyon's reaction to Danny's illness nothing short of admirable, which is one of the reasons he had felt so particularly dreadful about bollocking him so harshly for his admittedly insensitive sun/son joke. Indeed, when Danny had been diagnosed HIV-positive in January of last year, a little less than two years ago therefore, at first he had told only Kenyon, whom he had tried to swear to confidentiality; but, having found the burden of keeping such an apocalyptic secret from Rex intolerable, Kenyon had forced Danny to inform both his parents together, which unforgettably bleak conversation had taken place at Kenyon's instigation in the living room at Manor House Drive only a couple of days after Danny had broken the news to his chosen confidant. All four of them had wept unquenchably, Danny mumbling, "Sorry, Mum, sorry, Dad," again and again, the plaintiveness of his unending apologies excruciating for all of them.

Danny's doctors could not be sure when he had contracted the virus, but Jill had always been coldly certain that Three-Eight had been the culprit. That he may have been, but he had left Velite Radio Cars without warning or trace in July 1989, by which time he had fucked Danny a dozen times or so, never safely, and then was heard no more. Stupefied with bewilderment and melancholy, being told repeatedly by the Velite telephonists whenever he requested Three-Eight that he was not available, Danny had finally steeled himself to visit the Walm Lane base, as Three-Eight had always referred to it, so as to ask after his lover. "It's urgent, I really need to know where he is," he had told the poker-faced harridan behind the toughened glass screen, but she had replied, "Urgent it may be, sonny jim, but he's gone, left, quit, departed, not here any more, fucked off out of it, and we ain't got no idea where he is. Which word d'you not understand?"

The following month, on 24 August 1989 to be precise, Rex had been mightily impressed when Kenyon had buttonholed Danny, urging him that it was now time to have an HIV test, having noted the date in his diary as exactly three months to the day after their seminal *tête-à-tête* at the Holiday Inn Swiss Cottage, during which he had besought Danny always to use protection thereafter. But Danny had refused to be tested, even when Kenyon had pressed him, always finding an excuse to delay it, and had finally relented only in January 1990. Kenyon had forewarned Rex to expect the worst, sharing with him his suspicion that Danny's recalcitrance had been the result of his having begun to have a lot of sex the previous summer, with multiple partners, much or all of it unsafe. He had seen the signs, he had said. What he had not said, but had meant, was that Danny had confided in him that he had a cum fetish – a dangerous penchant indeed for a gay man whose role in anal sex was invariably passive.

After Danny had revealed his HIV status, and the tears of his nearest and dearest had been replaced, or rather augmented, by a call to action, whatever that might be, Rex had become upset and perplexed about it, mystified as to why his son had been so incautious. Jill's reaction had been repeatedly to vow to wreak violent revenge on Three-Eight, and Rex had had to try to explain to her that her certainty that Three-Eight was the villain of the piece was unfounded, untested and ultimately unhelpful. In turn, Kenyon had tried vainly to explain to her his theory that, having messed up his A-level exams and having thereby failed to win a place at any of the five universities he had nominated on his UCCA form, Danny had surely sought to cauterise his academic chagrin by replacing it with carnal *joie de vivre*, and had probably enjoyed an extremely reckless few months.

"Anyway," Margaret went on, "you have to understand that KS is a form of cancer. There isn't a cure at the moment, but the good thing is that there's more research being done into AIDS-related conditions than there's ever been done into any other diseases ever before. D'you want to hang around in case he wakes up sometime soon, or d'you want to come back later, or tomorrow?"

"His mother's coming tomorrow. But, yeah, I may come tomorrow, too, or Monday."

"Yes, that'd be good, I think."

Rex sat down very gently on Danny's bed, anxious not to wake him, then stared at him awhile. After a few minutes he spoke aloud, but very quietly. "Poor little darling Danny," he said. Time passed. "Poor little darling Danny," he repeated. More time passed. "Poor little darling Danny, I'll come and see you again tomorrow morning, I think, OK? Would you like that?" Danny did not stir. Rex continued to sit totally still until, again, he was disturbed by another ignoble and therefore unwelcome thought, this time a sudden, powerful and lusty gratitude for Kenyon's and his own rude health, thank god, their having tested negative when they had decided to move in together and thereafter having vowed to stay faithful to each other, for reasons of health as well as love, which promise they had both kept. Jill had often said that she would much rather she had AIDS than that Danny did. Rex could not be sure that he felt the same way. He stood up.

Suddenly he was aware that the boy in the next bed was looking at him, albeit through stony, lifeless eyes. "Hi," Rex said.

"Hiya," the boy replied.

"How're you doing, son?"

"Oh, you know, not too bad." His voice was husky but shrill, working class surely, cockney-ish perhaps, but Rex could not make out where from.

"What's your name?"

"Paul."

"Hi, Paul. I'm Rex. Nice to meet you properly. Obviously I've seen you on my previous visits, but we've never chatted before, because I've always been chatting to Danny, my son, but as you see…"

Paul completed Rex's sentence: "He's asleep, yeah. I'm often asleep, too, which is the real reason we've most probably not properly met."

Rex liked Paul's looks, fancied him if he was honest, although the idea of having sex with someone so obviously frail was an obscenity; it would be like fucking a robin. He smiled at the boy, who did not smile back. "Er, look," Rex ventured, "d'you mind if I ask you, er, how come you never have any visitors? Well, sorry, whenever I'm here you never have any visitors. Perhaps you sometimes do. Do you?"

"No."

"D'you mind me asking you why not?" Rex realised he was being nosy, but he had abruptly become both intrigued and incensed by the boy's apparent isolation.

"Well, no one knows I'm here."

"What d'you mean?"

"Just what I say: no one knows I'm here."

"How old are you?"

"Eighteen."

"What about your mum and dad?"

Paul emitted a sharp, harsh chuckle, then hissed, "Yeah, right." Suddenly, he was convulsed by a coughing fit. Rex fidgeted, wondering whether he should offer help, but what help could he offer? Should he fetch a nurse? The coughing would not stop. The boy coughed and coughed. There was no attenuation in his coughing, no end to it. It went on and on. Suddenly he fell silent, but his fit had exhausted him. He now lay skew-whiff, his eyes half-closed. Rex could not help thinking he looked like a cadaver.

"Are you OK?" he asked.

"Well, that's a fucking silly question, innit?"

"Well, I'm genuinely concerned, really. Can I get you anything? A glass of water perhaps?"

"Look, mate, OK, Danny says you're one of us, gay, which is fucking weird, but whatever, so I'll tell you. When I was fifteen, back in Herne Bay, my dad caught me and another boy wanking each other off in his shed. He went fucking ape-shit. Kicked the other lad out and beat the shit out of me. Then he threw me out on the street. I tried to go back, shouted through the letterbox to my mum and my big sister and everything, but they wouldn't fucking let me in. I think my mum would've done, but he wouldn't have it. So I ended up on the fucking street. I got cold and hungry. After a day or two sleeping rough I bunked onto a train to London, Charing Cross it was, and when I got here I started begging. In the end, cos I was only fifteen, a few chicken-hawks said they'd give me a bit more money if I let them fuck me. So I did. I kind of enjoyed it, to be honest, cos it was horny and they was a lot nicer than my dad, even though I knew they only wanted one thing. At least they didn't hit me, which my dad always did. So I went on the fucking Dilly, didn't I? It was fun, I had a few quid in my back bin, and I found a decent studio flat in behind Warren Street. It was good. But it fucked me up in the end. It's what got me in here."

"That's utterly appalling. Paul, I'm so sorry."

"It is what it is, mate. No point crying over spilt spunk. Your son's a good lad, as it goes."

"Thanks. Yes, he is. Such a good lad. The best. But can I ask you, er…" – Rex lowered his voice – "… why's he wearing that little tartan skirty thing. Sorry to ask you but, er, d'you happen to know?"

"It's obvious, innit?"

"Well, sorry, but I wouldn't ask if it was obvious to me. So, since he's my son, could you tell me, please?" Rex had not meant his reply to sound so schoolmasterly, but Paul seemed not to have minded it.

"He wants to look sexy. He fancies a couple of the other lads in here, that skinhead and that black guy…" – Paul pointed to his right and farther right – "… and he wants to pull if he can. And, as it goes, that little tartan skirty thing is called a mini-kilt. I wish I could still wear mine, but I can't, not now."

"Why not?"

"I can't wear mine cos I've got to wear a fucking nappy,

mate. I ain't got KS or CMV, like what Danny's got. No, I've got chronic fucking diarrhoea. And I can't hardly eat nothing cos I've got thrush all down my throat, which is fucking agony, as it goes. AIDS is fucking shit, mate. If it don't get you one way, it gets you another."

CHAPTER 26

AN APPENDAGE ON THE UPPER
RIGHT-HAND SIDE OF THE OLDER MAN'S TORSO

When Rex arrived home he phoned Jill, anxious to speak to her before she had become too drunk to engage properly. Although it was only teatime, he had left it too late. Nonetheless, he succeeded in confirming that she would visit Danny tomorrow, which knowledge he obtained by virtue of her tearing a strip off him for wasting her time by duplicating Kenyon's efforts. "Your boyfriend's just rung me to tell me the exact same thing," she slurred. "Are you two checking up on me or something? D'you think I'm about to, er, not visit my fucking son or something? Fuck off." She slammed down the receiver.

Rex went into the kitchen, where he found a note: "I've phoned Jill. She's confirmed she's on Danny duty tomorrow. I'm going to the gym. I'll be back by 6.00pm. Love you. K xxx"

Rex made himself a cup of tea, took it into the living room, switched on the telly, and tuned it to BBC2, on which channel was showing live coverage of the first Grand Slam Cup semi-final from Munich. He lolled on the sofa and began to watch it. David Wheaton was playing Michael Stich. Neither player interested him – they were both dark-haired whereas Rex had become an unwavering fan of blonds – and, although tennis remained one of his favourite sports, his attention wandered. After a while he nodded off.

*

Meanwhile, three miles due west, at Manor House Drive, Jill was sitting on the living room floor, her back braced against the sofa, drinking neat uniced gin and eating Twixes. She was wearing new tracksuit bottoms, bought at her request by Kimberly, having recently outgrown her old ones. Kimberly's father had died in the summer, and her mother had returned to Galway for good. Since she had done well in her A-level exams, was now reading sociology at City University, near Farringdon, which was an easy half-hour tube journey from Willesden Green, it had been decided that, when Danny had developed what was colloquially but Kimberly thought mercilessly known as "full-blown AIDS", she would move to 67 Manor House Drive permanently and free of charge, ostensibly to help Jill with Danny, but more accurately to look after both of them. She liked it. Being needed – and appreciated – felt good.

"I've run you a bath," she said briskly, entering the living room. "Go on, I'll have made us spag bol by the time you come down again."

"I don't need a bath, darling."

"I didn't say you did, but it'll do you good. Go on, I've just run it for you, with Badedas and everything. Then we can watch a video together. I'll go out and get us one."

"OK, thanks," said Jill, and Kimberly helped her stand up. She tottered up the stairs unaided, although Kimberly followed her all the way to the en-suite bathroom in what used to be her and Rex's bedroom, arms outstretched, ready to catch her should she fall.

It was only in the past month or so that Jill had let her drinking get completely out of hand. Prior to that, Danny had been living at home, albeit decreasingly hale and increasingly gloomy, but she had nonetheless managed to observe her self-imposed no-alcohol-before-6.00pm rule, although it had been difficult when she had had to close her antiques shop, its losses no longer shored up by Rex's casual beneficence. In truth she had not been unhappy to let it go. She hated being at work when Kimberly was at uni and Danny was home alone. But when Danny had been admitted to the Broderip, she had found that, unless she was visiting him, she suddenly had nothing to do all day and all evening except hit the gin. Even so, she never drank on the mornings of her Danny-duty days, allowing herself only two or three large gin 'n' tonics at the Fitzroy Tavern on Charlotte Street immediately before braving the Broderip, as she termed it. Emotionally drained by her visits, she invariably began to deluge her sorrows as soon as she had arrived home afterwards, however. Indeed, on bad days, she often revisited the Fitzroy for a couple of stiffeners before hailing a taxi, and there had been quite a few bad days lately.

Kimberly jogged to the video shop, selected the first romantic comedy they had not yet seen – *Betsy's Wedding* – trotted home, tidied up, hid the gin, and began to boil the spaghetti. She drained it, tipped a jar of Ragù Bolognese into it, stirred it and simmered it. She then ran upstairs to collect Jill, who, as was not unusual, had fallen asleep in the bath. Kimberly roused her, hauled her out, towel-dried her, handed her her dressing gown, helped her on with it, and escorted her down the stairs into the kitchen, where she stood leaning ponderously but silently against the fridge door. Kimberly dished up, grated cheddar atop both plates, then set them on the kitchen table next to two glasses of Shloer.

Jill had sobered up a bit, but she appeared to be looking for something. "Where's my gin?" she asked.

"You've finished it."

"No, I don't mean my glass, I mean the bottle. Where's it gone?"

"We've got wine," said Kimberly, indicating the Shloer. Jill sipped it, farted, began to eat, and said no more.

*

"Hi, you in? How was he today?" shouted Kenyon, letting himself into the flat. Rex shifted on the sofa, and half-awoke. "Oi, lazy bones, wake up, how was Danny today?" Kenyon went on, dive-bombing the sofa so as to jolt Rex awake.

"Ah, not so good, sweetheart, truth be told. I think his KS is a tiny bit worse, on his legs anyway if not on his face, thankfully, and he was very sleepy. I didn't get much out of him, to be honest. He snoozed most of the time. He said hi to you though."

"That's nice. You see my note?"

"Yeah, thanks for checking up on her."

"No prob."

"I actually spent more time talking to that very skinny lad who's in the bed next to Danny's. Danny was kipping so much of the time, you see. His name's Paul. He's a lively one, but his life's been tragic." Rex told Kenyon Paul's story.

"There but for the grace of god go I," said Kenyon when Rex had finished.

"Well, hardly, sweetheart. You escorted for a comparatively short time, always discreetly and prudently, and you never sold your arse on the Dilly like he did. Also, you didn't do it at fifteen."

"No, but still."

"Well, there's no 'but still' to it, really."

"OK, Rex, you must be right, you always are."

"Sorry, sweetheart. How was the gym?"

"It was fine." Kenyon lit a cigarette.

"Actually, another thing, Danny was hardly wearing anything today, just a tiny mini-kilt. I couldn't work out why, especially as it showed all his lesions on his legs and back, not that I saw his back because he was lying on his back throughout the time I was there. But still. It was odd, I thought. So I asked Paul if he knew why Danny was wearing only this bloody mini-kilt, and he said it was so's he'd look sexy, so's to pull. I found that so poignant. You know, that he'd still be trying to pull, and look sexy, when he's as thin as a rake and his body's so, well, unsightly."

"He's still cute, Rex. He'll always be cute. And he's still got the same cheeky little smile."

"Thanks, sweetheart. Yes, he's still got that. Kiss me." Kenyon complied and, noticing that Rex's eyes were moist, he meticulously kissed them dry, one after the other. "Thank you. You're so sweet. I'm sorry I'm sometimes a bit snappy. It's just Danny. He's my son. He's only twenty, for fuck's sake. And he's still obviously got a libido, even though his body is now so ravaged, and the only guys he can try to pull are fellow AIDS patients, all of them terminally ill. It's so utterly fucking sad."

"I know. It's shit. It's the shittest thing ever. It's so fucking unfair."

"It is."

Kenyon decided to change the subject. "Anyway, d'you fancy the Shahbhag, like we said? I've booked for 9.15pm cos I thought we might want to watch *Mrs Warren's Profession* on BBC2. It's a George Bernard Shaw play about prostitutes, probably pretty good, possibly quite interesting anyway. It's got Michael MacKenzie in it. He's hot. It finishes at ten past nine."

"Yup, fine."

*

Kimberly washed up, then loaded *Betsy's Wedding* into the VHS player. Jill made no effort to watch it, but instead draped the full length – and width – of her body onto the sofa and quickly fell asleep. Kimberly then relaxed, finally, and easily managed to enjoy the movie, even though Jill was snoring loudly throughout it and in truth she thought it was rubbish.

*

Mrs Warren's Profession had been good but not great, and Kenyon had rated it higher than had Rex. But Rex had enjoyed watching it all the same, not least because Kenyon had held his hand and popped a seedless grape into his mouth every ten minutes or so, which Rex had thought adorable.

At the Shahbhag, now, despite being unassisted by the distraction of telly, they managed to put up a decent impression of enjoying themselves, which performance they were enacting for each other's sake. Rex paid the bill, as always, dropping two £20 notes on the table in front of him, then said, "Listen, Kenny, I know I said I didn't want to go out with any of your mates tonight, but actually I wouldn't mind now. I'm a bit low. I could do with a bit of a laugh and a few more bevvies. And it *is* my fortieth birthday, after all." He had had only three half-pint glasses of Kingfisher, and no laughs.

"Good. I'm pleased. As it happens, I ran into Paolo at the gym. He and Rich aren't going to the William IV after all. They're probably going to LA, Paolo said. I didn't mention it cos you said you wanted a quiet one. But it *is* your fortieth, as you say, so let's join them. It's only 10.45pm now. If we grab a cab we'll be there at just after 11.00pm, and we don't have to stay there very late. Anyway, I've got work tomorrow, as you know."

"Fine. Let's have a few drinks in LA with the boys and try to leave by 1.00am at the latest, OK?"

They walked out into the street, where it was now distinctly chilly, sub-zero certainly, and Kenyon hailed a black taxi. "The London Apprentice, 333 Old Street," he said, and they both stepped in. The driver grunted, then exhaled slowly and extravagantly, in recognition of the fact that they had asked to be taken to a notorious gay bar, Rex thought. Kenyon did not notice.

*

The Broderip's lights had been turned out for the night. "You awake, Danny?" Paul whispered.

"Yeah."

"Can I ask you a question?"

"Yeah."

"What'll you miss most when you're dead?"

Danny thought for a while. "How many things am I allowed?"

"What d'you mean?"

"Can I choose three things?"

"Course you can."

"OK. Playing football, Three-Eight and my mum. No. Scoring goals, Three-Eight and my mum. What about you?"

"Just my mum."

*

Rex and Kenyon arrived at the London Apprentice to find it packed. For many years Earl's Court, seven miles south-west of Old Street, had been London's go-to district for gay men in search of sex, much of it centring on the Coleherne Arms on Old Brompton Road, a cruisy boozer colonised in the '70s by clones and leather queens, still the staunchest regulars, but also patronised more recently by a newly confident band of openly gay celebs such as Derek Jarman, Ian McKellen, Rupert Everett, Kenny Everett and Freddie Mercury. The streets around it were cruisy, too, especially after closing time, and the men who walked them in search of companions to go home with were often arrested and charged with obstruction, soliciting, importuning or even conspiracy to corrupt public morals. In the past Rex had often driven down Earl's Court Road or up Warwick Road, which were one-way in opposite directions, and he had been tempted to stop if he had spotted a particularly likely lad. But he had never dared. Cottaging had always seemed easier, quicker and safer.

Soho had always been a gay mainstay, too, and remained one, albeit more boozy than cruisy, its mother lodes Comptons on Old Compton Street and Brief Encounter on St Martin's Lane. However, in recent years the London Apprentice, in EC1, had become the city's most ascendant gay bar, its two levels almost always full of men and boys of all shapes, sizes, ages and colours, enjoying one another's company in all sorts of ways. Tonight was such a night.

"Where d'you think Rich and Paolo will be?" Rex shouted above the hubbub of jukebox and banter.

Kenyon looked at his watch. "Probably down here still," he replied. "I'll get us a drink." Kenyon pushed his way to the bar, quickly caught a bartender's eye, and ordered a pint of Hofmeister for Rex and a double vodka 'n' orange for himself. They walked around the bar in search of their friends, but could not find them. They secured a bit of floor space next to a pillar, against which Rex leaned, and sipped their drinks in silence, Kenyon smoking, their desire to chat trumped by their disinclination to yell against the din. Even so, occasionally they ventured a sentence or two, so as not to look dreary among the garrulous throng.

They finished their drinks. "Come on then," said Kenyon, "let's see if they're up there." If downstairs in LA was boozy, then upstairs was cruisy – with knobs on. As they climbed the stairs and entered the main room, which was unlit and therefore illuminated only by what light was emanating from the street lamps through the frosted-glass windows this cold and foggy December night, their eyes took a few seconds to adapt. It was always like that here: a sensation opposite from that of emerging from a matinée cinema into bright daylight.

Soon they saw that the crowd, which was large, had parted to provide a central space in which two men had taken it upon themselves to entertain the others. The bigger of the two, a muscular bearded clone of about forty, wearing a black leather bulldog harness and black leather boots but nothing else, was bending forwards against a chair, his bare arse raised. His younger companion, a scally-looking skinhead, in blue jeans and white T-shirt, was kneeling behind him, and was applying large quantities of lube to the object of his mission, before coating his right hand, wrist and forearm in the stuff, pointing his fingers together in the manner of Italian footballers mocking a referee's decision, then slowly working his way in. Fisting was something that neither Rex nor Kenyon had ever wanted to try, although in abstract it was horny, but they watched alongside the dozens of others, some of whom were openly masturbating.

Eventually, despite having made impressive headway, the skinhead tired of his exertions, and yanked his arm out of his mate. He then took off his T-shirt, threw it onto the floor beside him, pulled down his jeans – it turned out he was wearing no pants – and for ten minutes fucked him efficiently, with signal precision, his cock never slipping out despite the speed and length of his thrusts, which appeared neither to speed up nor to slow down. Eventually he pulled out and came voluminously over his comrade's buttocks. There was a ripple of applause from those spectators who still had both hands free. The skinhead then picked up his T-shirt, wiped his dick, hands and right forearm on it, put it back on, pulled up his jeans, and walked off. The other man bent over again, indicating his readiness for a repeat.

"No condom, you noticed?" said Rex.

"Yeah, crazy," Kenyon replied. "I know he pulled out but pre-cum can be as dangerous as cum."

Rex was suddenly gripped with anger. He marched up to the fistee, who was still in position but had not yet attracted a replacement accomplice, and crouched down in front of him, addressing his face rather than his butt.

"Why d'you let that guy fuck you without a condom?" he asked.

"*Je suis français. Pourriez-vous répéter s'il vous plait?*" came the reply, spoken courteously and without a posture shift.

"Er, sorry, er, *pourquoi n'avez-vous pas utilisé un préservatif?*" Rex essayed.

"*Parce que le plaisir est tout.*"

Rex walked back to Kenyon, who looked vexed. "What the fuck, Rex?" he asked. "What did you say to him? Why did you even speak to him?"

"I asked him why he was happy to risk his life by letting strangers fuck him up the arse without a condom, of course."

"For fuck's sake. It's none of your business. What did he say?"

"He's French. He said, '*Parce que le plaisir est tout.*'"

"What's that mean?"

"It means 'because pleasure is everything'. Playing with fire, is what it really means. It's fucking depressing."

The crowd had intermingled now, and a number of men were copping off in pairs. Rex and Kenyon retreated to a far wall, and leant against it. One of the couples approached them, a man and a boy, both shirtless, and at first Rex feared they would suggest a foursome, for Kenyon had already attracted not only licentious attention but also wandering hands, some of which he had batted away, but by no means all, even shooting a sexy smile at the odd handsome groper. "I'm only messing, Rexy," he had said at one point. "I'd never actually do anything." And he never had, with the result that his suitors had always drifted away before too long, albeit not as quickly as Rex would have liked.

The boy pulled his trousers and pants down, bowed low, and with both hands braced himself against the wall, cocking his arse deftly upwards as he did so. The man got his cock out, a hefty one, and slid it in. Kenyon whispered, "That nipper's had quite a few dicks in him already tonight, no doubt about it. That's a decent-sized schlong but look how easily he took it. He's probably having his rent paid." Rex could not tell whether Kenyon's jargony barb was correct – that the youngster was a rent boy – but he studied the couple carefully nonetheless, although in the half-light it was difficult. The lad was twenty at most, perhaps younger. His collaborator was at least fifty, but he had the ashen, wasted visage of a man twenty-five years older than that. Suddenly, on the upper right-hand side of the older man's torso, Rex noticed an appendage, thwacking rhythmically against his chest as he thrust backwards and forwards. Was it a pendant? A crucifix perhaps? No, it was not. Indeed, Rex now saw that it was not hanging from his neck, but from an indeterminate point on his right breast. Abruptly, Rex recognised it as a thoracic catheter. Jason, one of Danny's Broderip confederates, had one. He had had it fitted – permanently – in an effort to treat a pneumothorax, a lung infection common in HIV-positive patients, especially those suffering from pneumocystis pneumonia, as indeed Jason was.

"Look, Kenny, look!" Rex howled. "A thoracic catheter. You know, a fucking chest tube. That old guy's positive – obviously – and he's fucking that kid without a condom. D'you think the kid's seen it? D'you think he knows?"

"Fuck. I dunno," Kenyon replied.

"Should we tell him, d'you think?"

"Rexy, it's none of our business."

"No, I know, but…" – but Rex did not finish his sentence, because it was clear that the older man was now coming, and as he was doing so he was pushing deeper into the boy. He stayed in a while, then pulled out, rasped two words – "Cheers, baby" – pulled up his pants and jeans, then walked away.

Rex ran after him. "Excuse me, mate, sorry, I know it's none of my business, but you're obviously positive…" – he indicated the thoracic catheter – "… so what the fuck were you doing fucking that kid without a condom?"

"Who the fuck are you?"

"I'm no one. Well, I'm a human being with a brain and a conscience. It would appear that you aren't."

"Listen, you pissy queen, I'm a free spirit, with a free will. We all are. You are. That boy is. Anyway, look at me…" – he attempted then aborted a pirouette – "… he obviously knew I was positive, so he obviously wouldn't have let me fuck him without a condom if he wasn't positive himself."

"Are you fucking sure about that?"

"As sure as I need to be, girlfriend. Now leave me in peace. Actually, why don't you fuck off and have a wank?" He turned on his heel and sauntered off.

But Rex was not done yet. He went in search of the boy, and quickly found him. He tapped him on his bare shoulder and said, "Excuse me, son."

"Yeah?" the youth replied, turning around, and smiling seductively.

"Son, look, you shouldn't let strangers fuck you without a condom."

"That's OK. I've got condoms. You can fuck me right now. I charge a tenner with a condom, twenty without."

"No, no, no. I don't want to fuck you. Well, I wouldn't mind – you're a sexy lad – but, no, that's not what I meant. I meant you should never allow men to fuck you without condoms. You need to keep yourself safe from HIV."

"Yeah, I know. Everyone knows that. If a guy's positive, I always make sure they wear condoms."

"How d'you know they're positive? Or negative, for that matter?"

"Look, mister, no one wants to die of AIDS. Guys who are positive always wear condoms. Guys who are negative don't need to, obviously."

"So you're telling me that the fact that a man is willing to fuck you without a condom is all the proof you need that he's negative?"

"Yeah, basically."

"Did that guy – the guy who just fucked you – did he tell you he was positive?"

"No, he's negative."

"How d'you know?"

"Cos he didn't ask to use a condom."

Rex walked back to Kenyon, hugged him tight, and began to cry. "Let's go home now, sweetheart. Rich and Paolo obviously aren't here. Come on. I can't bear this."

"OK, Rexy, yeah, let's just go home to bed."

"Yes, please. I could murder a fuck."

CHAPTER 27

Rex and Kenyon both awoke early-ish on Sunday, despite having finally fallen asleep at just after 2.00am, Rex because he had slept fitfully and not at all after about 6.30am, and Kenyon because he had to be in West Sussex by 10.30am to photograph a cow for *Cattle Management*, a RED title, which necessitated an 8.45am departure.

Kenyon's alarm went off at 7.45am. Rex reached over him and switched it off. "Where are you off to today, sweetheart?" he asked him as he did so.

Kenyon yawned, stretched and scratched. "A farm in a village called Greatham," he mumbled.

"Right. You driving?"

"Yeah. You going to the office today?"

"No, it's Sunday."

"Oh, yeah, sorry, I'm still half asleep."

"Actually, I want to go to the hospital again today. I know Jill's on Danny duty, but he was so sleepy yesterday, so, yeah, I'll go and see him later this morning, I think."

"Good. Give him my love. I'll be home for dinner. It won't be a long shoot but I'll have to take the films to get processed at Metro in Clerkenwell straight away cos it's for the cover and they need to lay it out tomorrow apparently."

"OK. What mag is it?"

"*CM*."

"OK."

They kissed. Kenyon showered, dressed, shouted, "Bye," then lugged his bulky camera bags down the stairs and loaded them into his jet-black Range Rover, which Rex had bought him brand new a few months ago as a present for having successfully passed his MA. Rex took a shower, dressed, and let himself out of the flat. Since he and Kenyon had moved to Haverstock Hill, they had let expire their memberships of South Hampstead Tennis Club – to Nigel's moderate disquiet – and had instead joined Globe Tennis Club, behind Belsize Park tube station, which he now walked past. They rarely played tennis in the winter, and never when it was frosty underfoot, as it was today. Besides, Kenyon had become a serious gym bunny, and trained at the Armoury in nearby Pond Street four times a week. Scantily clad or, better still, naked, he now looked even more glorious than he had when they had fallen in love more than two years ago, Rex thought, so much so that he had caught himself wondering for whose benefit Kenyon's sculpted pecs, bulbous biceps and hard, undulating abs were being honed. He did not fear that his boyfriend was being unfaithful to him, precisely; no, not that; but it was clear that he was enjoying the growing number of admiring glances that his increasingly heavenly body was now attracting.

Rex did not like gyms. He thought exercise should have a purpose. Sport counted; lifting weights that did not have to be lifted did not. Brisk walking counted, too, and, although he still loved driving, he did a fair bit of walking now, too. He had decided to walk this morning. If he stopped for breakfast at his favourite café, the Goodfare, on the corner of Parkway and Arlington Road in Camden Town, he would arrive at the Broderip by the time staff and patients would be expecting to begin receiving their keenest visitors.

En route he bought a Caramac and a Lilt, for Danny, and the latest *Autocar & Motor* to read while eating his "two on two" – two poached eggs on two slices of granary toast – and as a result he lost track of time a bit, engrossed as he was in the first UK road test of the new Mercedes-Benz 400SE. When he arrived at the Middlesex, slightly later than he had intended, and a tad liverish therefore, he found Liam, Danny's London Lighthouse "buddy", smoking on the steps outside.

"Hi, Liam, all OK?"

"Hi, Rex. Liam Wallace, London Lighthouse," came the reply, annoying to Rex, since they had met a number of times and he therefore knew Liam's surname and voluntary occupation, appreciated the latter, and was certain he would never have reason to use the former.

"Yeah, yeah. Honestly, there's no need to keep saying 'William Wallace, London Lighthouse' like you're some nerd on *University Challenge*. I know who you are. Anyway, all OK?"

"It's Liam Wallace, not William Wallace."

"OK, OK, OK. If you hadn't kept bringing Wallace into it, I'd never have called you William. Sorry, Liam…" – he now raised his voice a little – "… but is everything OK with Danny? That's Danny fucking Davis, alright?"

"Yes, everything's OK. Danny's much livelier than yesterday, which is good. I just popped in to see him quickly because I called to ask how he was yesterday and they said he was very drowsy, but as I say he's better today."

"Good. Yes, that's basically why I'm here today, too. He was extremely drowsy yesterday, I thought. Jill's on Danny duty today, but I wanted to see him today, too, because yesterday he was a bit too *sotto voce* even to converse."

"Eh?"

"Never mind. Thanks, Liam. You do good work. I'm very grateful. We all are. See you soon. Bye."

Liam dropped his cigarette, stubbed it out with the toe of the monkey boot on his right foot, said, "Thanks, Rex, that's much appreciated, see you soon," and strolled away. Rex walked on into the hospital, and up the stairs into the Broderip.

He marched briskly through the ward, and made straight for Danny's bed. When he arrived at it, he saw that it was empty, crumpled sheets rucked halfway down. A nurse he did not recognise caught him up. "Are you Mr Davis?"

"Yeah."

"Danny's in the bathroom, that's all, nothing to worry about," she said. "He said you'd be visiting this morning."

"Did he? I didn't tell him. Well, maybe I whispered it to him yesterday while he was asleep."

"He may not have been asleep, you know. He may just have been resting deeply. They often hear things in that state, I've found."

Rex nodded, and sat on Danny's bed. In so doing he found himself facing Paul's bed. Paul was not around either, but his bed was not empty. Rex stared at the occupant – a man of about thirty-five, wan, thin, but otherwise not too unhealthy by the look of him – and after a while he greeted him. "Hi, I'm Rex," he said, but the man only nodded and just discernibly smiled. Rex wondered why Danny was taking so long. The nurse he had not recognised was writing notes on a pad nearby. Rex walked over to her. "Excuse me, sorry, where's Danny?" he asked her.

"He's in the bathroom still. He'll be back in a mo."

"OK. And Paul?"

"Sorry, Paul?"

"Yes, Paul. The young lad who's in that bed…" – he pointed – "… the bed next to my son's."

"Oh, I'm sorry, Mr Lee passed away in the night."

"Mr Lee?"

"Yes, Paul Lee, the young man who was in that bed before. Did you know him?"

"I did, yes. I certainly did. I, er, I…" but Rex found that he could not speak more.

CHAPTER 28

A NOTHING, A TRIFLE, A BAGATELLE, A TRINKET, A CURIO,
A KNICK-KNACK, A BAUBLE, A BIBELOT, A GEWGAW

Jill seldom drove these days, fearing with good reason
that she was rarely under the drink-drive limit, even
in the mornings. Indeed, when she had last tried to start
her Volvo, which now lived alone in the Manor House
Drive garage, it had had a flat battery. She had become
a regular and valued customer of Cheetah Minicabs
of Willesden High Road, not only travelling with their
universally West Indian crew of drivers herself but also
commissioning them to bring her gin whenever she
ran out late at night, and Chinese takeaways, and, on
one occasion, in despair, even summoning one of their
number to heave a sofa from one side of the living room
to the other. To her surprise, he did so willingly, charging

her the minimum fare of £2.00, explaining that it was "a great job" because it had taken only three minutes and had used no petrol. She wondered whether she was the only person who had realised that minicab drivers were the modern equivalents of bob-a-job boys; she did not know.

Today, Cheetah's telephone receptionist had said, "Sorry, love, no cars for at least an hour. Sunday morning's a busy time, you see." Jill had toyed with the idea of waiting, but it was already 11.00am, and she was anxious to get to the Broderip.

"No, goodbye," she said, put the phone down, then turned to Kimberly. "No minicabs, darling," she said.

"Really? You could go by tube, I s'pose?"

"No, no, no. I can't bear the tube."

"I'll help you, go with you, I mean. I wanted to go with you today anyway."

"That's very kind of you, dear, but no tube."

There was a silence. "We could always try Velite," said Kimberly.

"I'll never use that company, never."

"Why not? We know Three-Eight doesn't work there any more. You need to get to the hospital, and you won't take the tube, so…"

"Oh, well, OK," Jill replied after a pause. "Pass me the phone book."

"I know the number by heart: 452 9000."

Jill dialled. "Hello? Yes. May I have a minicab, please? As soon as possible. I'm at 67 Manor House Drive and I want to go to the Middlesex Hospital, Mortimer Street."

The telephone receptionist chuckled. "Not Finsbury Park this time, eh? Is this an SJ? Three-Eight has left, love. You'll have to pay if you want a cab."

"What d'you mean? Of course I'll pay."

"OK, it's just that your address is on our list of SJs. Some drivers like an SJ from time to time. Your address is one of Three-Eight's SJs, but he's left, as I say."

"What's an SJ?"

"You're kidding me, right?"

"No. Please tell me."

"Sex job."

Jill blinked. "Er, no, look, I want a minicab and I'll pay the fare in the usual way, in cash, I mean."

"OK, no problem, five minutes. Bye, love."

Jill turned to Kimberly and said, "What an extraordinary thing."

"Yeah, I heard," Kimberly replied.

*

As Danny inched his way from bathroom to bed, feeling his way along the walls so to do, still wearing only his mini-kilt, he looked brighter and fresher than he had yesterday, Rex thought. They hugged. "I'm so, so, so sorry about Paul," Rex mumbled, but Danny responded only by hugging his father more tightly. Finally, after about a minute, they released each other, and Danny groped his way back into bed.

He said nothing for another minute, but when he spoke his voice was firm, if quiet. "Dad, he was my mate.

We always chatted in the night, whispering about this and that. We always done that recently. We done it last night. And then when I woke up, he never. He never woke up, I mean. He'd just slipped away. He was only eighteen."

"I know, son. It's dreadful. I was chatting to him only yesterday, when you were asleep. Here, have these." He placed a Caramac and a Lilt on the bedside table, then, remembering that Danny probably could not identify them, added, "Lilt and Caramac, as usual."

"Cheers. Yeah, I heard some of you and him talking." He folded his arms. "Dad, I'm going to die, too, you know that, don't you?"

Rex could not think how to reply. There seemed little point in challenging this stark, bleak utterance, since it was certain to be true. Besides, it was also in Rex's view a magnificently valorous thing to say, and therefore deserved respect – reverence even – rather than a fortifying pleasantry. Nonetheless, he could not bring himself to answer with simple agreement. "Look, son, no one knows," he said eventually. "There's more research being done into HIV and AIDS than has been done into any other disease ever before."

"They've been trying to find a cure for cancer for a hundred years, but they ain't managed it. Why's AIDS going to be any different?"

"It may be. We don't know."

"Even if it is, it'll be too late for me. I'm probably iller than Paul was. I ain't got long, Dad. You know I ain't got long. I've got KS *and* CMV."

"I know, son." Rex wondered why neither of them was crying, but they were not. He looked away. Gradually, realising by degrees that one of these conversations would be their last, perhaps this one or perhaps not this one but almost certainly one of the next few, he decided to say more now than he had ever dared say before. "Son, I want to tell you something. It isn't going to be easy to say, but the nature of our communication has changed now. We have important things to say to each other, and, yes, it's true, perhaps a limited time in which to say them. So, yes, you're probably going to die. There, I've said it. Margaret says she hopes you're going to get a bit better again soon, and that you'll be able to go home again in a little while, or perhaps to my and Kenny's flat, and that'd be fantastic, obviously. But your courage deserves an honest reply, and, yes, you've got a terminal disease. The death of a young person is the most tragic thing in the world. Literally, there's nothing sadder. There's nothing worse. There's nothing more unfair. You've done nothing to deserve this. OK, you've had some unsafe sex, but who hasn't? You've been one of the unlucky ones. And I have to say that I…" – and now Rex's tears came out in a torrent, coursing down his cheeks as he battled on with what he had to say, minding not that his voice was cracking – "… er, I think the way you're facing it is the bravest and most impressive thing I've ever witnessed in my whole life. You're my son. My kid. You're twenty but you'll always be my little boy. My darling little boy. It seems only yesterday that I first took you to Arsenal, that I first taught you how to play tennis, snooker, all that. I bitterly regret not watching you play football more. Why didn't I do that?

I'd give everything I own to see you score a goal, now, and yet I hardly ever went. Why the hell not? I'm sorry I haven't always been a brilliant dad, son. I do love you, though, I really do, and I'll only forget your courage in the face of this terrible illness the minute I die."

"Thanks, Dad. You've been fine. It's been fun." They stared at each other awhile, neither able to see the other's face clearly, the one hampered by tears, the other by cytomegalovirus retinitis. Finally, Danny spoke: "When did you know you were gay, Dad?"

"All my life, son. All my life. I'm not going to lie, not now, not to you. It'd be obscene to lie to you now. I got your mum up the duff when I was eighteen. Nine months later you popped out. In between we got married. You kind of had to do that in those days. When I was young, in my teens, I shagged a few birds, because it was what lads did. It still is, of course. But, for me, it was also camouflage. If people thought I was a bit of a Casanova, which they did actually, then they wouldn't work out I was gay. It was so disgraceful in those days, being gay, I mean. I remember reading an article in my mum's *Sunday Mirror* when I was a nipper, ten or eleven, I s'pose. I'll never forget it. Its title was 'How to spot a possible homo'. Can you imagine? In the end I think I convinced myself I was straight, in adulthood, I mean, what with having your mum, and you of course. It's better now, being gay. Well, it was until all this, until AIDS, I mean."

"Yeah, AIDS is shit. I hate having it, I really do, but there ain't nothing I can do about it. It was horrible being shouted at in the street. That was the worst bit. You know,

'Fuck off and die, AIDS face,' all that kind of thing. Mums grabbing their kids and screaming, 'Kids, stay away from that freak.' It's better in here, to be honest. I don't know if I want to go home, or to your flat, actually, ever, not now, not with this." He waved a floppy hand at his face and legs. "Is Mum coming today?"

"She is, son, yeah."

"Good. Please pour me a glass of Lilt." Rex busied himself with the task. "So, Dad, there's something else on my mind, too. I ain't going to be able to say goodbye to Three-Eight. I don't know where he is. He just disappeared. The people at Velite don't know where he is. He could be dead for all I know. He's positive, after all."

"Well, you don't know that for sure."

"I do."

"How?"

"Because he's the only man who's ever come up my arse. So I got this off him. So he must have it, too."

"Really?"

"Yeah, really."

"But Kenny says…"

"What's Kenyon say?"

"Well…"

"Dad, don't beat about the bush. You don't have to be shy with me about sex stuff. Me and you are both gay anyway."

"True." Rex shrugged. "Look, Kenny says you told him you like cum."

Danny shook his head. "I do. But I like it on my face. Not up my arse, not even in my mouth really, but all over my face. That's what really turns me on. I love being fucked but I don't care whether my arse actually takes a load or not. Anyway, since Kenyon first told me all about HIV and AIDS, at the Holiday Inn Swiss Cottage, I always made the guys who fucked me use condoms, always, every single time. The only one I never used condoms with was Three-Eight, cos I was in love with him, or I thought I was, and I wanted it to be, you know, intimate. And you can't get pozzed up by getting cum on your face."

"So it was Three-Eight who infected you then, son? Definitely? That's what you're saying, right?"

"No, I infected myself. I've talked about it a lot with the guys here. I talked about it a lot with Paul. I pozzed myself up by letting Three-Eight come up my arse. I wanted his cum cos I wanted it to be special, to feel like we were really making love, not just having sex. But I don't think he loved me. In fact I know he never. He was just a horny guy, and he was positive, which I never knew, and in fact I think he never knew neither, cos he ain't educated or even intelligent to be honest. I know it's harder for tops to get infected, but he was totally a top, I can't imagine him ever letting anyone fuck him, so he must've got infected by fucking someone. It does happen, although it's much rarer than bottoms getting it."

"But Three-Eight was the one, son. He was the one who gave you this. That's what you're saying, correct?"

"Dad, yeah, technically. But who cares? Shit happens. Shit's happened. I should've made Three-Eight use condoms when we fucked. I always did with all the others. It's my fault, not Three-Eight's. And I reckon he left Velite, and disappeared off to fuck knows where, because he finally realised he was positive. He's probably dying now, or dead. I keep hoping he'll be admitted here, to this ward, I mean, but…" He shut his eyes and neither of them spoke for half a minute. "I heard Paul's last words, Dad. We were chatting, whispering, in the middle of the night. He asked me what I'd miss most when I'm dead. It was a funny question, he knew that, he was clever with words like that, because obviously I won't miss nothing when I'm dead cos I'll be dead, but it was a good way of asking it. He meant, 'What d'you love most in the world?'"

"What did you say? How did you answer, I mean?"

Danny paused. "Well, I said, 'Scoring goals, Three-Eight and my mum.' I'll miss you, too, Dad, obviously, but that's what I said. And then I asked him what he'd miss most when he was dead, and he said, 'Just my mum.' Then we went to sleep. So his last words were 'Just my mum'. And his mum'll never know that, cos she don't know he's here, or was here, and she don't know he's got AIDS, or had AIDS, and she don't know he's dead. And she never will."

"That's so sad, but in a way so beautiful, too."

"It ain't. It's so shit, is what it is."

"Yeah, sorry."

A silence developed, quite long, and it was broken by Rex. "Son, there's something else I need to tell you. I didn't think I was ever going to tell you it, because there seemed to be no need to tell you it, or actually there seemed to be an urgent need *not* to tell you it, but that's all changed now, because of the tragic situation we find ourselves in. As you so bravely said a little while ago, we may not have much time. I don't know how I can even frame such a sentence as 'We may not have much time' without cracking up, but it appears I can. People cope with shit like this. We're coping. We are. It's like Auschwitz. Many of the old German Jews you see in Cricklewood, or Golders Green, men and women, must have been in Auschwitz or one of the other concentration camps, but they coped. Like, I was queueing at the customer relations counter at Woolworth's in Kilburn High Road a few years ago, I can't remember why, and I overheard this old Jew in front of me talking about Auschwitz with his grown-up daughter, and when his turn came to make a complaint it turned out he wanted to get his money back on a faulty toaster. And the assistant wouldn't have it, for whatever reason, and the old boy went on and on and on about it long after most people would've given up. Obviously, he was within his rights to persist, but I couldn't help thinking: *You've survived Auschwitz, for fuck's sake, and now the thing that matters most to you in the world is getting a refund on a poxy toaster.* But that's life. Human beings are odd animals. They're very brave when they're tested by hardship, which they rarely are; they cope; and time is a great healer. So he'd got over Auschwitz, and the toaster mattered more now. In your case, though, you're being unbelievably brave when tested by hardship, and by god you really are being tested, and you're coping, but there may not be time enough to be that great healer." He began to cry again.

"It's OK, Dad. I'm sorry I done this to you and Mum, especially Mum. You'll be OK when I'm gone. You'll be sad, but you'll be OK, and Kenyon's a good boyfriend for you. Mum won't be OK though. She ain't even OK now. OK, she's got Kimberly at the moment, but that ain't going to last for ever. Kimberly'll meet someone, and move out, and then Mum'll be on her own with Mr Gordon and Mr Schweppe. Well, she don't bother with Mr Schweppe much these days. Look after her, will you? For me, I mean."

"I will, son, I promise you that…" – he looked down at the floor – "… but, anyway, as I say, there's something I want to tell you. Something happened on Saturday April 22nd 1989. I'll never forget the date – and, when I tell you why, you'll remember what happened on that date very well, too, I'm sure. It was the day your mum found out you'd been cottaging on Harrow Road rather than playing football."

"Yeah, how could I ever forget?"

"Exactly, yes. Well, Jesus, I can't believe I'm actually going to say this, but I fucking am. I fucking am because I fucking have to. Shit. Anyway, here goes." He shut his eyes and grimaced. "So, well, it so happens that I'd been cottaging that day as well, also on Harrow Road, and, well, it turns out that mine was one of the five cocks you sucked through that glory hole that day."

"You what? Fucking hell, how d'you know?"

"Because after I'd come, I was washing my hands, and then you let yourself out of the cubicle next to the one I'd just been in, and you walked past me out into the street. I saw you, but you didn't see me. I nearly died."

Danny frowned, shrugged, and then, to Rex's alarm, began to laugh irrepressibly. "That's actually very funny,

Dad," he said after a while, cackling as he spoke, "and, you know what, I couldn't give a fuck. So I sucked your dick. Who cares?" Suddenly, astonishing himself, Rex was sniggering, too, then giggling, then, as Danny began to shake and caterwaul, Rex began to emit great belly laughs. And now they were both roaring with laughter, together, and Rex realised that everything mattered but nothing mattered, and he knew more certainly than he knew anything that he had been right to tell Danny his great dark secret, a secret that in the sharing had become a nothing, a trifle, a bagatelle, a trinket, a curio, a knick-knack, a bauble, a bibelot, a gewgaw.

CHAPTER 29

A TENSE, OTHERWORLDLY, FAUX-CHEERY RICTUS

As they neared the Middlesex, Jill asked her Velite driver to take her and Kimberly to the Fitzroy Tavern on Charlotte Street, as had become her habit. Once she had ensconced Jill into a booth, Kimberly took a fiver from her and ordered a double gin 'n' tonic and a Diet Coke, which they drank together in silence. "Get me another one, please, darling," said Jill, long before she had finished her first. Kimberly obliged.

They then walked to the hospital, very slowly, Kimberly guiding Jill by the arm. They mounted the stairs, Jill stopping for a breather on each landing. They then braved the Broderip.

Jill spotted Rex, ignored him, and lunged straight for Danny, whom she hugged soundlessly but extravagantly, slumping on his bed as she did so. "Hi, Danny, it's me –

Kimberly – and your mum," Kimberly had called out as they had approached, so as to save Jill the shock of not being seen clearly by her son, nor therefore recognised by him, for Jill had not properly taken on board that Danny was now what the medics called "partially sighted". Rex stood up. Kimberly heaved Jill's torso perpendicular, so that she was sitting on the edge of Danny's bed. "Hello, darling," she said finally.

"Hi, Mum," Danny replied, a vivid grin overtaking his ghoulish countenance.

"He's much better today than yesterday, Jill," said Rex, "aren't you, son?"

"Yeah. I was sleepy yesterday. I can stay awake and chat today. It's funny how it goes."

"Well, Jill, maybe I'll head off now, to leave you two – you three – together. OK, son?"

"You don't have to go on my account," said Jill. "Happy birthday for yesterday, by the way."

"Thanks. No, I know, but I've been here a couple of hours already, and you're on Danny duty today, I'm just here as an extra, and maybe I'll try to pop in tomorrow with Kenny if I can finish work in time. He'll be on Danny duty. I'll trundle off now if that's OK. Give me a big hug, son." They embraced, then Rex left. He did not look back. He wanted to, but he feared Danny might interpret his backward glance as a desire for visual closure. Besides, he was crying, which he did not want his son to see. But as he descended the staircase he cursed himself. He could have turned around, he realised too late, because of course Danny could not have seen him do so.

He wondered why – why specifically now – he was crying. He did not always cry on leaving the Broderip. He had never done so before, in fact. The answer, when it came to him, startled him. He was crying not because of the profound significance of their conversation – on the contrary, despite its intense poignancy, it had consoled him – but because he had caught himself momentarily wishing that Danny would hurry up and die, so that he, Rex, could be freed from the tyranny of dreading his death, and that horrid realisation had shocked him to tears. "You're a shit, Rex Davis," he whispered as he walked out into the street.

"Darling," said Jill, holding her son's right hand with both of hers. She wanted to say more, but somehow she could not. There was a long silence. Jill's eyes filled, but she managed to stave off her tears by forcing her face into a tense, otherworldly, faux-cheery rictus. She sat like that for a while, then pulled from her handbag a small Tizer bottle, from which she took a swig. Kimberly could see that it contained not the lurid red fizz depicted on its label, but instead a colourless liquid. Danny did not spot the discrepancy.

"Darling," she said again. Danny smiled, pulled her hands gently towards his lips, and kissed them. He wanted to tell Jill some of the things he had told Rex, but, despite the fact that he loved his mother more than he loved his father, he felt he could not. She would likely fly off the handle at the merest mention of his feelings for Three-Eight, and she would surely become hysterical if he talked about his own dying. On the other hand, no one had ever been more important to him than this woman, nor would her status in his life ever be usurped now. She was the one. She had given birth to him, had fed and nurtured him when Rex had not been bothered with an infant, had raised him, had fussed over him, had washed his smalls, had made his packed lunches, had given him Lemsip when he had had colds, had painstakingly cleaned his muddy football boots, had helped him with his English and history homework, had doted on him throughout, had then been distraught when she had found out that he was gay, and, now, had been driven to alcoholism, obesity and depression by his AIDS diagnosis.

"I'm sorry, Mum," he began. "I'm sorry about all this. I'm so, so, so sorry. I know you wanted grandchildren. I know you wanted me to…" – he swallowed – "… do things I ain't never going to do now. But I'll always love you."

Jill began to weep. Kimberly placed a hand on her shoulder. Jill opened her mouth a couple of times, but no words emerged. "Your mum loves you very, very much," said Kimberly, "and she doesn't want you to feel bad."

"No, that's right, Kimberly, thank you, yes, I definitely don't want you to feel bad, darling," Jill whispered between huge, heaving sighs. "No, absolutely not. And, yes, I love you, I always will, and I'm proud of you, too, enormously proud."

"Thanks, Mum. That means a lot. I love you, too. Thanks for coming." He began to cry, too.

Jill knocked back another slug from her Tizer bottle. Why could she not think of more to say, to her only son, to the boy who had been for the past twenty years by an order of magnitude the principal focus of her life? "Oh, shitting shit!" she shouted suddenly, loud enough to turn heads in and around other beds, then said no more.

"I love you, Mum. Thank you for everything. But I'm tired now. Maybe I should get some sleep."

Jill blew her nose. Kimberly helped her up, then stopped, turned, and said, "Why did you have so much unsafe sex, Danny?" Jill looked simultaneously affronted and intrigued.

"I don't know if I had *so* much unsafe sex, actually, Kimberly," he replied.

"Yes, you did. You were always going off to Finsbury Park with Three-Eight, and, after he left you, you carried on going there on your own. You told me. You used to tell me everything, remember? You used to go there and meet random guys and have sex with them in the bushes. You know you did."

Danny toyed with the idea of reminding his old friend what she also knew, which was that he had always had safe sex on such expeditions. Indeed, he had bumped into and had even befriended some of the Terrence Higgins Trust volunteers who used to arrive most evenings with buckets of condoms and lube, which they placed strategically at points closest to where the tree cover allowed men to rut discreetly, each bucket illuminated by a battery-operated night-light attached. He had even had sex with some of them, safe of course. But he decided not to remind her of all that, despite wondering why she had selectively forgotten it, or had pretended to, because to do so would be to finger Three-Eight as his infecter. He knew Jill bitterly disapproved of Three-Eight, and that had always been and still remained a great sadness to him. Even so, he could put up with it. What he felt he could not cope with was his mother loathing his beloved with every synapse of her being. He wished he had told Rex to keep from her the revelation that Three-Eight had been the sole agent of his infection. He made a mental note to speak to Kenyon about it tomorrow.

"OK, darling, we'll head off now. See you again very soon," said Jill. Kimberly took her arm, and they began to walk away from Danny's bed. Jill took a couple of steps towards the door, then staggered, tripped and fell. Kimberly hauled her up, assisted by Jason, who had been watching from his bed, and in whom the effort triggered a short but violent wheezing fit. Jill looked about her, aware that she was the centre of attention, and embarrassed about it. She was unhurt, but she felt the need to say something. She cleared her throat.

"This, this, er, this is like the First World War," she began. "It's like the First World War in that men and boys are now dying of AIDS as soldiers did on the Western Front three-quarters of a century ago. But, unlike the heroes of the Somme and Ypres, who were rightly revered and decorated, you men and boys who are dying of AIDS – I'm sorry but it's true and we all know it – are facing your deaths often despised and rejected, and sometimes entirely alone. What a wicked waste of wonderful life. How did Tennyson put it in *The Charge of the Light Brigade*? Er, let me remember, yes, 'Theirs not to reason why, theirs but to do and die'. You poor, poor darlings. You're all heroes, every last one of you…" – she turned to Danny, paused, then smiled – "... and I'm as proud of my brave and beautiful son as any mother in the world."

She and Kimberly walked out of the Broderip to the sound of all twelve patients and two of the nurses clapping. A few of them stood up to do so, one of them Danny.

CHAPTER 30

THE JUST-DISCERNIBLE LUKEWARMTH
OF THE TIMID WINTER SUN

Although he had not admitted it to Rex, and probably would not, Kenyon enjoyed Danny duty. He had become one of the Broderip's coterie of migratory beefcakes, whose visits were looked forward to by all but those patients who were too ill to notice him. He felt as though he imagined celebrities must feel when engaged to open brand new supermarkets, in amongst a subordinate throng yet also apart from them, shinier than them, and adored by them. He privately disparaged his exalted Broderip status as frivolous, shallow even, but it was also undeniable. And yet, like Dave Lee Travis cutting a ribbon tied across the automatic doors of a brand new Safeway, admired and cheered for doing it despite its being not only a triviality but also a cinch, he allowed himself to be fêted, hugged, pecked on the cheek even. Moreover, unlike DLT, he assumed, he was happy to present his arms to be groped and caressed by men hideously infirm, taking pleasure in the smiles that suffused their pockmarked faces as their fingers kneaded his hardy, healthy biceps. He had even taken to wearing cap-sleeved T-shirts and the like on Danny-duty days so as to facilitate such inspections, and to going to the gym before his visits, so that his muscles would be suitably pumped in preparation for them.

Was he being narcissistic, he wondered? Yes, he was, a bit, certainly, but he did not think it mattered much, and his concerns had been allayed somewhat just last week when, perhaps sensing the coyness of his contentment, Margaret had sidled up to him and had whispered, "Don't worry, they love it when you come in, it cheers them up, and it's sweet of you to let them paw you like that. But are *you* OK with it?" Kenyon had assured her that he was absolutely fine with it. He had not added, although it was the case, that he had been surprised that she had even allowed for the possibility that he might dislike the attention, when his fear had been that the pleasure he took from it was conspicuous and might be looked upon as silly; but it was not.

He was not working today, despite its being a Monday. He had run to the Armoury, had weight-trained intensively there, had jogged home again for a breakfast of coffee and a cigarette, and had then taken the Northern Line from Belsize Park to Goodge Street. He had strutted the seven minutes' walk to the Middlesex, enjoying the just-discernible lukewarmth of the timid winter sun.

As he entered the Broderip, he saw Liam, who spotted him and walked over to him, meeting him a couple of wolf whistles in. "Hi, Liam Wallace," said Liam.

"I know. Hi everyone." Kenyon bowed theatrically in all directions. "So, Liam, how's Danny?"

"Asleep."

"OK." Kenyon walked over to Danny's bed, sat down on the chair beside it, and looked at him. He thought he was even thinner than when he had last seen him, which had been only a few days ago, and there was a yellowy waxiness to his skin that was new. He wanted to ask him about his seminal recent conversation with Rex. He was interested to probe the revelation that he had had unsafe sex with no man other than Three-Eight, not least because it clearly signified that he had taken on board the advice that he had given him at the Holiday Inn Swiss Cottage, which pleased him. Would he also ask him about his cheerfully undramatic reaction to Rex's Harrow Road cottaging confession? He might. Indeed, he wanted to. He felt that he was the natural helmsman of Danny's gay tiller, the custodian of his moral gay compass even, and he had therefore received the news from Rex with mixed emotions. In the telling, Rex had couched Danny's rollicking reaction as a wonderful relief, had chuckled often, and had used the word "closure" a lot. Kenyon could see the positives, of course he could, but he also felt slightly piqued. If anyone should have been able to steer Danny through his discovery of that ultimate busted taboo, he felt it should have been himself. He had sometimes envisaged being the one whose sexy savvy had been a godsend in the eventuality that Danny had somehow found out about it, and had become traumatised by it, but AIDS had transcended all that now. Rex had said, "Everything matters but nothing matters," more than once in bed last night, spooning him and nuzzling him as he had said it, and, in their pillow talk, they had agreed that Danny – weak, supine and acquiescent as he was – was also now magically impervious to scandal, not only resistant to its power to cause emotional upset but also immune from its propensity to wreak reputational damage. In a way, he was home safe: he would never be troubled again. In that sense, Kenyon almost envied his situation, and yet it was a dire and grisly tragedy, of course it was, and in every other sense he did not envy it at all.

Danny was still asleep. Kenyon decided to visit some of his fans. He strolled around the other eleven beds, and chatted flirtatiously with those of their occupants who were awake, and especially with Jason and his quartet of hunky visitors, who were all migratory gay totty like himself. When he returned to Danny's bed, Liam was sitting beside it. "I'm going to head off now. He seems peaceful enough," he said, and Kenyon bade him farewell.

A copy of the latest issue of *Time Out* was on Danny's bedside table, and Kenyon flicked listlessly to the "Lonely Hearts" pages, whose densely leaded classifieds he scanned with brisk professionalism. He challenged himself to find a coded escort ad within a minute, and did so even faster than that: "Handsome tanned muscular straight-acting gay guy 21 WLTM generous gentleman for friendship and fun. GSOH more important than looks. Box 4561". Kenyon smiled at "GSOH"; clearly the advertiser had wearied of his diet of horny dullards and was pining for a client with a good sense of humour. Having to spend a whole evening having sex with a very boring man was quite a lot worse than getting your kit off for a very ugly one, Kenyon remembered. Apart from anything else, the bores would never be rushed.

Danny shuddered. Kenyon looked at his face, and realised that he was dreaming, his eyeballs darting about erratically under his closed eyelids, his breathing fast and loud. He took his hand, and fancied he felt thin, bony fingers exerting a tiny degree of reciprocal grip; but he could not be sure. Soon Danny was once again more tranquil, less fidgety, his breathing slower and quieter. Kenyon withdrew the duvet a foot or so, and watched his scrawny chest heaving as he inhaled and exhaled.

Then it stopped moving. Kenyon reached for Danny's wrist, felt for his pulse, and was mightily relieved to find that it was present; strong even. But he was still not breathing. Kenyon was not only panicked but also torn: should he stay or should he call for help?

In the end he did both. Still holding Danny's hand, in such a way that he could feel his pulse, which was throbbing strongly, he yelled for help. "Margaret, here, quick!" he shouted. The staff nurse did not appear. "Help, someone!" Kenyon shouted. Jason bounded over, his thoracic catheter bouncing against his bare chest as he did so. "Danny's not breathing," Kenyon told him, "get a nurse, a doctor, someone, now, now, now, fucking now."

In less than half a minute Jason returned, with Margaret, by which time Danny was breathing normally again. As Jason, panting, draped a skinny arm around his neck, Kenyon explained what had happened, wondering as he did so whether Margaret would believe him, since Danny now appeared imperturbably serene. "They often do that," she said, smiling encouragingly. "Sometimes you think it's their last breath, but the pulse is still there, like you said, and then suddenly they gulp the air back in hungrily, like they were only playing with you."

"Yeah, that's exactly what he just did now. He can't have breathed for at least half a minute, maybe more."

"Sometimes it's a minute and a half," Margaret replied.

"So what does it, er, mean, Margaret?" Kenyon asked.

"He's poorly. Yes, I'd say he's poorly. He's waxy, isn't he? But the doctor was here this morning, and he didn't seem…"

"Was he awake then, for the doctor, I mean?" Kenyon asked.

"I don't think he's been awake this morning, no, has he, Jase?"

"I don't think so, no," Jason replied. "She's been just like this all morning. You know, dozing. But she was like this the other day, too, and then the next day she had a long chat with her dad, with your boyfriend, I mean, and then she was asking me where all her CDs were, cos one of the other girls had borrowed them, and she was all 'Oi, buy us a Lilt and a Caramac' and all that. And then today she's sleepy again. Tomorrow she'll probably be shouting the odds and demanding Caramacs and Lilts again."

"Margaret, what's the significance of 'waxy'?" Kenyon asked.

"Well, sometimes their skin changes like that towards the end. As I say, he's poorly," she replied, her diction gentle.

Kenyon tutted. "Why d'you keep using that word, 'poorly'? Is that code for he's going to die?"

"Well, he *is* going to die, Kenyon. He's terminally ill. I don't know when. Could he die today? He could, yes. Could he live a few more days? Yes, he could."

The word "days" hit Kenyon hard. He swallowed. He had expected her to say "weeks". But, no, days only. Days at best. And perhaps not even days. Perhaps today was the day. Danny stopped breathing again. Margaret leant over and felt for his pulse. "Strong," she said. They waited. Jason slid a hand up the back of Kenyon's T-shirt and squeezed his right shoulder. Kenyon tensed it obediently. Danny began to breathe again.

"Maybe I should ring Rex?" said Kenyon. "Yeah, I think I'll pop down to the card-phone and ring Rex at work. I think he should visit today. And, yeah, thanks for reminding me, Jase, I'll buy a Lilt and a Caramac while I'm down there, so's he can have them when he wakes up." Kenyon leant forward and kissed Danny on the forehead, noticing the distinctive texture of his skin as he did so; it was a bit like kissing the top of an opened tin of Vaseline; "waxy" was the *mot juste*. Jason went back to his bed, his four beefy acolytes making way to allow him to climb in. Danny began to make quiet humming noises – "Mmmmmm mmmmmm mmmmmm" – but his breathing was steady and so was his pulse. He was dreaming again, Kenyon figured. He hurried downstairs.

There was no queue for the card-phone but Rex's direct line went straight to answerphone. Kenyon replaced the receiver and dialled the main switchboard number. He asked for Rex's PA, Ursula, who plainly did not like him much. She told him that her boss was at an off-site meeting and would be back in an hour or so. If it was urgent, she would send out for him, she said. Kenyon decided to say that it was not, since, well, it was not, actually, was it? Worrying, perhaps, but urgent? No.

He walked across the polished lino to the hospital shop, and bought a Lilt and a Caramac. He also bought an apple, which he began to eat as he walked back up the stairs, holding the Lilt and the Caramac in his free hand. As he re-entered the Broderip, he saw that Margaret was sitting on the side of Danny's bed. He was pleased that she had not left him alone. As he neared them, Margaret stood up. "He's gone, Kenyon, just now. It was extremely peaceful. I was with him, holding his hand. He just slipped away."

Kenyon's eyes pricked but did not at first fill. He might not have cried at all, but when Margaret hugged him, then wept herself, he could not hold back the tears. He dropped his apple, half eaten. "How *could* he have just died? He was kind of OK."

"It sometimes happens this way, Kenyon. Sometimes they don't want to go in front of their nearest and dearest. I've often noticed that. I don't know if it's for the best or not. He didn't suffer. I was with him. I was holding his hand. He was taking good breaths, but the gaps between them were getting longer, like earlier but a bit longer even. One of the gaps went over a minute. I was going to fetch a doctor when, gently but suddenly, he raised his head slightly, maybe only an inch, made another of those 'Mmmmmm mmmmmm mmmmmm' noises, then managed to gasp what he must have been trying to say all along – 'Mum!' – then gulped a mouthful of air as though he was taking a bite out of an apple. Then there was a slight gurgling sound, and, well, I know what that is. I'm so sorry."

Kenyon stared at the ground. "Poor little darling Danny," he said.

Margaret pressed on, but her voice was straining. "I'm telling you all this because it's important that you know it all. You'll have to tell it all to Danny's mum and dad. They'll want to know every detail, believe me. I reached for his wrist to feel for his pulse, and it was there, but faint, and then I felt it fade to nothing under my fingertips."

"When did it happen?"

"I'd say three minutes ago, four maybe."

"Really? Are you sure he won't breathe again then? Earlier he didn't breathe for ages but then he burst back to life, kind of thing."

"He has no pulse. He's gone." She wiped her eyes. "Kenyon, you must make sure Jill knows that her son's last words – his last word actually – was 'Mum'. It'll break her heart when you tell her, but it'll sustain her in the years ahead."

They hugged again. Kenyon put the Lilt and the Caramac on Danny's bedside table.

CHAPTER 31

A PAIR OF CHINOS HE HAD NOT WORN
FOR YEARS AND HAD FORGOTTEN HE HAD

When Rex returned to the RED office from his off-site meeting, Ursula forgot – or perhaps neglected – to give him the second of Kenyon's messages, which had been that he should telephone him at the Broderip with the utmost urgency. Rex therefore made a few calls and wrote a couple of memos, bade Ursula goodbye, and drove off. He briefly considered detouring via the hospital, but he figured that no news must be good news, and, after all, he had visited not only yesterday but also the day before, so there was really no need. Besides, he had already decided that he would go tomorrow, which was down as a Liam-only day on Kenyon's rota.

So Rex drove home. When he arrived, Kenyon was not there, still at the Broderip, utterly distraught. He had not yet phoned Jill, despite Margaret's gentle urgings that he must, because he wanted to tell Rex first. But he could not track Rex down.

Rex made himself a cup of tea, began to drink it while standing at the kitchen counter, and went through the post: a Barclaycard bill, a letter from a Porsche dealership offering him a free track day, and a handwritten envelope, mauve, whose neat capitals he recognised.

He opened it and read what his mother had written.

Dear Rex,

I hope your well. You're father has had a hip operation but is baring up well. My tinitus is a bit worst but one mustn't grumble.

We're going to move to Gibraltar. The climat will be better for us. We've sold the house. We got a good price for it. We'll be going in the new year. We'll rent at first but we'll then by. I'll write again to give you are address when we know were we'll be.

Please pass on are regards to Jill and Danny. We hope their both well.

Regards,

Mam

PS: I saw this short artical in the Liverpool Echo. I thought you may find it intresting, disgusting of course, as the man concerned is an old boy of your school in your year I seem to recal.

Rex shook the envelope and a small newspaper cutting – what editors would call a nib, short for "news in brief" – floated onto the floor. He picked it up and laid it on the kitchen counter. He took a sip of tea, then read it. "Wallasey man to face trial for gross indecency. Christopher James Harrow, 40, an accountant, of 3 Claremount Road, Wallasey, is due to go on trial at Liverpool Crown Court on April 27th next year, accused of committing an act of gross indecency. Harrow was arrested after the offence allegedly took place in the gentlemen's public convenience on the promenade at New Brighton, Wirral, last month."

Rex read it again, and again once more.

He then went to his and Kenyon's bedroom, where he took off his suit, hung it in his wardrobe, and changed into a sweatshirt and a pair of chinos he had not worn for years and had forgotten he had. He walked back to the kitchen, and stared out of the window. The traffic was heavy on Haverstock Hill below. He put his hands in his pockets, and found a piece of paper in one of them. He took it out and looked at it. It was a note in Jill's handwriting: "Rex, Sorry about being so blotto last night. See you tonight. Don't show Danny this message. Love, Jill xxx". He could not remember when Jill had written it, or why.

He laid Jill's note on the kitchen counter beside the *Liverpool Echo* cutting, and read them both again.

He began to cry.

"Poor little darling Harry," he whispered.

The phone rang.

It was Kenyon.

 Matador